I0552034

SEE ME

The Donovan Family Series (#8)

MARGARET WATSON

Copyright © 2016 Margaret Watson

All rights reserved. No part of this book may be reproduced,
scanned, or distributed in any printed or electronic form without
permission. Please do not participate in or encourage piracy of
copyrighted materials in violation of the author's rights.
Purchase only authorized editions.

This is a work of fiction. Names, characters, places, brands,
media, and incidents are the products of the author's imagination
or are used fictionally. Any resemblance to actual events, locales,
or persons, living or dead, organizations or businesses is entirely
coincidental.

ISBN-13: 978-1-944422-29-5

TITLES BY MARGARET WATSON

CHAPTER 1

Gabriella unlocked her front door and stepped inside, pleased she'd made it home a little earlier than usual. As a teacher's aide for a special education class, she often had to stay late to help a student. No one had needed extra help today, and she hadn't wasted time getting home.

She wouldn't pick up her daughters for over an hour. Bella would go straight from Lane Tech High School to Spencer Elementary School, to help with the tae kwon do club. And Cece, her ten-year-old, had an after school program today at Spencer for students who wanted to learn French. So Gaby would have time to study for her own class that evening.

Pediatric nursing. Her mouth relaxed in a smile. Her favorite subject in nursing school.

Dropping her purse on the hall table, she shrugged off her coat and tossed it over the newel post of the staircase. Stilled.

Something was wrong.

The cool smell of spring rain and damp earth swirled through the air. As if she'd left a window open. Or the back door.

All the windows had been closed and locked when she left this morning. She'd double-checked the back door, too. She did that every morning before she left for work.

Her hand shaking, she reached into her purse and curled her fingers around her phone. Pulling it out, she fumbled to press 911 as she crept toward the kitchen at the back of the house.

Maybe she was being paranoid. It was possible she'd forgotten to close the window above the sink. Sometimes Bella opened it, to lean close to the screen and peer into the garden. Her older daughter liked to watch the birds at the backyard feeder.

She edged through the tiny dining room she'd made into an office, then froze. Not paranoid.

Someone was in the kitchen. Opening drawers. Closing them. Not even trying to be quiet. Backing away, she was half-way across the living room when her 911 call connected.

"What is your emergency?" asked a nasal female voice.

The noise in the kitchen stopped. Gripping her phone, Gaby turned and ran for the door. A hand grabbed her braid, yanking her painfully backward. When she put up her hands instinctively, hard fingers closed around her wrist. Her phone flew through the air, landing on the floor with an ugly crunch and sliding beneath the coffee table.

"Where is it, bitch?"

Gaby sucked in a breath. Spun around to see her ex-husband glaring down at her. *"Julio?"* She hadn't seen him since the day he was arrested at Spencer school, not even when she'd signed the divorce papers. In the year that had passed, he'd become more muscular. Wider. Harder. He'd clearly been working out in Cook County Jail.

Sweat poured down her sides as she tried to swallow her terror. Her stomach heaved, but she managed to choke back the nausea. She couldn't show any weakness in front of him. "What are you doing here? What happened? You're not supposed to be out of...out of there."

His fingers wrapped hard around her wrist, grinding her bones together. "You can say it, Gaby. Why am I out of that hell hole?" He tugged her closer, rage twisting his expression and darkening his eyes. "Just lucky, I guess. They opened the door this morning and said I was free to go. I went."

"Then why are you here?" She didn't dare glance at her phone. She hoped the 911 dispatcher was listening, though. That she'd send the police. "What are you doing in my kitchen?"

He squeezed her wrist, sending pain arcing up her arm. But she refused to cry out. Refused to let him see her pain. That just excited him.

His mouth thinned when she merely stared at him. "You keep money in the house. I need it. Where is it?"

"You think I'm stupid enough to keep money in here? After you stole it the last time?"

"Yeah, I think you're just that stupid." He slapped her, moving so fast that his hand was a blur. Her head snapped back and stars burst behind her eyes. "So get me that money." His already painful grip on her wrist tightened further, and she bit the inside of her cheek to keep from crying out. "Maybe, if you behave yourself, we'll have a little fun before I leave."

His eyes glittered as they swept up her body. Stopped at her breasts. She had to steel herself to hold his gaze. "You always were a good lay."

"Fine." She didn't have to pretend to let her voice quiver. "I'll give you my cash if you promise to leave immediately."

"You don't want to have a little fun in the sack?" He grabbed her breast, crushing it hard enough to bring tears to her eyes. "Maybe I can talk you into it."

He was moving her toward the stairs so easily. Like she weighed no more than a doll. Horror swept over her. She knew what happened next. "Don't...don't you want that money?"

"I'll get it later." He shoved her to the bottom of the staircase. "Once we've had our fun."

Gaby scanned the room, looking for a weapon. Anything that could stop Julio.

There. On the table by the door. The heavy glass bowl that held her keys – a wedding present from Julio's aunt.

She'd only have one chance. She had to make it good.

He pushed her toward the stairs again, and Gaby pretended to stumble. She must have surprised him, because he let go of her wrist.

She put her hands on the table, as if using it to pull her upright. When Julio grabbed her right wrist, she lunged for the bowl with her left hand. Swung it around and smashed it into his face.

Blood spurted out of his nose, and he dropped her hand to cover it. "You bitch!" he screamed.

Gaby smashed the bowl into the side of his face. He staggered, his knees bending, but rose up, murder in his eyes.

She swung again, but as he reached for the newel post to steady himself, his fingers gripped the coat and it fell away. As he floundered, she gripped the bowl with both hands and swung as hard as she could.

With a sickening, hollow thud, the bowl connected with the side of his head. In slow motion, he collapsed on the floor, his legs folding beneath him like an accordion. He sprawled half-on the stairs, blinking but otherwise unmoving.

Gaby scrambled for her phone. Clamping it in a desperate grip, she stepped over Julio's body and threw open the door. It banged into his shin. Hard. It must have opened a cut on his leg, because blood darkened his jeans, and the copper smell of it filled the air.

Pressing a hand to her stomach, as if that could hold back the nausea rolling through her, she slid through the opening and ran down the steps. "Are you still there?" she asked, her voice wobbly.

"Yes. Police are on their way." Gaby began to cry.

"Can you tell me what's going on?" the dispatcher asked, her voice calm and impersonal. Exactly what Gaby needed.

"Julio. He's in my house. He tried...he tried to rape me. Wanted my money."

"Is this your address, Ma'am?" The dispatcher recited numbers and a street. It took Gaby a moment to process.

"Yes," she managed to get out between wrenching sobs.

"The police will be there in less than a minute," the dispatcher said. The click of computer keys filled the silence. "Is he still in the house?"

"I hit him," she said, hiccupping a sob. "In the head. With a bowl. He fell down. I ran outside."

"Can you go to one of your neighbors until the police arrive?"

"I'll...I'll see if anyone's home."

They wouldn't be. Everyone on her block worked. Most of them had two jobs. None of the parents could afford to stay home with their kids. But she needed to be away from the house. If Julio woke up and came after her, he'd kill her.

She'd seen her death in his eyes.

She was three doors down from her own house when she heard the sirens. Moments later, a squad car turned onto her street. Another one followed closely behind. As the police jumped out of the squad, she ran toward them.

"Are you Gabriella Stefano?" one of the officers asked.

"Yes. My ex-husband is in there." She pointed at her house with its still-open front door. "He's supposed to be in prison. I don't know how..." She stopped. Swallowed. She had to get control of herself. "I hit him," she said, a little more calmly. "With a glass bowl. More than once. He finally fell down, and I ran out the door."

A female officer cupped her elbow. "Why don't you sit in the back of our squad car while we check the house?" she said, her voice kind. "For your own safety."

"I..." She glanced at her house and shuddered. Safety?

She wasn't sure if she'd ever feel safe again. "Okay." Her legs trembled, and her chest tightened. "I'd like to sit down."

The woman helped her into the back of the squad car, then leaned in. "I'm going to lock the door, just in case. You won't be able to open it from the inside. Are you all right with that?"

Gaby didn't want to be locked in the back seat of this car. But she nodded. She couldn't get out. But that meant Julio couldn't get in.

Once she was inside the squad car, all four officers drew their guns. Two of them edged down the narrow sidewalk between her house and the one next door. The other two walked up to the front door.

They shoved the door open and ran into the house. Gaby listened, but she didn't hear any sounds. No shouting. No yelling.

No gunshots.

She gripped the arm rest in the door of the squad car, staring at her house. Wondering what was happening inside. Finally, after what seemed like hours, the woman came out of the house and opened the door of the squad car. She squatted next to it, her face level with Gaby's.

"He's gone," she said. "There's blood on the floor, and we found the bowl you used to hit him, but it looks like he ran out the back door. There are drops of blood across your kitchen floor." She scanned Gaby. "Are you bleeding?"

"No." Gaby wrapped her arms around herself. "No blood."

Julio was gone? Terror had short-circuited her brain, and it wasn't processing. She couldn't focus on anything besides the fact that Julio had gotten away. He wasn't in prison, and the police hadn't caught him. He was free to come back and terrorize her again.

And he would. He would be back.

Oh, God. The girls. He could come back and hurt Bella and Cece.

Last year, while Gaby had been at the grocery store, he'd tried to strangle Bella. The girl hadn't told her mother, afraid Julio would punish her for ratting him out.

Gaby closed her eyes and tried to breathe around the frantic terror that filled her chest and cut off her air. Lightheaded, she gripped the armrest as she swayed on the vinyl seat of the police car.

Julio blamed Bella for his arrest. What would he do to her if he found her?

"My girls." Gaby pushed the words out of her frozen chest. She grabbed the police officer's arm. Held it tightly, willing the woman to focus. "He might...he might try to hurt them."

"Where are they?" the officer asked. She dislodged Gaby's fingers gently, then grabbed her radio.

"At...at Spencer Elementary school. Bella is helping Ms. Taylor with her tae kwon do club. Cece is at her French lesson. In the accelerated language program." Gaby wrapped her arms around herself, trying to hold it together. "That's where Julio was arrested. He might go there. He might try to hurt Ms. Taylor, too."

The officer, L. Weldon according to her name badge, cocked her head. "Is that Raine Taylor? Engaged to Connor Donovan?"

"Yes. That's her name. Raine Taylor."

"And your girls are at the school with her."

"Bella is. Cece is in the French class."

Officer Weldon reached for her radio, and Gaby tapped the woman's arm. "If Detective Jennings is available, could you ask him to get them? He knows Bella and Cece. They know him. They might not be as scared if Alex got them."

Weldon cocked her head. "You know Jennings?"

"Yes." Gaby flushed as she pictured the tall, blond detective. "From before. When Julio was arrested. He knew Bella from the tai kwon do club. He comes over to check on us once in a while."

"I'll call the station, see if he's around."

She stood up and walked away. Gaby heard her murmuring on the phone. She glanced over her shoulder at Gaby, then turned and continued talking.

A minute later, she was back. "Jennings is going to get the girls from the school. He'll meet us at the station." She touched Gaby's shoulder. "He's going to call me the moment he has them, so you'll know they're okay. All right?"

Gaby took a deep, trembling breath and let it out slowly. "Okay. That's good. I trust Alex."

The officer squeezed her shoulder, then dropped her hand. "I know you're worried about the girls, but Jennings is on his way to the school. He'll be there in less than ten minutes. I still need your help. Are there any guns in the house your ex-husband might have taken?"

"No." Gaby shuddered. "No guns." Thank God. What if Julio had found a gun? She would probably be dead.

"It looks as though he was searching for something in your kitchen. Any idea what it might have been?"

"Money," she whispered. "I used to keep some cash in the freezer."

"Not any more?" Officer Weldon asked.

Gaby shook her head. "Julio found it before. Stole it. After that, I put it where he couldn't find it."

"Maybe not such a good idea to keep money in the house. In case he comes back."

"He *will* come back," Gaby said, wrapping her arms around her waist. "Not for my money, though. He'll come back because I won. That will eat at him." Yes, Julio would be back. He couldn't bear being bested by a woman.

Her heart fluttered like a frightened bird. She wanted to pack the girls in her ancient Toyota and run. Take off and disappear until Julio was in jail again.

She couldn't. The girls needed to go to school. And so did she.

"Is there someone you can stay with?" Weldon asked.

"I don't know. Maybe. I'll figure something out." She

couldn't endanger any of her friends. Or her family members.

The police officer scribbled something in a small notebook. Then she touched Gaby's hand. As if apologizing in advance. "Can you tell me exactly what happened?"

Her chest clenched as the memories swept over her. She closed her eyes. Counted to ten. This was important. She had to get it right.

She recounted the story, from the moment she walked into the house until the cops arrived. Finally she said, "He's supposed to be in prison. He got a fifteen-year sentence. How did he get out?"

Officer Weldon frowned at her. "What do you mean, he's supposed to be in prison?"

"He was arrested a year ago." Gaby forced herself to breathe deeply. She had to focus. Alex would take care of the girls. She had to do her part, as well.

Another deep breath, and the tightness in her chest eased enough for her to speak more easily. "Julio assaulted Ms. Taylor at the school. Spencer School. A year ago. He tried to beat up the cops who were arresting him. He's been in Cook County Jail ever since. His trial was a month ago. He was convicted and sentenced to fifteen years. So how did he get out of prison?"

"Holy hell." Weldon shoved her hand through her short reddish hair and stood up. "Hey, JJ," she called to one of the other cops. "We have a problem."

CHAPTER 2

Alex sat at his desk, reading a report he'd just finished about an interview with a murder suspect. He made a few corrections and hit 'save'. He was pushing away from his desk to get a cup of coffee when his cell phone rang.

"Jennings," he said as he closed the file.

"Hey, Jennings. Lisa Weldon here. I'm at Gabriella Stefano's house. She had a break-in."

His heart lurched, then began pounding. He stood so fast that his chair caromed into the wall behind him. "Is she okay?" He patted his pocket for his car keys. "What happened?"

"Ms. Stefano is fine, but there's a situation. The guy was her ex. Julio Abrietto. She's afraid he's headed to Spencer School. That's where her daughters are."

"I'm on my way to Spencer." The words were out of his mouth before Weldon finished speaking. "Abrietto is supposed to be in Cook County Jail. On his way to prison. How the hell did he get out?"

"No idea. I'll find out, though."

"You take care of Gaby. I'll have someone here look into it." He ended the call, shoved his phone into his pocket and scanned the bullpen. There. Connor Donovan. His fiancée taught at Spencer. Raine knew Bella.

"Donovan," Alex yelled as he ran toward the other detective's desk. Connor was scowling at his computer, but his head jerked up when he heard Alex.

"Jennings. What's going on?"

"Just had a call from Weldon. She's at Gaby Stefano's house."

Connor frowned, as if trying to place Gaby.

"Bella's mother. From Raine's tae kwon do team."

"Right." Connor nodded, recognition morphing into concern. "What's wrong?"

"Her ex, Abrietto, is out of Cook County. You hear anything about that?"

Connor's eyes narrowed. "Hell, no. The guy's supposed to be transferred to Joliet this week."

"He wasn't. Can you get on the horn and find out what happened? I'm heading over to Spencer."

"Will do." Connor dropped back into his chair, rolled it to his desk and snatched up the phone as Alex ran for the stairs. "Once I get this figured out, I'll be right behind you," Connor called as Alex headed for the stairs.

Alex waved, but he didn't turn around.

Alex threw on the siren and lights as he sped toward the school. Time stretched out and slowed. Dread drummed through his body with every beat of his heart. Bella. Cece.

Gaby.

It took seven minutes to get to Spencer School. Felt like seventy.

He turned off the siren when he was a couple of blocks away, but he kept the lights on. He didn't take a deep breath until he'd parked in front of the school and run inside, his hand on his gun.

There were two girls in the long hall, chatting as they stood at their lockers. The door to the principal's office was open, but Anna Lieu, her secretary, was gone. Through the open door behind Anna's desk, Alex saw Pat Lewinski, staring at her computer monitor.

"Dr. Lewinski." He skidded to a stop in front of Anna's desk.

The principal looked up from her computer. Smiled. "Detective Jennings. What…" Her smile fell away. "What's wrong?"

"You need to lock down the school. Right now."

As he turned to leave, he saw the principal stand up. "What is it?"

"Bella's father. Somehow escaped from Cook County. He went to their house. Might be on his way here. Follow your lock-down protocol."

He ran to the gym, his fingers tightening on his gun. As he yanked the door open, his gaze scanning the gym for signs of Abrietto, he saw only Raine and Bella standing on the mats. Raine was demonstrating a tai kwon do move. Bella was gesturing with her hands, the way she always did when she asked a question. The rest of the girls were gone.

Bella looked over at him and her face lit up. "Alex," she called with a shy smile. "Hi."

"Hey, Bella. Raine." He forced himself to walk slowly. To relax his shoulders. Abrietto wasn't here. If he had been, Raine and Bella would be terrified. Not calm and smiling.

"Where's the rest of the team?" he asked as he approached the mats.

"Changing in the locker room," Raine said. She nudged Bella's shoulder. "Bella wanted to work on a move we showed the girls today."

Alex didn't miss the way Bella glowed at Raine's inclusive 'we'. "Yeah?" he forced himself to say. "Did it go well?"

"It's a new move," Raine said. "It'll take a while."

"Bella, why don't you change your clothes," Alex said. "I need to talk to Ms. Taylor for a minute."

"Okay," the girl said happily, tucking a lock of her dark, wavy hair behind her ear. "I want to talk to Katya anyway."

Alex watched Bella run to the locker room and push

through the door. Then he turned to Raine. "I'm assuming you haven't had any trouble this afternoon."

"What kind of trouble?" she asked, her smile falling away.

Alex glanced at the door. "Bella's former stepfather somehow escaped from Cook County Jail. He showed up at Bella's mom's house."

Raine sucked in a breath. "Is she okay?"

"Yeah, but Abrietto got away. She's afraid he's headed over here. Keep the girls in the locker room for a few minutes. Mrs. L is locking the school down. I'm going to get Cece. I'll be right back." He kept his hand on his gun as he turned and jogged toward the doors.

Two minutes later, he stood in front of a classroom door on the second floor of the building. A volunteer was speaking French to a small group of children, from first graders all the way up to eighth graders. Cede Stefano, a fifth-grader, sat in the first row, rapt.

When the teacher asked a question in French, Cece's hand was the first one in the air. Her dark, wavy hair, so much like her mother's and sister's, hung half-way down her back. Tangled. As if she'd played hard and recess and hadn't combed it out.

He hated to interrupt. He knew how much Cece loved this class. Loved learning French. When she'd found out he spoke the language, she'd run up to him whenever he stopped by the house, chattering away in surprisingly good French.

Gabriella Stefano had managed to raise great kids, in spite of the abusive jerk she'd married a few years ago.

A jerk who was supposed to be locked up for the next fifteen years.

Drawing a deep breath, wriggling his fingers to loosen them, he rapped on the door and stuck his head inside. "Bonjour, Madame. Excusez moi?"

Every head in the room swiveled toward him. "Alex!" Cece beamed at him.

The teacher murmured something to Cece that he couldn't hear, then hurried to the door. She tucked a strand of dark hair behind her ear as she closed the door behind her.

"May I help you?" she asked in a cool voice.

He showed her his badge. "Detective Alex Jennings. I need Cece Stefano. Her former stepfather has escaped from prison and may be headed to Spencer. Mrs. Lewinski is locking down the building, but I need to have Cece and Bella where I can see them." He wasn't letting them out of his sight until they were face to face with Gaby.

The teacher studied him for a long moment, then scrutinized his badge. She pulled her cell phone from her pocket and pressed a button. "Mrs. Lewinski, this is Chantal Renoir. There's a man at my door who says he's a Chicago police detective. He wants to take Cece Stefano with him."

Her gaze flickered to his as she listened. Her shoulders tensed as she said, "Thank you, Pat. Yes. I'll keep the rest of the students occupied."

Ending the call, she nodded at Alex. "I'll get her."

Alex nodded back. "Thank you for double-checking."

The woman's eyes softened. "Take care of her," she said.

"I will."

Moments later, Cece hurried out the door, her backpack dragging along the yellowed hardwood floor. It looked as if it weighed twice as much as the short, slender child. "Alex!" she said, grinning, her eyes sparkling. As if seeing him was a special treat. His heart twisted in his chest. There was a place in hell reserved for men like Abrietto, worthless pieces of shit who abused women and kids.

The asshole would have to go through him to get to these children or Gaby.

"What are you doing here?" Cece bounced along beside him, her backpack thudding against the floor. He took it from her and slung it over his own shoulder.

"I'm taking you and Bella to meet your mother." Thank

God the kid wasn't speaking French. He wasn't sure he could keep it together if she was questioning him in her adorable French accent.

Cece frowned. "Mommy has school tonight. She's supposed to be doing her homework."

"She's probably working on it now." He didn't want to scare Cece. He'd let Gaby explain what had happened. And he'd be there to help her.

"Okay. Is Bella still doing her Kung Fu Panda thing?"

Alex muffled a snort of laughter. "I think she's finished. She was talking to Ms. Taylor when I left them."

Alex turned into the stairwell, raising his hand to signal Cece to be quiet.

Nothing. No breathing noises in the staircase, no sounds drifting up from the first floor. No tension in the air.

Drawing a deep, relieved breath, he started down the stairs, holding out his hand for Cece. She gripped it, completely trusting. As they crept down the stairs, he had a flashback to another time he'd run down a set of stairs with a child.

Afghanistan. A house on the outskirts of a tiny village in the mountains. That time, the child was in his arms. Whimpering from the pain of broken ribs and a gunshot wound in his thigh. He'd survived the massacre of his family by rolling under a bed.

Alex had covered the boy's mouth with his hand, trying to prevent his sobs from alerting the Taliban fighters he could practically smell in the field behind the house.

But he felt every one of the boy's painful inhalations. Every tiny jerk of his body against the pain.

That child had survived. Alex's team had gotten him out of the village, onto a chopper and back to their base, where his wounds had been tended by a doctor. Alex had been airlifted out himself before he found out if they'd managed to find any of the kid's relatives.

Alex snapped back to the present. Cece wasn't injured.

Wasn't going to be.

When they emerged onto the first floor, the hall was deserted. He hurried toward the gym and opened the door. Their footsteps echoed in the empty gym as they walked toward the locker room. Before they reached it, Alex heard the chatter of the teens on the team – high-pitched. Giggling. The occasional squeal.

Completely normal.

Taking a deep breath, he stuck his head in the door. "Raine?"

She appeared from around the corner, smiling when she spotted him with the younger girl. "Hey, Cece. Why don't you go find Bella?"

He put his hand on Cece's shoulder to keep her with him. "Any other way into the locker room?" he asked Raine in a low voice.

"Nope. Just a few windows, but they're made of those wavy glass blocks with a tiny screen in the middle."

"Great." He squeezed Cece's shoulder, then let her go. "Cece, why don't you get the rest of the girls? We'll all play basketball for a while."

Cece scrambled toward the locker room door, and Raine nudged his shoulder. "Never figured you for a Disney Princess guy," she said, poking the backpack and lifting one eyebrow.

"Go ahead and mock. All the cool cops have Disney Princess backpacks."

Her smile fell away. "Have you heard anything?"

"No." He glanced around the gym. "I'll be right back. I want to make sure the school doors are locked." He wouldn't be out of sight of the gym door.

* * *

An hour later, all the kids had been reunited with their parents and Alex herded Bella and Cece toward his car. As soon as they were in the back seat, belted in, Alex pulled away from the curb.

"What's going on, Alex?" Bella demanded. "You said you were taking us to meet Mom. Why did it take so long?"

What the hell was he supposed to say? What would Gaby *want* him to say? He wasn't their parent. If it was up to him, he'd tell them exactly why it took so long. He'd warn them about Abrietto.

But he didn't have the right to tell them what had happened. He didn't want to terrify them. It was up to Gaby to explain to them.

"Your mom is waiting for you at the station," he finally said. "She's fine. I'll let her fill you in."

"Is someone hurt?" Bella demanded, leaning forward as far as the seat belt would allow. "Dead?"

This fear, this jumping to the worst possible conclusion, was Abrietto's fault. His poisoned legacy to these two children. Alex clenched his jaw, but managed to squash his anger enough to say, "No one's hurt or dead. As far as I know."

"Then why are we going to your police station?"

"Your mom will explain, okay?"

"Do you think I'm a baby?" Bella demanded. "That I can't handle it?"

"Of course not." He rolled to a stop at a red light and closed his eyes. Just this once, he wished Bella wasn't so smart. So quick.

A car honked. He opened his eyes to a green light, and the car lurched forward into the intersection. "We'll be there in three minutes. Your mom will explain."

Bella huffed in the back seat, and Alex concentrated on arriving safely at the station. After he parked in the lot, he led the girls through the back door and up the stairs toward the bull pen.

He spotted Gaby, sitting at his desk. In his chair, and his stupid heart lurched. She looked like she belonged there. Like she was claiming him and his space.

He was an idiot.

Mia and Quinn were with her, Mia perched on the edge of the desk. Mia was laughing and gesturing, and Gaby smiled and nodded, but she looked…distracted. As if her mind was elsewhere.

"Mommy!" Cece shouted, dashing toward her, and Gaby turned to look, exhaling as if she'd been holding her breath since she walked into the station. Her shoulders relaxed as she stood to sweep Cece into a fierce hug.

She grabbed Bella when her older daughter got close and squeezed her tightly. She held both children for a little too long, her eyes closed, her face pressed against their shiny, dark hair. Gaby's own wavy hair, a perfect match for her daughters', spilled over her shoulders.

Finally, when Bella began to squirm, Gaby let them go. Bella straightened her purple long-sleeved tee shirt and glanced around furtively, as if assessing whether anyone had seen her hugging her mom. Trying to decide if the cops in the room thought she was lame.

Reassured when it looked as if no one was paying attention, Bella rolled her shoulders. Stuck out her chin at Gaby. "What's going on, Mom? Why did Alex come to Spencer and drag Cece out of her French class? Why did we have to hang around for so long after practice?"

"Mommy! Your hair's not in a braid," Cece said, reaching up to touch the rippling waves.

Gaby smoothed a hand over it, a flash of fear in her eyes. He'd ask her about that later.

"I felt like wearing it down after I got home," she said. Her tone of voice was casual, but he heard the tension beneath her words. "I must have braided it too tightly this morning. It hurt a little."

"You're changing the subject," Bella said, stepping closer to her mother. "What happened?"

Gaby shot him an anxious look, as if unsure what to tell her daughters. Alex wanted to sweep *her* into *his* arms and make sure she was okay. Find out what that asshat had done to her. But he couldn't do it in front of her kids.

Hell, he didn't have the right to do that at all. He was merely a friend of the family. The guy who'd held her hand after Abrietto had been arrested and her life was falling apart.

So he sucked in a breath, forced a casual smile and nodded at Gaby. "Hey, Gaby."

"Alex." She smiled at him, but her mouth trembled. "How…what…" She wanted to ask him what to tell the girls. He saw the plea in her eyes.

"How about we get out of here?" he said. "Maybe grab a pizza. We can go to that place the girls like." The one with the arcade, so he could give the girls tokens and talk to Gaby while they were playing.

Both girls' faces lit up. Between working as a teacher's aide and paying for her college courses, Alex was pretty sure Gaby's budget didn't include going out for pizza. Maybe he'd distracted the girls enough to put off their questions until he and Gaby could talk.

"Okay." She swallowed and glanced at her watch. "But we have to go now. I have class tonight."

Alex frowned. She was going to class? After what had happened? Maybe it wasn't as bad as he'd thought. Alex let out the breath he'd been holding all afternoon. "Let's go, then. You can call and order pizzas on the way."

Twenty minutes later, the girls standing at games in the arcade where Gaby could see them, Alex took her hand. Her fingers trembled beneath his. "Can you tell me what happened today?"

CHAPTER 3

Gaby's hand trembled when Alex laid his fingers over hers. His expression softened, as if he thought she was trembling because of Julio's attack earlier.

That was part of it. But the biggest reason was Alex himself. Touching her as if she was precious. Important.

As if he wanted to reassure her.

It had been so long since a man had touched her with...care.

She slid her hand from his, knowing she needed to focus on Julio. What had happened. How to protect Bella and Cece from their former step-father.

Disappointment flickered across Alex's face. She'd hurt him. She fluttered her fingertips over his hand lightly, all she could allow herself. "Thank you, Alex. For going to Spencer. Making sure the girls were okay." She swallowed. "I feel foolish that they had to lock the school down. I'm not sure Julio would even think of going there."

"No." Alex leaned closer, his blue eyes laser-focused. On her. "Don't feel bad about that. You were right to tell Weldon about the girls being at the school. And *I* told them to lock the place down." He curled his fingers around hers again, making every nerve beneath her skin burn. She slid her fingers away from his and into her lap, cupping the place his caress had set fire to her skin.

"The kids who were still in the school were fine." Alex continued as if he had no idea how his touch affected her. "Once Pat Lewinski reassured them that it was just a precaution, they acted like it was a big party." He squeezed her shoulder. "Can you tell me what happened with Abrietto?"

Gaby drew in a deep, steadying breath. If she didn't want Alex to know how scared she'd been, how helpless she'd felt, she had to keep it together. She would *not* fall apart in front of him. "I had just gotten home from Stella School," she began.

Ten minutes later, she finished, "And then the cops showed up." Alex had taken her hand again halfway through her uncomfortable recitation. His fingers were reassuring. Steady. She never wanted to let him go, but she gently drew her hand away and took a shaky breath. "What do I tell the girls?"

Alex reached out, then let his hand drop. "I don't have kids," he finally said. "So I could be way off base. But I think you need to tell them Abrietto somehow got out of jail. They need to know he might come around again. That they have to be careful. Watch what they do, where they go."

"I can't tell them what he wanted…" She swallowed the remembered terror. "What he tried to do."

"Of course not. They don't need to know that. But I think you can tell them you defended yourself. Scared him away. They need to know you stood up to him."

"Because I didn't stand up to him before." The shame of what had happened with Julio, and even worse, what she'd done to Bella, made her close her eyes. But it couldn't erase the images that played on an endless loop in her head. "I was such a bad example to them. That's something I can never erase from their memories."

Alex shifted his chair closer. "Gaby." He lifted her chin. "Listen to me. Yeah, you made mistakes. We all do. But you did the right thing in the end. You divorced him. He ordered you to pay for his defense attorney, but you didn't do it. You and the girls all went to therapy. Don't let what happened in the past taint what you did today. Standing up to Julio? Defending yourself? You should be proud of that."

Somehow he'd taken her hand again. As if he knew, even when she resisted, that she wanted to cling to him, to wrap her fingers around his and let his strength flow into her.

Before she could make a fool of herself, their waitress appeared with two large pizzas on a tray. "Our food's here," she said, slipping her hand out of Alex's and standing up. "I'll get the girls."

Fifteen minutes later, the girls had each eaten a few pieces of cheese pizza. Gaby had managed to choke down one piece of pepperoni and mushroom. Dropping the crust on her plate, she drew a deep breath. "Bella, Cece, you need to know what happened today. Why your school was on lock down."

Bella narrowed her eyes at her. "I knew something fishy was going on." She switched her gaze to Alex, and Gaby cringed at the angry, sulky look she gave him. "Why didn't *you* tell me at the school?"

"It was something you needed to hear from your mother," he said calmly. "And if I'd told you, the other kids at the school would have figured out something was wrong. Which would have been better? Everyone freaking out? Or everyone staying calm and having fun?"

If Bella stuck her lower lip out any farther, a plane could land on it. But Gaby knew better than to tell her that in public. So she bit her tongue and waited.

Finally, Bella said grudgingly, "Better that everyone stayed calm."

"Yes. Much better."

Gaby took a breath, let it out slowly. Time for her to take charge and tell the girls. "Julio came to the house today."

She outlined what had happened, trying to minimize her terror and emphasize that she'd defended herself. That he'd run away. "If he's smart," she concluded, "he won't come back. He'll know we're looking for him, and that we'll call the police if we see him. But you both need to be careful until they catch him."

Alex nodded at Bella. "You have a phone, right, Bella?"

"Yeah," she said around a mouthful of pizza.

"Make sure you keep it with you. Cece, how about you?"

"I don't get a phone until I'm in seventh grade," she said with a pout. "Most of the kids in my class already have one."

Gaby rolled her eyes, but her shoulders relaxed. Cece wheedled and whined about a phone all the time. Somehow, hearing the familiar complaints today, after everything that had happened, cheered her up.

"Keep it up, Cece, and it will be eighth grade before you get a phone."

Her younger daughter opened her mouth to respond, caught Gaby's eye and shoved her pizza in her mouth instead. Smart girl.

"We have some old phones at the station that we use for emergency situations," Alex said. He glanced at Gaby. "I think this counts as an emergency. Could I get one for Cece until Julio is back where he belongs?"

Truthfully, Gaby would feel better if she could get hold of both girls any time she needed to talk to them. "Thank you, Alex. That would be great."

"I'll bring one by tomorrow," he promised.

Gaby glanced at her watch. "We have to go," she said. "I need to get to school."

The girls stood up and Gaby nodded toward the bathroom, reminding them to go wash their hands. When they had disappeared into the ladies' room, Alex turned to

Gaby. "Who stays with the girls while you're at school?"

"Bella normally watches Cece."

"I'm not sure that's a great idea right now. Maybe you should skip school tonight. Stay home with them."

Gaby's stomach twisted tighter. "I wasn't going to leave them at home. They're coming with me." They would sit in the back of the room and do their homework. Read a book when they finished. It wasn't what she wanted, but she didn't have a choice.

"You can't skip class one night?"

"I already missed one when I had to take Cece to the urgent care. If I miss another class, my grade goes down."

"Okay," he said slowly. "Then how about I stay with them? They'd be at home, and they'd be safe. And you could concentrate on your class."

"Thank you, Alex. But I couldn't let you do that."

She wasn't going to lean on Alex – she had to learn to manage on her own. As a wife at nineteen, she'd leaned on her husband. Then she'd leaned on Julio. She was an adult, for God's sake. From now on, she was managing her own life.

"I'll be happy to stay with them. We'd have a good time." He tilted his head, watching her.

She remembered the way her hand tingled when he touched her. This is what had gotten her in trouble before. Leaping before she figured out her next moves. Jumping in too soon, before she'd thought everything through.

Alex wasn't an abuser. She'd spent enough time with him to realize that. He'd been helpful after Julio was arrested. He'd come over regularly, usually bringing pizza. He was great with the girls.

Not just the girls. The electricity that crackled between her and Alex was sexual awareness. Their attraction had hummed beneath the surface for the last year, the constant subtext to his visits. Although he'd been coming over less frequently lately.

He made her stomach jump and her heart pound. Who

wouldn't be interested in the tall detective with the wide shoulders, the blue eyes, the wavy blond hair? The sweet, thoughtful man who had been so kind to them after Julio was arrested?

He was interested, as well. But he'd never acted on it. Never said or did anything out of line. He was a friend of the family. Nothing more.

Even though in her secret dreams, she wished he was.

"I can't let you stay with them, Alex," she said with a sigh.

"Why not? Sounds like a win-win for all of us."

She puffed out a breath. "Hardly a win for you. I have...I have to learn to manage on my own. Not to let people do things for me. That's how I got in trouble with Julio. In the beginning, I took what he offered, without a thought. When things got bad, I let it go on. I made so many wrong choices. Every time I didn't throw Julio out when he..."

He put his hand over her mouth. "Gaby, stop."

His hand smelled of almonds. Something sweet underlying it. Soap, probably. The kind you'd find in a restaurant. Or a police station.

She closed her eyes and inhaled once more, fixing his scent in her memory, then pulled his hand away from her mouth before she did something stupid. Like kiss it.

She couldn't take what she wanted. Even if it was only an offer to watch the girls for her.

She opened her eyes to find him watching her again. Studying her with those blue, blue eyes, as if probing for her deepest secrets.

"Why do you stop me from speaking the truth?" she asked, her voice calm. Her marriage to Julio was the shame that clung to her like the sticky strands of a spider web. "I should have divorced Julio the first time he hit me."

"You think I haven't made mistakes, Gaby?" His expression darkened, as if old, unwelcome memories swirled in their depths. "Everyone does. You learn from it, get over it and move on."

"Some things are easier to get over than others." She spotted the girls coming out of the washroom and stood up. "Thank you for dinner," she said. "This was...great. The girls loved it."

"And you, Gaby?" His gaze bored into her. "Did you love it, too?"

"I always like pizza. And it was nice, not having to cook." She turned and slung on her coat to get away from the intensity in his eyes. "The girls and I will make you dinner one night."

"Sounds great," he said, standing as well.

"Get your coats on, girls," she said to Bella and Cece. "We need to get home and pick up the car. You're coming with me to class tonight."

Right on schedule, Bella rolled her eyes. "I hate going to class with you. Those desks are uncomfortable. And your professor is completely lame."

Gaby raised her eyebrows. "Because she says hello to you in front of the class?"

When Bella scowled, Cece piped up. "I like going with you," the girl said, bouncing on her toes. "Your teacher lets us chew gum in class. That's awesome."

"It doesn't matter what you like or don't like. Alex is going to take us home so we can get the car." She glanced at him to make sure, and he nodded once. "You'll bring your books so you can do your homework."

As the girls shrugged into their coats, Alex drew her away and put his hand on her arm. "Please reconsider," he said, his voice low. She appreciated that he didn't ask in front of the girls. "Let me stay with them while you go to school?"

"I know you have better things to do." She had to bite her lip to keep from saying yes.

"Nope. Was planning on getting some takeout and watching the 'Cats game. Seeing if Marino, that hot rookie, is as good as everyone says he is. Hanging out with Bella and Cece sounds like a lot more fun."

"Yes!" Cece tugged on her hand as they walked through the parking lot. "Say yes, mommy. Please. I want to stay home with Alex."

Apparently, they hadn't been quiet enough.

"Yeah, Mom, why can't Alex stay with us?" Bella asked. "He's my friend. I haven't seen him in a while. I want to watch the 'Cats with him."

Alex didn't say a thing. He didn't push. Gaby closed her eyes, surrendering to the eagerness in the girl's eyes and her own relief at not having to drag them to school with her. "All right. Just this once. But we're going to owe him a couple of dinners."

Alex flashed the smile that never failed to cause butterflies to flutter in her stomach. "I'll take it. Home-cooked meals in exchange for hanging out with Bella and Cece? I'm making out like a bandit here."

He wasn't gloating. Wasn't getting all cocky about muscling his way through a crack in the wall she'd erected. It wouldn't happen again, though.

As they stepped into the parking lot, Alex's smile disappeared as he scanned the parked cars. The sky was the royal blue of dusk, and shadows lurked between the cars. His alertness, his tension, made Gaby's anxiety swell.

Was this what it was going to be like until they caught Julio? Was she going to jump at every shadow? Cringe every time she heard a sudden noise?

She wanted to tell herself she was stronger than that. Wanted to believe that Julio was smart enough to stay away from her. But she knew neither was true.

Julio blamed Bella for his arrest – Raine Taylor, her tae kwon do coach, had goaded him into a fight because she'd seen the bruises on Bella's neck. He blamed Gaby for leaving him in jail instead of paying his bond.

He wanted to punish both her and Bella. Raine as well.

And Gaby wasn't strong enough to face the monsters that lurked in the shadows. She was getting there, one agonizing therapy session at a time. But the guilt she carried would never completely disappear.

She wasn't sure she wanted it to. Because if she forgot what she'd done, she might do it again. Hurt her children again.

Cece and Bella had lost their father to a drunken driver. After struggling with Antony's death, she'd allowed an abuser to enter their lives, their *home*, with all the chaos and pain that came with that.

Her children had been hurt far too much in their young lives.

She couldn't, *wouldn't* forget what happened when she let her impulses control her. She'd lock them down so deep that they couldn't threaten her family again.

Starting with the feelings Alex Jennings stirred in her.

CHAPTER 4

Alex muted the television and turned to the girls. They all sat on the couch, Bella on one side of him, and Cece on the other, the empty popcorn bowl in front of them on the coffee table. Both girls stared at the television as if riveted by the 'Cats game. He couldn't tell if it was genuine interest, or merely an attempt to avoid bedtime.

"You guys need to go to bed," he said after glancing at his watch. "Your mom will be home soon, and she won't be happy I let you stay up this late."

"Not yet," Cece begged.

"I want to see how the game ends," Bella protested.

Alex bit the inside of his cheek to keep from smiling. Cece's eyelids had been drooping for the last half an hour, and he'd caught Bella stifling several yawns.

Bella knew a lot about baseball – she'd apparently been paying attention when they'd watched games last summer and fall. Tonight, she'd been attentive to the game and asked a lot of questions.

Cece had been thrilled she got to stay up past her bedtime. Alex had only a tiny spasm of guilt – he was pretty sure Gaby wouldn't blame him for distracting the girls until they were tired enough to fall right to sleep.

"Just one more inning?" Bella tried to look pitiful, but spoiled it by yawning again.

"Nope. You have school tomorrow. You were supposed to be in bed an hour ago." He raised one eyebrow as he waited for them to head upstairs. Finally, with Bella rolling her eyes, they tromped up to their bedrooms.

Once they disappeared to the second story, he left the television muted. He didn't need the commentators to know what was happening in the baseball game.

Instead, he listened to the girls' chatter as they got ready for bed. Cece giggled as she dashed into the bathroom first, ignoring Bella's outraged shriek. Bella pounded on the door and yelled at her to hurry up.

A few minutes later, their feud forgotten, Bella went into Cece's room. Bella's voice drifted down the stairs as she read to her younger sister. Before long, the floor creaked as Bella returned to her own room, and it took only a few minutes before silence settled on the house.

Alex glanced toward the second floor where the girls were, he hoped, asleep. In spite of Abrietto and everything that had happened in the past year, Cece and Bella seemed to be happy, well-adjusted kids. Although Gaby probably had a tight budget, with paying for nursing school and caring for two kids on a teacher's aide's salary, Bella and Cece were really lucky. As far as Alex could see, they'd won the parent lottery.

His smile faded as memories of his own childhood escaped from the box where he kept them locked away. No one had ever needed to remind him to go upstairs to bed. He'd run to his room as soon as dinner ended, only breathing deeply once he'd escaped the tension swirling around his silent, reserved parents in the dining room.

In his room, he'd had his own television and game console. His sister had had the same. Sometimes she'd sneak into his room to watch TV with him, or play a game.

But Theresa had mostly hidden in her room, as well.

Gaby's obvious love for her children, and the way she always wanted them close by, was completely different from the way he'd been raised. His wealthy, distant parents weren't around much, completely absorbed by their jobs and the charities they supported.

The housekeeper, Nonna, had been his and Theresa's substitute parent. She was the one waiting for them when they got home from school. Nonna always greeted them with a smile and a hug, listening raptly as he and Theresa took turns telling her about their day.

Until the afternoon she was gone when he and Theresa arrived home from school.

His mother had been there, instead. She'd told them they were old enough to manage on their own after school. Thirteen-year-old Alex and ten-year-old Theresa had begged their mother to let Nonna come back. Theresa had sobbed when her mother replied flatly that Nonna was gone for good. Alex and Theresa were getting too attached to Nonna. The Italian immigrant wasn't the kind of role model her children needed. She would come home early from work to supervise them.

Gaby didn't supervise her children. She loved *them.*

Alex had sniffled. Wiped his eyes surreptitiously. *A Jennings didn't cry,* his mother had snapped at them. Her mouth thinning, she'd told them to go to their rooms and start their homework.

Alex had left home and enrolled in the Navy as soon as he graduated from college. Theresa...

He jumped up from the couch and headed into the kitchen, shoving the memories away. He could examine them all he wanted – it wouldn't change a thing. Instead of brooding over old news, he needed to focus on things he could control – what he could do to help Gaby. Make sure her house was secure.

The kitchen was a mess – fingerprint dust on the counters, drawers hanging open, the back door broken. Abrietto must have kicked it in. Two hinges had been torn from the wall and the door listed crookedly, held up by the final hinge. The cops who'd responded to the call had braced it with a kitchen chair. The night sky was visible in the gap between the door and the jamb, and a stream of chilly air cooled the kitchen.

Alex moved the chair, opened the door just wide enough to slip through, and went to the garage. In the dim light provided by the bare lightbulb in the ceiling, he scrounged a few pieces of scrap lumber, a hammer and some nails. Returning to the house, he set them on the floor beside the door. As soon as Gaby was home and inside, he'd nail the door shut.

Lowering himself onto the couch again, he ignored the baseball game and glanced at his phone. Ten-thirty. Gaby would be home any minute.

He smothered the anticipation that tightened his chest. He was a jerk for even thinking about Gaby that way, after what had happened earlier with Abrietto. She'd been traumatized, for God's sake. Completely shaken. Alex needed to be a friend. Supportive. Helpful. Cheerful.

Completely non-threatening. Non-sexual.

He couldn't be the guy who spent his nights fantasizing about Gaby and her dark, wavy hair. Her deep green eyes. The curves he'd dreamt about touching so many times.

The rumble of the garage door opening made him jump off the couch and open the back door, being careful not to break it completely. The garage light glowed through the window on the side of the building, spreading a golden radiance over Gaby's garden and the tiny sprouts barely poking up from the soil.

Hand on his gun, he ran down the steps and scanned the backyard. A dark cat slinked through the bushes, jumped on the fence and dropped into the next yard. Lights burned in about half of the houses – in this working-class neighborhood, people went to bed early.

No footsteps in the alley. No noise from the neighboring houses. The cat had disappeared silently – Alex couldn't even hear it rustling the leaves beneath the bushes.

As soon as the side door in the garage opened, Alex hurried toward Gaby. She flinched when she spotted him. Sucked in a breath as if getting ready to scream. But her shoulders relaxed when she realized who it was.

"Alex," she sighed. "You didn't have to come outside to meet me. It's chilly for April."

He wanted to do so much more for her than meet her outside the garage. Pushing that thought away, he allowed himself to brush a hand over her shoulder. "And miss the chance to show off for you?" he said lightly. "I wasn't about to let you walk through this dark yard alone."

She stilled for a moment, and he swore he felt heat shimmering off her. Was she blushing? Then she rolled her shoulders. "You don't have to show off for me, Alex," she murmured, her voice barely more than a whisper in the cool, still night air. "I already know…"

Her throat rippled as she swallowed the rest of her words. He really wanted to know what she'd begun to say, but he kept his mouth closed. He wouldn't push. He'd been holding himself back since the first time he met her, and he'd continue to hold back until she was ready to think of him as more than a friend.

"You're going to have to slide through that small opening in the door," he said as they reached her porch. "It's broken. Once we're inside, I'm going to nail it shut. It's too late to get someone over here tonight to replace it, but I'll call a guy I know first thing in the morning."

Gaby studied the door as it listed to one side, held up by a single hinge. "Julio did that."

"Yeah. Asshole kicked the door in. It'll be fixed tomorrow, though." He'd make sure she got a sturdier door and a stronger lock, too.

"You don't need to worry about the door," she said as she slid inside. "I'll call someone in the morning and take a personal day tomorrow."

She probably wouldn't get paid for it, either. He

followed her inside, then closed the door and used a two-by-four to nail the door in place. Once he was finished, he set the nails and hammer on the kitchen counter.

"Why don't you let me handle that?" he said. "There's a guy we always use to replace doors and locks at..." He stopped abruptly. He was an idiot. He hadn't thought this through.

"At what?" She tilted her head as she waited for him to continue.

"At crime scenes," he said reluctantly.

Gaby glanced around the kitchen, biting her lip. "You don't have to be afraid to say it, Alex. That's what my house is now. A crime scene."

Getting a new door was the first step in replacing Gaby's memories of the dirty, ransacked room and how it had gotten that way. "You need a new door installed tomorrow so Julio can't break in again. My guy will be able to do it."

"You think he's coming back, don't you?" she asked as she dumped her messenger bag over the back of a chair. She slung her jacket onto a peg in the coat rack, then rubbed the back of her neck. As if trying to erase that deer-in-the-headlights sensation he knew she was feeling.

"If he's smart, Abrietto will stay as far away from you as possible." It wasn't an answer, but Gaby knew the truth as well as he did.

She snorted a tired laugh. "He's not smart, though. Julio is too hot-headed to think things through. If *I'd* escaped from jail, I'd get as far from Chicago as I could. He has a couple of cousins in Florida. He should have gone there."

She closed her eyes, then glanced at him. "He's not going to Florida, though, is he?"

"No," he said gently. "I don't think he is. But you're right about him – he's all impulse and temper. Which is why we'll catch him sooner rather than later."

He put his hand on her back to nudge her toward the living room. "Come watch the end of the 'Cats game with me. You want a beer?"

She glanced toward the refrigerator. "I'm so tired. I feel like a wet rag, limp and wrung out. As if I'll start to cry any moment. If I have a beer, I'll pass out while I'm crying."

"Maybe you need to just pass out. Leave this day behind." He opened the fridge, pulled out two bottles of Goose Island Green Line. "Although I'm a little disturbed that my company will put you to sleep."

A genuine smile lit her eyes briefly. "Never, Alex. I wouldn't fall asleep on you."

"Then sit and relax for a few minutes. Watch the end of the 'Cats game. Let me tell you about what great kids you have." He herded her gently toward the other room, where the baseball game flickered silently on the television.

She folded herself into the couch with a sigh. "That's one thing no one has to tell me. I know how lucky I am to have Bella and Cece. They've been through a lot, but they're still sweet, down-to-earth kids."

"You're a really good mother, Gaby. Yeah, Bella's a typical teen-aged girl, all attitude and lip. Just like my sister at her age. But underneath that attitude, Bella's a sweetheart. And Cece? She's completely adorable. She was trying out her French on me again tonight. I'm going to have to brush up, or I'm going to embarrass myself around her."

"Thank you," Gaby said quietly.

"For what? Liking your kids? Believe me, Gaby. It's not a hardship."

"For being such a good role model for them. For showing them that not every man is like Julio." She swallowed. "They were so young when Antony died. Bella was seven, and Cece was only three. Cece barely remembers him. And Bella's memories are fading, too."

What was he supposed to say? That he'd love to continue to be a role model? That he wanted to be more than a casual friend? To all three of them?

He took a long drink of his beer and let his hand drop to the couch cushion. Gaby's hand was inches away, her fingers spread flat on the cushion, and he wanted to reach for it. To slide his fingers over that silky skin. To press a kiss to her palm. Instead, he curled his fingers around the beer bottle and watched the Pirates make the final out of the game. The 'Cats won, 8 to 7.

He wished the game had gone into extra innings. Given him an excuse to stay longer. Maybe find the guts to inch closer to Gaby's hand.

Gaby set her half-empty bottle on the coffee table, next to the popcorn bowl. "Thank you for staying with the girls, Alex. I really appreciate it."

That was his signal to leave. He glanced toward the nailed-up door in the kitchen. It wouldn't take much for someone to kick that door in again. "Why don't you let me stay tonight?"

She froze, staring at him. The faint tinge of red on her cheeks told him where her mind had gone.

He hadn't meant it that way. But he was damn happy to see that was where her mind went. Maybe...

No. "On the couch," he said quickly. "If I leave you alone in this house, I won't sleep anyway. I'll be up all night, thinking about that broken door."

"You already spent your evening here," she said. Her gaze darted from his eyes to his mouth. Jerked back to his eyes. That hint of pink darkened in her cheeks.

Forcing himself to ignore it, he took another drink of beer to moisten his suddenly dry throat. "Doing the same thing I would have done if I'd been at home." His bottle rattled on the table as he set it beside hers.

"I feel as if I'm taking advantage of you, Alex." She grabbed her bottle and stared at it for a moment, then began to pick at the label.

He leaned closer, catching a hint of ginger, rising fresh and delicious from her skin. "Please, Gaby. I want you to take advantage of me."

He held her gaze, and color suffused Gaby's face. She knew exactly what he meant. She swayed closer, her eyes darkening as her pupils grew larger. When she blinked slowly, there was only a small rim of green and gold around the black.

His voice was a low rasp from his suddenly tight throat. "I know you have a lot going on. I'll wait until you're ready." He leaned closer, though, pulled toward her by an inexorable force.

Gaby didn't move away. She stared at him, her mouth slightly open, her chest rising and falling too fast.

He pulled back just in time as he heard the quiet thump of footsteps on the stairs. When he turned, Bella stood there, watching him and Gaby. She scowled at them, her gaze flicking from Gaby's face to his.

"What are you guys doing?" she demanded.

Gaby leapt up, grabbing the beer bottles and the popcorn bowl. "Watching the Bearcats win their game," she said evenly. "I wasn't about to kick Alex out before he saw how it ended." She paused with the bowl clutched to her chest. "Why did you come down, Bella? Is something wrong?"

Bella's scowl turned harder. "I heard voices. I wanted to make sure nothing was wrong."

"Everything's fine, baby," Gaby said with a soft smile. "Go on upstairs. I'll come kiss you goodnight in a few minutes."

"I'm not a baby," she glowered as she turned and flounced up the stairs.

"I need to go," Gaby said. "She's upset."

"Then I'm going to crash on your couch." He touched her mouth as she began to speak, then curled his fingers into his palm at the burn. "For my sake as much as yours. Please, Gaby. I was telling the truth. I won't be able to sleep if I'm worrying about you."

"I should say no." She studied him for a long moment, then her gaze darted toward the kitchen and the broken door. "But I'll feel better, knowing you're down here. I'll get you a pillow and some blankets."

She turned and disappeared up the stairs, returning in a couple of minutes with a pillow covered by soft blue cotton and two thick, gray blankets. She set them on the couch, then took his hand.

"Thank you, Alex. You're...you're a lifesaver. I'll see you in the morning."

She leaned closer, as if to kiss him, then reared back. She stared at him for a long moment, her eyes wide and shocked. Then she fled up the stairs, disappearing without another glance.

CHAPTER 5

Alex sat on the couch, listening to the sounds drifting down the stairs. Murmurs of voices – one of them Gaby's. Even in a crowd, he'd be able to pick out her voice. Something in his head was uniquely tuned to her soft, low tones.

The other had to be Bella. That sulky, huffy voice definitely belonged to a teenager.

The voices stopped, and doors closed. Water pipes rumbled, and he wondered if Gaby was taking a shower. Closing his eyes to block out the images his mind conjured, he buried his face in the pillow.

A faint scent of ginger rose lightly. Gaby. She'd given him a pillow from her own bed.

Cursing silently, he tossed the pillow onto the couch, threw the blankets over it and lay down. Footsteps moved across the floor, directly above him. Gaby. Getting ready for bed.

Pushing the images that thought conjured out of his head, he squirmed on his lumpy bed. His feet hung over the arm of the too-short couch. If he bent his knees to fit, he was twisted like a pretzel. He shifted on the pillow, and

Gaby surrounded him. He stilled, hoping that would help. It didn't. Finally, surrendering to the impulse, he buried his face in the pillow and breathed deeply. Imagined Gaby lying beside him.

He lay awake in the dark house, his body aching, too aware of his surroundings to fall asleep. The house had gone still and silent, but he was still revved.

It wasn't because he was afraid Abrietto would sneak in if Alex fell asleep. He'd wake instantly if he heard an unusual noise, courtesy of his years as a SEAL. That hyperawareness never really went away.

And yeah, the couch wasn't built for someone his size. His cramped legs felt as if they'd been folded into a box. That wasn't keeping him awake, either. Compared to some of the places he'd slept, this uncomfortable, too-short couch was luxurious.

He'd fallen asleep in holes on top of mountains in hostile territory, surrounded by Taliban fighters. He'd slept in snow and rain. Mud. The blazing heat of the desert sun. So why was a couch in a living room in Chicago such a problem?

It wasn't the couch. It was Gaby, surrounding him every time he moved his head on the soft cotton pillowcase. The knowledge that she slept in her bed right above him.

The memory of sitting beside her, drinking beer, watching television wasn't helping, either. For a few moments, they'd been like an ordinary couple, chilling out after a long day. Doing mundane, ordinary things. The kinds of things most people did without thinking twice.

He and Gaby weren't an ordinary couple. She was trying to recover from an abusive marriage. Repair her relationship with her daughters. And now terrified because her ex-husband had somehow gotten out of Cook County Jail.

And him? He was the cop who was trying to protect her. The man who wanted more than just a friendship with Gaby.

As thoughts chased themselves like squirrels around his brain, he rolled off the couch and pulled the cushions onto the floor. Grabbed more cushions from a couple of chairs and laid them out in a row. Then he lay down again, telling himself that now he had no excuse to toss and turn.

But he listened to the creaks and groans of the old house far into the night. Felt the drift of cool air every time the nailed-shut back door shifted. Finally he sat up and reached for his phone. Matt was used to getting calls late at night. And Alex wouldn't be able to sleep until he got hold of his old friend.

* * *

Gaby rolled out of bed as the weak early morning sun spilled pale light into her bedroom. She hadn't slept well – images of Alex, sleeping on the couch right below her, kept her awake for far too long. Taunted her with images of what could never be.

She'd almost kissed him last night before she headed upstairs to bed. She'd jerked back at the last moment, but the impulse had almost pushed her to make a huge mistake.

She knew Alex was interested. She wasn't stupid. She knew the signs. Recognized the attraction simmering between them.

Still, he'd been a perfect gentleman every time she'd seen him. Asking how she was doing. Talking to the girls. Bringing them pizzas. Letting Cece practice her French with him. Teaching Bella about baseball.

Doing all the things friends did for each other.

But the heat in his gaze wasn't that of a friend. Neither were the taut wires of electricity tugging her toward him whenever he was in the room.

She steadfastly ignored them. Pretended she didn't notice his glances. Tried not to react to the tiny touches that made her shiver.

She'd always been impulsive. She'd fallen in love with

Antony at first sight in college. Jumped into a relationship with him without hesitating. Ended up dropping out of school a year before graduating, pregnant with Bella, to marry Antony.

Did she regret it? No. How could she? She'd gotten Bella and Cece from her marriage to Antony. He'd been a sweet boy, and she'd loved him.

And then Julio. He'd been charming. Strong. Concerned about her. She'd leaped again, and look what had happened. He'd gone from strong and concerned to controlling, Then to abusive.

What had she missed?

She was *so* done with impulsive. *So* over jumping into relationships without looking or thinking. She would never do that again.

Not even with Alex.

Especially not with Alex.

She'd never been friends with a man before, but Alex was her friend. She wouldn't ruin that by making another impulsive decision.

Splashing water on her face, she brushed her teeth, put on her make-up, got dressed for school. Glancing at her watch, she smiled. She had time to make breakfast for the girls and Alex before they had to leave.

As she started down the stairs, doing a mental inventory of her refrigerator, a sound from the kitchen made her stiffen. The back door opened, then closed. Voices murmured quietly, too softly for her to hear.

Glancing over the railing, she spotted the blankets she'd given to Alex, folded neatly on the couch. The pillow rested on top of them. He wouldn't have left without saying goodbye. He had to be one of the people in the kitchen.

Who would be in her kitchen with Alex this early in the morning?

Trotting down the stairs, she hurried to the kitchen. Cold air swirled around her, and it reminded her of coming home yesterday and realizing someone was in the house.

She froze. Wrapped her arms around her waist. Stared at the kitchen door, dread pooling in her stomach.

It wasn't Julio. Alex wouldn't be talking to him.

"Gaby?" Alex appeared in the doorway, his welcoming smile fading when he saw her. "What's wrong?"

She took a deep breath, let her hands drop to her sides and stood straight. "Nothing." She'd been foolish to think, even for a moment, that Julio was back. But just for a second, those memories had swallowed her.

She forced a smile. "Good morning, Alex. I was just going to fix some breakfast for all of us."

He studied her for a long moment, and she could tell she hadn't fooled him. Sympathy flickered in his eyes. "You heard us in the kitchen. It reminded you of yesterday, coming home to an intruder. I'm sorry."

"Don't be." She dragged in another breath, forced herself to smile. "I knew it was you."

"No, my fault. I shouldn't have asked Matt to come over so early. I should have waited and checked with you first."

Gaby leaned to the side to see around him. "Who's Matt?"

"The guy I told you about last night. The one who repairs doors for the police department. I called him last night, after you went to bed." His gaze darkened and he looked away quickly. Too quickly to see her eyes narrow. "Let me introduce you."

She followed Alex into the kitchen and saw a tall, solid man unscrewing the last hinge on her battered back door. He dropped the screws and the hinge into his tool belt and lifted the door to the side. Cold air rushed into the room.

"Matt, this is Gaby Stefano. Gaby, this is Matt Reardon."

Matt turned and nodded at Gaby. "Nice to meet you, Ms. Stefano. Alex told me what happened yesterday. Sorry I had to come over so early, but I have a full schedule today. This was the only time I could make it."

"Thanks, Matt. I appreciate that you made time for us."

She backed into the dining room, and Alex followed her.

When they were far enough away that Matt couldn't hear them, she straightened her spine and held Alex's gaze. "It was kind of you to call him, but you shouldn't have inconvenienced him. I told you I'd take a personal day."

"Yeah, I know you did. But Matt said he could do it right away. So I told him what kind of door and lock you needed, he brought them over, and he'll be finished before you have to leave. So you won't have to take a day off." He nodded at the kitchen table. "I asked him to bring bagels and coffee for all of us, too."

"Alex!" She stared at him, mortified. "You asked your friend get up this early to fix my door? *And you made him stop for bagels on the way?*"

He watched her warily. "I thought you'd appreciate having one less thing to worry about. About not having to make breakfast until you had a chance to clean up your kitchen."

She'd forgotten about the mess in the kitchen. She took a deep breath, held it, then let it out. "Okay, right. I forgot about the dirty kitchen. But you shouldn't have done any of that. At least not without talking to me about it first."

"We talked last night," he said, looking bewildered. "I told you I'd handle it."

She replayed the conversation in her head, then sighed. "You asked me to let you take care of it. I didn't say yes. I didn't intend for you to have to deal with this. It's my house. My ex-husband who kicked the door in. My responsibility to take care of it."

"What did I do that was so wrong?" He looked puzzled. As if she was speaking an unintelligible language.

"You did too much," Gaby said, smoothing her hands down her legs.

"But we're friends." He tilted his head as he studied her. "Friends help each other."

"And you've done so much." She sighed again. She didn't want to hurt Alex. But she didn't want to take advantage of this…this dance they were doing. "I accept plenty of help from you, Alex. You took us out to dinner yesterday. Stayed with the girls while I went to school. Slept on that hideously uncomfortable couch last night, so I wouldn't have to worry about Julio. You've done so much for us over the past year, and I appreciate it. More than you can possibly know. But I need to learn to deal with…with *stuff* myself. Not lean on anyone else. That's what got me into trouble before."

He moved closer, until she could smell her soap on his skin. Her toothpaste on his breath. "I'm doing what any friend would do, Gaby. You had a rough day yesterday. An upsetting, scary day. You're allowed to lean on someone after a day like that. Leaning on a friend doesn't make you weak."

Alex wanted to be more than a friend. His blue eyes were deep pools of tenderness and…and something she refused to name. Something she wanted, as well, but couldn't allow herself to have. "I have to learn to stand by myself before I can allow myself to lean on anyone."

She hesitated, then touched his shoulder. His shirt was soft beneath her fingers. Warm from his skin. She wanted to burrow beneath the smooth fabric and slide her hand along his chest. Feel the strength of his muscles. The pounding of his heart. She wanted to have the right to touch him. The right to lean on him.

But she couldn't. Not now, and probably not for a long time.

"I spent my whole adult life leaning on a man. First my father. Then Antony. After he was killed, Julio. I can't lean on anyone else until I know I can stand by myself. Until I can trust myself not to make another bad decision."

She swallowed. "Especially not you, Alex."

His eyes clouded with hurt. "Why especially not me?"

"Because it would be too easy to lean on you." *Because I want it too much.*

He put his hand over hers, brought it to his mouth.

Kissed her palm, then began to draw her closer.

Stilled. Glanced toward the ceiling. Let her go.

She heard it, too. The girls were stirring. They'd be down in a few minutes.

"Now's not the time for this discussion, Gaby. But we will be having it. Sometime when we're not going to be interrupted."

She managed a short nod, her throat thick with all the words she couldn't say.

Before either of them could speak, Bella spoke from behind them. "What's going on? Why are you guys whispering?"

Gaby forced herself not to leap away from Alex. Thanked God that he wasn't still holding her hand. Turning around, she said, "'Morning, Bella bug. We were trying to speak quietly so we didn't wake you and Cece up. One of Alex's friends is fixing the door in the kitchen."

Bella clomped down the stairs, her gaze shifting between her and Alex. "I heard him pounding. That's what woke me up."

"Sorry, baby, but the door had to be fixed before we could all go to school. And Mr. Reardon brought some bagels. Is Cece up yet?"

"Yeah," Bella said, her mouth pinched. "I heard her getting dressed."

"Please run upstairs and tell her to hurry if she wants a bagel."

Bella held her gaze for a beat too long before she swiveled and headed upstairs. Before Gaby could brush past him into the kitchen, Alex put his hand on her arm.

"Do you keep extra house keys in the kitchen?"

She sucked in a breath. She hadn't even thought about that. "Yes," she whispered. "In one of the drawers."

"Would Abrietto know where they were?"

"He might. I never tried to hide them."

"Why don't you check and see if they're where they belong."

Fear tightened in her stomach like a fist, and Gaby hurried to her odds and ends drawer. She yanked it open and searched through it. The keys were gone.

CHAPTER 6

Gaby's fingers scrabbled through the pens and pencils, matchbooks, tiny calculators and rubber bands in the drawer as she checked again. Once more. The silver ring holding three keys had to be here. She was probably looking right at it.

After touching almost everything in the drawer, she finally slammed it closed. "They're gone," she said, dread settling on her chest like an anchor, threatening to drag her deep into terror. "Julio must have taken them."

Alex nodded at Matt. "You have those extra locks?"

"In my truck."

"Do you have time to install them?"

"I'll get right on it," he said, turning the deadbolt with the key. He glanced around her kitchen, then tapped a spot on the wall a couple of feet from the door. "Is it okay with you if I put a hook for the key here?" he asked. "No one will be able to reach it if they smash in the glass, but it'll always be handy if you need it in a hurry."

Gaby glanced from Matt to Alex. Both men watched her patiently. Alex held her gaze, his head tilted. As if he expected her to insist on doing it herself.

Which would be completely stupid, since Matt was here and it would take him about a minute to nail in the hook. "That would be great, Matt. Thank you."

She turned to Alex. "What do you mean, 'the other locks'?"

"Abrietto has the keys to your front door. Your basement door," he reminded her. He watched her warily, as if waiting for an explosion. "You have to change the locks," he continued when she didn't say anything. "Matt has locks with him. He can have them changed out in less than an hour." Alex's voice held both frustration and irritation.

She stared at him. He stared back, as if daring her to refuse.

She wanted to refuse, but Alex was right. Refusing because of pride, so that she could take care of it herself, would be really stupid. So she nodded once. Turned to the man watching uneasily, his hammer poised to tap a hook into the wall. "Thanks, Matt. I really appreciate that. If you'll give me your invoice, I'll write you a check."

Matt's gaze flicked to Alex. Hard to mistake the panic in his eyes.

Alex cleared his throat. "I, ah, already paid for it," he said. "I was afraid I'd forget in the rush to get the door installed and get everyone off to school."

"That was a good idea," Gaby said, nodding but clenching her teeth. Alex wasn't going to pay for damage that *her* ex had done to *her* house. "Matt, do you have a copy of that invoice?"

Matt's gaze shifted from her to Alex. Back to her. "Sure, Gaby." He reached into his tool box and pulled out a piece of paper. Handed it to her.

Gaby studied the crumpled invoice. Five hundred dollars. Her stomach twisted tight. That was a lot of money. She and the girls wouldn't be ordering takeout for a while, and there'd be a lot of rice and beans in their future. "Thanks, Matt," she said, folding it and sliding it into her bag, still slung over the back of the kitchen chair. "I'll settle up with Alex later." She glanced at Alex, and he nodded.

"We'll talk about it later," he promised.

"We will," she retorted. There was a lot of 'later' going on this morning.

Gaby turned to find Bella standing in the doorway from the dining room, watching them with a tiny smile as her gaze shifted from Alex's face to Gaby's. Gaby frowned. Was Bella *happy* she and Alex were fighting?

She reached for the bag of bagels. "Bella, why don't you get five plates so we can have breakfast, then pour milk for yourself and Cece. I'll get silverware."

The knives and forks clattered onto the table, then she found the jar of capers in the refrigerator. Plopped the jar on the table and set a fork next to it. Grabbing the carafe from the coffee maker, she said, "I'll start more coffee. You were both up so early, I'm sure you can use another cup."

After an uncomfortable breakfast, with Bella glaring at her and Alex, Cece chattering away and Alex mostly silent, Matt escaped. Gaby sent the girls to brush their teeth and get ready to leave for school. When they were safely upstairs, she turned to Alex.

"I'm sorry I was so pissy about Matt and the door and the locks." She tilted her head and studied him. When he merely waited, his expression unreadable, she drew in a deep breath. "I was upset because you asked Matt to come over without checking with me. I was upset because you paid him."

Her gaze shifted to the drawer where her spare keys should have been, and she sighed. "I was upset because I feel helpless. I don't like feeling that way."

Alex's cool blue eyes softened a little. "I get that, Gaby. But I was only trying to help. So was Matt. This is an emergency, and I wanted to make sure your house was secure before you left for work."

He sighed and ran his hand through his hair, making it stick up in unruly waves. "Maybe I feel guilty on behalf of the police department because some idiot let Julio out of jail."

"Why would you feel guilty?" She tilted her head, studying him. "You had nothing to do with it. Neither did the Chicago Police Department."

"I should have checked in with the jail more often. Make sure they knew how dangerous Abrietto is."

"That's not your job," she said quietly. "And speaking of Julio, you never told me what happened. How he got away."

His eyes hardened. "Connor Donovan checked into it yesterday. He called me first thing this morning. The jail called it an 'administrative error'. A guy with a name similar to Abrietto's was supposed to be released yesterday. The dumbass deputy pulled out Abrietto instead. Turned him loose without double-checking."

"That's not your fault, Alex." Gaby let her irritation bleed away. "You didn't let him go."

"No, but a guy who doesn't belong in law enforcement did. You could have been killed because of his mistake." His jaw worked as he stared at the drawer where her extra keys should have been. "No way in hell was I going to leave your house until I knew Abrietto couldn't get back in here."

What had happened to the easy camaraderie they'd had last night? The connection that had felt so solid? So strong?

Gaby sighed. She'd tossed it away with both hands when she'd let pride and prickliness take over this morning. "Thank you, Alex," she said quietly. "You've been nothing but kind to us since yesterday, and I've been an ungrateful whiner."

"I'd never say that, Gaby," he said, leaning closer. The soft expression in his blue eyes made her want to close the distance between them. "I get it. You need to feel as if you're independent. But even the strongest person needs help sometime. And right now, with Abrietto loose? You need all the help you can get.

"And here's a heads-up. I'm gonna step on your toes

again before he's caught."

Gaby took a chance and laid her hand on his arm. He didn't yank away from her, and that was a good sign. "Forgive me?"

His eyes were as blue as a cloudless summer sky. Full of emotion. Caring. Concern. "Of course," he murmured, putting his hand over hers. Sliding his fingers between hers for a long moment. "We'll talk tonight, and you can write me a check for the door and the locks."

He squeezed her hand, smiled, then let her go. "I'm gonna have to insist on paying for the bagels, though. The girls and I pretty much cleaned out your popcorn supply last night. Now we're even."

It would take a long, long time before she and Alex were even. She opened her mouth to tell him so when Bella stepped into the kitchen. Her older daughter looked at Alex, then at her mother, her mouth thinning. "We need to leave, or I'll be late for school."

Alex let Gaby go and stepped back. "I was just heading out," he said to Bella. "Want to watch the Bearcats again tonight? See if the Marino kid gets another hit?"

Bella scowled. "I'm going to have a lot of homework tonight."

Alex shrugged. "Okay. You can join us if you have time. Otherwise, I'll continue Cece's baseball education."

"Whatever." Bella's jaw clenched as she grabbed her jacket from the coat rack and yanked it on. "I'll wait in the car."

"Not a good idea, Bella," Alex said, moving in front of her. "I'll walk all of you out when you're ready to go."

"I'll just take the bus, then," she said, heading toward the front door. "I don't want to be late."

Gaby followed her daughter into the other room, irritated and embarrassed. "Bella, what's wrong with you?" she whispered. "Why are you being so snotty with Alex?"

"Leave me alone, Mom. I need to get to school," Bella retorted as she reached for the front door.

What was this about? Gaby slid in front of her. "Don't be ridiculous. This is the time we normally leave. If you take the bus, you'll be half an hour or more late. You'll get detention and miss tae kwon do. Is that what you want?"

Bella stared at her mother for a long moment. Gaby could see the indecision in her eyes – spite her mother by taking the bus, or miss the sport she loved?

Finally she shoved past her mother and yelled up the stairs, "Come *on*, Cece. We're gonna be late."

Gaby followed Bella back into the kitchen. While the girl put on her shoes, Alex raised his eyebrows. Gaby shrugged. She had no idea what was going on with her older daughter.

As soon as Cece danced into the kitchen, all three of them followed Alex out the back door. He rested his hand on his gun, and Gaby drew both girls close to her. Cece wrapped an arm around Gaby's waist. Bella didn't shrug her off.

Gaby didn't relax until they pulled out of the alley, waving goodbye to Alex and driving toward Bella's school. She was sitting in the front seat, with Cece in the back. When they stopped at a light, Gaby glanced at Bella. "You want to tell me what was going on back there?"

Bella stared out the window for a long moment, and Gaby was afraid she wouldn't answer. Finally, though, she swung around to face her mother.

"Alex is *my* friend," she said, her eyes glittering. Was she close to tears? "I knew him first. He came to my tae kwon do meets before you even met him. Now you're trying to steal him."

"*Steal* him?" Gaby stared at Bella, stunned, until the car behind her honked impatiently. She started into the intersection with a jerk. "I know you met him first, but don't you think we're all friends now? What's wrong with that?"

Bella sulked in the seat beside her, shooting her mother a dark glare. "I saw you last night. Looked like you wanted to be a lot more than friends." Her throat worked and she looked away. "You always pick the wrong guys. Look what happened with Julio. Now you're gonna have sex with Alex and ruin *my* friendship with him."

Gaby sucked in a shocked breath, her chest aching as if Bella had landed a kick on her sternum. When she could breathe again, she asked quietly, "Do you think Alex is anything like Julio, Bella? Are you afraid he'll hurt you or Cece or me?"

"No," she said, her voice sulky. "He's a good guy. Not that *you* would be able to tell the difference."

Her daughter's words were a hard slap in the face. Gaby blinked back tears and gripped the steering wheel more tightly. Finally, when she was sure she wouldn't break down and cry, she said, "You're right. I made a huge mistake with Julio, and we all paid for it. But that doesn't give you the right to be disrespectful, Bella. You may think you know everything about what went on with Julio, because we all lived in the same house, but you don't. You're a very smart girl, but you know nothing about adult relationships."

"You mean sex." Bella sneered at her mother. "I know all about sex. You gave me the *talk*. I took Health."

"You better not know all about sex, not for a very long time," Gaby shot back, her sadness vanishing, replaced by irritation. "You can ask me anything you want, but you'll do it in a respectful way. And Alex and I are not having sex. But we're adults, and if we *were* having sex, that would be between us. And certainly not something I'd discuss with you."

She pulled into the car pool line at Lane Tech. Bella reached for the door, but Gaby stopped her with a hand on her arm. "Bella, you need to be extra careful on your way from here to Spencer. Don't walk around with your earbuds in. Pay attention to what's going on. And try to walk with a group."

"Maybe I'll call Alex." Bella smirked, as if she was one-upping her mother. "Ask him to walk with me."

"That's a good idea." Gaby nodded at Bella. "Call him if you're at all nervous or concerned. I'm sure he'd love to walk with you to school, say hi to the other girls and Ms. Taylor."

Bella's eyes narrowed and she pressed her lips together. Gaby struggled to keep a straight face. Bella had expected her to say, 'Don't bother Alex.' But it was actually a good idea. She'd feel better, Bella would be safe, and Alex would be pleased to help Bella.

"I'll see you at Spencer, Cece," Bella muttered as she climbed out of the car and slammed the door. She headed toward the door, then disappeared into the building without looking back.

Cece leaned over the center console. "Bella was crabby this morning. Maybe she shouldn't have stayed up so late watching the baseball game last night."

Gaby angled around to press a kiss to her cheek. "We're all crabby sometimes, and you're probably right. Bella is tired." That might be part of it, but something else was going on with her older daughter. She smoothed her younger daughter's hair back, then tapped her nose lightly. "You stayed up just as late as Bella." She stepped on the gas as the parent in front of her began to move. "I hope you can stay awake for French this afternoon, *cara*."

* * *

Bella stepped off the bus that dropped her three blocks from Spencer and slung her backpack over her shoulders. She wasn't going to call Alex, even though she'd told her mother she would. He'd think she was a baby or something if she couldn't walk three blocks by herself.

She could take care of herself. She knew tae kwon do. If that asshole Julio showed up, she'd kick his ass.

As the bus pulled away, rumbling and belching smelly smoke, she glanced around once. Four other people got off the bus with her, but they all went in a different direction.

None of them were heading toward Spencer.

She swallowed and squared her shoulders. Shoved her ear buds back in her ears. Her mother didn't know anything. Bella would be able to hear Julio sneaking up on her, even with the buds in place.

She glanced from side to side as she walked past the drug store and the small market. Sometimes she bought a snack in there. She caught a glimpse of herself in the window, along with the deserted sidewalk. Turning away from the store, she walked a little faster. She wasn't very hungry today.

With Taylor Swift playing in her ears, she turned a corner and saw Spencer two blocks away. She took a deep breath. Two blocks was nothing.

As she got closer, she saw a few kids hanging out on the steps. They looked totally lame. A tiny voice reminded her that she'd hung on the steps, too, before she started tae kwon do.

Bella scowled. Her friends were iced. No one would ever call *them* lame.

After she crossed the final street, she let her shoulders relax. She was good now. Julio knew she did tae kwon do. He wouldn't mess with her. Picking up her pace, she hurried toward the front door. Turned up the volume on her music.

She was ten yards from the door when someone grabbed her backpack and yanked her backward. Hard.

CHAPTER 7

Bella flailed, struggling for balance as she felt herself tumbling backward. A shove forward stopped her fall, then someone grabbed her shoulders to steady her. Her heart thundering, gulping air, she tried frantically to recall some tae kwon do moves.

She wished she hadn't been so mean to her mother that morning. What if she never saw Mom again? Maybe Julio was going to kill her.

She swung around, trying to remember the kick she'd learned yesterday. Only to see her friend Piotr.

"Hey, Bellissima." The tall, lanky kid with long blond hair beamed at her, shoving his hands into his pockets.

"What the hell, Piotr? Yanking me backward like that?" She sucked in a steadying breath. Gripped the straps of her backpack to hide the tremble in her hands. "You're lucky I didn't kick your ass."

"Yeah, you're a big bad." Piotr slung an arm over her shoulder. She wanted to shake him off, but she took another breath, instead. She kind of didn't mind Piotr's arm around her. And he'd be insufferable if he knew how he'd frightened her.

"You know it." She slanted a glance at her friend, who was a year younger and therefore still at Spencer. "Better remember that next time."

Her friend grabbed her hand. Jiggled it up and down. "This thing licensed to kill?"

"That's totally lame," she said, but her hand felt good in Piotr's. "You're just jealous that Ms. Taylor doesn't have a program for the guys."

Piotr chattered about his soccer team, how much better it was than Bella's kicking and punching, and Bella began to relax. They got to the sidewalk up to the school, and she glanced across the street before they turned.

Julio stood behind a car, watching Spencer.

Staring at her.

* * *

"I'll be right there, Bella. Stay in the school."

Alex threw the gumball on top of his unmarked and flipped on the sirens. Three squads were on their way, as well, but he wasn't about to wait for them. He drove over a sidewalk when both lanes were blocked at the next intersection, then turned down the side street.

Turned off the siren. He wanted that shithead Abrietto to be standing outside the school when he arrived. He'd take a lot of pleasure in tossing him on the ground. Slapping on the cuffs. Hauling his ass back to Cook County Jail.

The front of the school was deserted when he arrived. No kids on the stairs, like there usually were. No one walking home. The neighborhood was eerily silent.

Abrietto was gone.

He couldn't be far, though, unless he'd jacked a car. Alex pressed his radio button. "Any report of a carjacking in the vicinity of Spencer School? Keeler and Montrose?"

The radio crackled as he pulled to the curb in front of the school. "No car jackings reported," the dispatcher said.

"Okay, thanks."

Alex swung out of his car, stood beside it and listened. Traffic hummed a few blocks away. A dog barked on the next block. Then another. Alex took off at a run in that direction.

Footsteps sounded in the alley, and Alex veered that way. He spotted a male running between two houses seventy five yards in front of him. He headed in that direction as he pulled out his radio, barking instructions to the dispatcher.

Twenty minutes later, he trudged back toward Spencer. No sign of Abrietto. The three squads were still searching for him, but the douche bag was probably gone. Now he needed to check on Bella and Cece.

The front door of the school was locked. He rang the bell, looked up at the camera and held up his badge. Moments later, he heard footsteps approaching.

Pat Lewinski opened the door just far enough to let him in, then locked it behind him. "Did you catch that bastard?" she asked.

"No." Alex clenched his teeth. He'd been so close. "Three squad cars are still searching, but it looks like he got away." Sweat rolled down his sides and back from all the running, and heat rolled over him in waves. He shrugged out of his coat and snapped it against the wall in frustration. "Saw him at one point, but he vanished."

Taking a deep breath, he straightened, struggling to control his anger. "Everyone okay here?"

"There were only a few kids outside, and the only ones in the school were in the enrichment classes and the gym," Pat said, patting his arm as if he was a kid she needed to reassure. "Only Bella Stefano and Piotr Kurowski know that anything's wrong. They promised not to say anything to the other kids."

"They in the gym with Raine?"

"Yes." Her mouth softened. "I kept them in the office for a little while. Bella was upset, and Piotr was confused. Bella filled him in, then she wanted to help Raine. I sent both of them to the gym. Nice kids."

"Yeah." Sweat cooling on his back made him shiver, and he shoved his arms back into his jacket. "I'm going to get an officer to stay here tomorrow. He'll be in front of the school in the morning, and again in the afternoon when the kids are leaving. I'll make sure someone covers the school until we catch that asshole."

He glanced at Pat Lewinski and closed his eyes. "Sorry, Pat."

"Don't apologize. I've called him far worse." She patted his arm again. "Go check on Bella."

"Did you call their mom?"

"I figured you'd do that," she said, a tiny twinkle in her eye. "Since you know Gaby."

"Yeah, I'll do that."

He waited for the principal to disappear into her office before he called Gaby. "It's Alex," he said when she answered. "Everything's okay, but Julio was in front of the school when Bella got here. I'll bring both her and Cece home."

Gaby gasped, then stuttered out questions, one after another. Alex finally interrupted her panicked voice. "Sweetheart, they're okay," he said gently. "I'll fill you in when I get home with the girls. I need to check on them now, though. You stay inside. Make sure your doors are all locked. Okay?"

Silence on the other end of the phone. Finally, Gaby said, "Okay, Alex. See you later."

Damn it. He'd called her sweetheart. And he'd said 'when I get home'. He closed his eyes and sucked in a deep breath. He'd been shaken. Scared to death, jumpy as hell since Bella called him. But that was no reason to forget every good intention he had. Every vow to take things slowly with Gaby. To be a friend. Nothing more. Not until she was ready.

Heading toward the gym, he called himself every name he could think of, 'idiot' being at the top of the list.

He brightened momentarily. She'd been rattled. Maybe she hadn't even noticed.

No. This was Gaby. She noticed everything.

They already had a few things to talk about tonight, after the girls were in bed. Maybe his slip of the tongue would be added to the 'later' list.

As he reached the door of the gym, he paused to phone Connor Donovan. "Hey man, Abrietto showed up at Spencer this afternoon." He paused as Connor swore into the phone. "Yeah. Not sure who he was looking for, but you might want to walk Raine out of the school and follow her home tonight. And if I were you? I'd drive her to school and pick her up until we catch this dirtbag."

Sliding his phone into his pocket, he opened the gym door. When he stepped inside, she saw that the girls were almost finished. They jogged around the perimeter of the gym while Raine and Bella talked on the mats. A blond kid perched on the bleachers, watching Raine and Bella.

Alex narrowed his eyes. No. The kid wasn't paying any attention to Raine. He was staring at Bella as if she were a gourmet meal and the kid was starving. Alex's hackles rose, and he started toward the boy.

Bella glanced at him and scowled, as if she could read his mind. Alex stopped. It wasn't his place to go all protective parent over Bella. Even though he wanted to.

Another thing to mention to Gaby.

He strolled over to the kid and sat beside him on the bleacher. "Alex Jennings," he said, holding out his hand.

"Piotr Kurowski." He studied Alex for a long moment. "You the cop Bella talks about?"

"Maybe." Alex narrowed his eyes. "What does she say?"

Piotr raised one shoulder. "Just that you come to all her team's meets. That you've been to her house a few times."

"Yeah, that's me." He rolled his shoulders, unsure of his role. He went with the easiest. "Bella tell you about the guy who was watching her?"

"Yeah." Piotr frowned. "Sounds like a bad scene. You

catch him?"

"No." Alex clenched his teeth again. "But we're still looking. Maybe we'll get lucky."

The kid's foot jiggled on the wood of the bleacher. Tiny thumps accompanied each jerk of his knee. "Are you, like, dating Bella's mother or something?"

Or something. "No. I know Bella through the team."

"Oh. Okay." The jiggling stopped. Had Piotr thought he'd have to face Alex if he wanted to take Bella on a date?

Christ. Could this be any more awkward? "You a friend of Bella's?" Alex asked.

"Yeah." The kid's foot began jiggling again. "We, ah, ate lunch together last year. She's a year ahead of me."

"So you're still here at Spencer." Okay. Alex breathed out more easily. Bella probably didn't see him very often.

"Yeah, but I'm applying to Lane for next year. Already took the test. Then me and Bella will be at the same school again."

Another morsel of information for Gaby. "Good luck," he said as Bella and Raine walked toward the bleachers.

Bella's gaze touched on Piotr and she blushed. She slid her gaze over to Alex. "Did you catch him?"

"No. But a bunch of cops are still looking for him." He stood up and drew her away from Piotr. "Do you remember what he was wearing?"

Bella frowned. "He was behind a car. Mostly hidden. A dark sweatshirt, I think. With a zipper." She shrugged. "I didn't see much."

"That's okay. You about ready to go? I'm driving you and Cece home."

"I have to change. Cece comes to the gym when she's finished. She'll be here in a few minutes."

"Okay. I need to talk to Ms. Taylor for a moment."

Out of the corner of his eye, Alex saw Bella say something to Piotr. The kid nodded, then leaned close to Bella. Too close. Alex was about to yank him away when someone touched his arm.

Raine.

"Hey, Alex. What's up? You going all Papa Bear on poor Piotr?"

"You know that kid?"

"Of course I do. He's in my class." She grinned, her eyes twinkling. "He stays after school a lot, too. In the gym. Says he might want to take up tae kwon do."

"Does Gaby know about this?"

Raine put her hand on his arm. "There's nothing to know," she said quietly. "It's a first crush for both of them, I'm guessing. Pretty innocent."

"Innocent my ass." Alex scowled, just barely stopping himself from glaring over at the two teens. "I was a fourteen-year-old boy once, myself."

Raine elbowed him. Hard. "Knock it off, Alex. After teaching for a few years, I have a pretty good sense of what's innocent and what's not. If I think they're drifting towards not-so-innocent territory, I'll let Gaby know."

Alex rubbed his upper arm where Raine's sharp elbow had caught him and grimaced. She was right. He was over-reacting about something that was probably completely innocent. Why *was* he so protective of Bella?

He glanced over his shoulder at Bella and Piotr, who were still talking. Maybe because she was vulnerable. Beneath the swagger and bluster was a scared kid who had suddenly been thrust into a frightening situation. The man who'd tried to strangle her had escaped from jail. Showed up at her school.

If Piotr could steer her back to normal, good for him.

Unless he stepped out of line. Then, all bets were off.

He turned back to Raine. "I'll take your word that there's nothing to worry about with that kid and Bella. But you let me know if I need to talk to him."

Raine tilted her head and studied him, a tiny smirk playing around her mouth. "You *are* going all Papa Bear. Something you want to share with the class, Alex?"

"Hell, no. And even if there was, you think I'm going to

blab about it in front of the kids? You know they all have ears like bats."

Raine's smirk faded, replaced by a delighted smile. "You know I think a lot of Bella. Gaby and Cece, too. If you and Gaby were...involved, I'd be thrilled for all of you."

Alex kept his face carefully blank. "Speaking of involved, I called Connor. Told him what happened. He's probably heading over here right now to walk you to your car and follow you home."

Her smile fell away. "He doesn't have to do that. I know how to defend myself."

"Yeah, you do, but why take the chance? I wouldn't put it past Abrietto to hide behind the dumpster in the parking lot and jump you when you left school."

"I'll be ready for him, then," Raine retorted.

"Come on, Raine. He was arrested for attacking you. You think he's going to play nice? God knows what he would have done to Gaby if she hadn't gotten away. And what if the asshole got a gun somewhere? I don't want to see you hurt again."

He softened his voice. "Look at it from Connor's point of view. I'd go nuts if Abrietto was after my fiancée." Gaby's face flashed in his mind, and he shoved it away. Not his fiancée. Not his anything. "Cut the poor guy some slack. Let him walk you to your car."

Raine sighed. "Sorry. Knee-jerk response. I know you're right. I don't want Connor to worry." She rolled her shoulders and a tiny smile curved her lips. "Part of the give and take of a relationship."

The door to the gym banged open, and Alex and Raine turned to see Cece skipping across the hardwood floor. "Take your kids home and watch out for Gaby," she said as she strode toward the locker room.

His kids.

Bella and Cece weren't his. He and Gaby weren't even dating, for God's sake. But as he watched Cece skip across the floor with her contagious grin, and Bella talking to Piotr, their heads too close, he wondered what it would be like to have the right to protect them. Love them.

To pick them up from school, ask them about their day as they drove home.

He had no idea how it would feel. His own parents had never picked him up from school, or attended school events. They were too busy with their own lives.

If he ever had kids of his own, they'd grow up knowing they were loved. Cared about. More important than any job or meeting or leisure activity.

Ten minutes later, on the ride back to Gaby's house, he realized how little he actually knew about raising kids. Bella leaned against the car door, studying him. "Alex?" she began.

He glanced over at her. Wasn't sure he liked the speculation on her face. "Yeah?"

"So you like my mom, huh?"

"I like all three of you," he said cautiously.

Behind him, Cece leaned forward as far as her seatbelt would reach.

"Not like that." Bella rolled her eyes at him. "I'm not stupid. I see the way you look at her. The way she looks at you."

"You do, huh?" He tightened his grip on the steering wheel, chanced a quick glance at Bella as he stopped at a stop sign. "How does she look at me, Bella?"

A disgusted frown furrowed Bella's forehead. "All sappy. It's sickening."

He was tempted to ask her if it was the same way she looked at Piotr, but he stopped himself in time. He knew better than to bait a teenager. Or worse, to tease one. "Is that right?" he said instead.

"You're just as bad. Mooning over her."

He glanced at her sharply, saw a hint of sadness in her eyes. Why? Didn't Bella want him to get together with her mother?

The thought made his heart ache.

But he didn't have time to analyze it now. "I do not moon anyone, Bella Stefano," he said, trying to turn it into a joke. "That kind of stunt would get me into big trouble at work."

"What's mooning?" Cece asked from the back seat.

Bella rolled her eyes again. "It's when you drop trou and flash your ass at someone."

"Ewww! Gross!" Cece flopped back into her seat. "Do you moon, Bella?"

"Of course not." Bella turned to her sister. "Mooning's lame. Only dickheads do it."

"Bella!" Alex glanced at her, shocked. "Don't say stuff like that in front of Cece." He sighed to himself. He'd hoped to distract Bella from her questions about him and Gaby. Instead, he'd created a completely different problem.

He had a lot to learn about kids.

"Like she hasn't heard worse at school?" Bella scoffed. "Wake up and smell the coffee, Alex. She probably heard the 'f' word in first grade. Just like I did."

"Maybe she did," he said wearily, regretting their lost innocence. "But you don't have to add to her vocabulary."

"Whatever." Bella leaned against the door and stared out the window. Conversation over.

God! Alex pinched the bridge of his nose. Another item to add to the long list of 'things to discuss with Gaby'.

He was pretty sure she wasn't going to like any of them.

CHAPTER 8

Alex eased his car to the curb and glanced at Cece in the back seat. Her hand was on the door, ready to open it. He hoped to God she wasn't rushing into the house to tell her mother about her new vocabulary word.

Bella was ready to bolt, too. Probably afraid his lameness was contagious.

"Stay in the car," he said, wincing when he heard the bite in his voice. All cop. Not enough reassurance. "For just a minute. I want to make sure your mom's home."

Bella swung around to face him. For a moment, the tough teen was gone. Her mouth wobbled a little. "You think he's here?"

"No." *God, he hoped not.* "But I have to check. Habit."

He was halfway out of the car when his radio squawked. "Armed robbery in progress." The dispatcher read off the address, and Alex froze. Two blocks away.

He pressed his response button. "Jennings here. I'm close. On my way in thirty seconds."

He ran up the steps and pounded on the door. Gaby must have heard the car pull up, because she opened immediately.

"What's wrong? Where are the girls?" She pushed him to the side and leaned out, searching for his car.

Exhaled when she saw Bella and Cece sitting in his unmarked. "Why are they still in the car?"

"Everything all right here?"

Still watching the girls, she said, "Yeah. No problems when I got home."

He turned around and signaled for Bella and Cece. As they scrambled out of the car, he said, "Keep the girls inside. Lock the doors. I have to respond to a call. Don't go anywhere until I get back."

He practically shoved the girls into the house, waited until he heard the locks engage, then raced back to his car.

A minute later, he pulled up in front of a currency exchange. A squad car pulled in behind him, another blocked off the street. Un-holstering his weapon, he ran into the tiny storefront.

The clerk behind the counter clutched his cell phone so hard his knuckles were white. A corner of the phone tapped a staccato beat on the counter – the kid's hand was shaking. "He ran." The clerk waved in a vaguely northern direction. "That way, I think? I couldn't see."

"What did he look like?" Alex pulled out his notebook as a patrol officer appeared in the door.

"Not real tall." The clerk swallowed, slipped the phone in his pocket and let his palm wobble in the air. "About like this."

Five-nine, five-ten. Alex scribbled in the notebook. "What else?"

"Ski mask covered his face. Maybe Latino, from what I could see. Brown eyes. On the stocky side, but not fat."

"Clothing?"

The clerk shrugged helplessly. "A black hoodie. Jeans."

"Anything else?"

"He had a gun. He was wearing blue rubber gloves. Tight ones. Like doctors use when they're around blood." He frowned. "One of the fingers kind of flopped around.

Like it was missing?"

"Which hand?" Alex clenched his fingers around the pen.

The clerk stared into the distance for a long moment. "Left," he said, nodding. "The gun was in his right hand. It was the other one. I saw the floppy finger when he reached over the counter." The clerk swallowed hard. "He pointed the gun at my head. Said to give him all the money I had. And we had a lot. Today's payday. Lots of people come in to cash their checks. Once I gave him the money, he made me get down on the floor. Face down. With my hands on my head." He swallowed again, and his hands trembled. "I thought he was going to shoot me. I was praying. Then I realized he was gone. So I got up and dialed 911."

Alex glanced at the uniformed officer, nodded at him. The young cop dashed out of the store, got in his car and took off. He'd comb the area, but Alex figured the robber had slipped through their fingers. Based on the meager description, he'd have to be walking down the street in his ski mask for them to find him.

"Okay," he said. "Tell me how much money he got. And describe the gun."

* * *

Fifteen minutes later, Craig Schultz, one of the robbery detectives, walked into the currency exchange. Alex gave him the details that the clerk had relayed, although Craig would question him again. But instead of turning to the clerk, Schultz frowned and nodded at the door.

Once they were outside, Schultz said, "Someone with a missing little finger used blue latex gloves before. Not recently, but that detail stuck in my brain – blue gloves and a missing finger is kind of unique. I think it was at currency exchanges, too. After I talk to the clerk, I'll take a look at my cold cases."

"How long ago are we talking?" Alex asked, the hair on the back of his neck lifting.

Schultz shrugged. "I'd have to check. A year, at least."

"Do me a favor, Schultz, and give me a call when you find out. Might be related to something I'm working on."

"Yeah?" The other detective tilted his head. "Blue latex guy connected to a homicide?"

"Not a homicide. Something's setting off alarm bells. I'll tell you if I'm a genius or full of shit after you give me some dates for those armed robberies."

"You got it." Schultz nodded at Alex. "Appreciate you taking that call. I was tied up on a home invasion."

"No problem. I was in the area."

A few minutes later, Alex pulled to the curb in front of Gaby's house and sat in the car, listening to the engine ping as it cooled. He didn't want to upset her, but she needed to know that a currency exchange only two blocks from her place had been robbed.

Abrietto had been at Spencer. Spencer school was less than a mile from the currency exchange. Abrietto knew the area.

Bella said Abrietto had been wearing a dark sweatshirt with a zipper. A sweatshirt with a zipper was usually a hoodie. The kid in the currency exchange said the robber was wearing a black hoodie.

Alex didn't want to jump to conclusions, but he'd never been a big believer in coincidence.

The good news was, based on the clerk's description of the robber's gun, it was most likely a realistic toy.

The bad news was, if Julio *had* been the robber, he now had more than enough money to buy the real thing. The clerk estimated the robber had gotten more than ten thousand dollars.

Alex knocked at the door, and Gaby opened it almost immediately. "What's wrong?" Her face was sheet-white. "Was it Julio?"

He closed the door carefully and spotted Bella right behind her mother. Watching him with frightened eyes.

"It was an armed robbery. At a currency exchange on

Montrose. No one was hurt, and the robber got away," he said, trying to sound reassuring. "I needed to respond because I was the closest officer."

Gaby sagged against the newel post on the stairs. "So it wasn't Julio."

"We don't know who it was," Alex said carefully. "He wore a mask, so the clerk didn't get a good look at him. Wore gloves, too, so no fingerprints. The bottom line? Unless he's a total idiot, he's far away from here by now. The area's crawling with cops."

Bella gripped one of the spindles on the staircase. Alex saw her hand shaking before she tightened her fist around the wood. "Was it that place a couple of blocks away?"

"Yeah, that's the one."

Bella took a deep, shuddering breath. "There was a robbery at that same place a couple of years ago," she said, her voice almost a whisper. "I remember because one of the kids in my class had a cousin who worked there. He said his cousin wet his pants." Color flooded her face and she stared at her hand on the spindle. "Gordon got teased for weeks about having a cousin who wet his pants."

Had Bella been one of the kids teasing Gordon?

"Kids can be mean sometimes," Gaby said. She reached out and squeezed her daughter's shoulder.

Bella shrugged her off. Didn't look at either of them.

"You're wondering if it's the same robber, aren't you?" Gaby asked, watching Bella. Gaby's fingers were twisted into the fabric of her bright yellow apron.

Bella tensed. Shrugged. Her knuckles turned white on the spindle she gripped.

"That's not very likely," Alex said, keeping his voice easy. "Two years is a long time. And currency exchanges get robbed more than other kinds of stores. They usually have lots of cash." He watched Bella swallow. She had to be shaken up. First Julio appears at her school. Then a currency exchange close by gets robbed.

"The good news is, once they have their money, they try

to get as far away as possible. So I doubt there's anything to worry about."

"Thanks for explaining," Gaby said, letting go of the apron. Smoothing out the wrinkles. "Bella was worried."

"No, I wasn't." Bella scowled and let go of the wood. "I just wondered why Alex had to go rushing off."

"I'm a cop," he said, trying to keep it light. "That's what cops do."

"It's weird that the same place was robbed again."

"It happens." He glanced at Gaby and was relieved she looked less worried. Less tense.

"You okay?" he asked her.

"I'm fine."

Bella turned and began running up the stairs. "Bella?" Gaby asked. "What's wrong?"

"Nothing. You guys are talking now. I'm going upstairs."

Neither he nor Gaby spoke until they heard a door slam. Finally Gaby shook her head. "She's been so grumpy lately."

"Do you know why?" Alex glanced up the stairs, wondering if Bella was listening to them.

Gaby motioned toward the kitchen, and he followed her into the next room. Gaby turned, leaned against the counter and sighed.

"She's jealous that you're spending time with us," she said, her cheeks turning a delicate shade of pink. "She thinks you're her friend, and that I'm stealing you from her."

"*Stealing* you?" Alex stared at her, horrified. "I don't...I wouldn't..."

"Alex." Gaby put her hand on his arm. "Stop. Of course I know that. And Bella doesn't think of you as a potential 'boyfriend'." She glanced toward the stairs and lowered her voice. "She's got a friend at school. Piotr. She talks about him a lot – I think she has a crush on him.

"I think Bella's feeling possessive because she knew you first. You were her friend, and now we're all your friends."

She twisted the apron fabric around her finger. "I think it's all wrapped up in what's going on with Julio. He escaped and showed up here. Threatened me. Today he threatened Bella."

He opened his mouth to correct her, and she laid her fingers across his lips. "He might have only watched her, but that's a threat. You know it as well as I do."

Her hand dropped away, and he wanted to put it back. To kiss her palm. But Gaby wasn't looking at him. She was staring out the window into the back yard. "I made a bad choice the last time I got involved with a man, and Bella paid the price. Bella knows you're attracted to me, and...and I'm..."

"I know," he said. He didn't want to let her to say it. Force the issue with her. "We talked about it in the car on the way home."

"Oh, God." She spun around, a horrified expression on her face. "What did she say?"

"That you get all sappy when you look at me. And that I'm mooning over you."

"She said that?" She stood straighter and glared in the direction of the stairs. "That won't happen again. Bella and I will be having a talk."

"Gaby, don't." He grabbed her wrist as she took a step toward the door. "She'll be mortified. Angry at me for ratting her out. Pissed off at you because you confronted her. She'll shut down. I don't think you want that. I certainly don't."

She glanced over her shoulder at him. Studied his face. Her shoulders slumped. "You're right. I'm sorry she put you on the spot like that."

"Don't be," he said, letting his hand slide from her wrist down to her fingers. He twined their hands together, squeezed gently. "I was pretty happy to find out you're all sappy about me."

"Sappy is a stupid word," she said, easing her hand away from his. "I like you, Alex. But sappy? That makes me sound like a silly, fluttering woman."

"You're the least silly woman I know. And I've never seen you flutter."

"And you won't," she muttered.

Heat roared through him, making *him* flutter. And sooner or later, Gaby would, too. "Don't make promises you're not going to keep, *cara*." His voice was a low, husky rumble, and Gaby froze. Stared at him.

He cupped her face, let his thumb skate over her mouth, then let her go.

They stared at each other for a little too long. Neither of them spoke. But he suspected the longing in Gaby's eyes was reflected in his.

Finally she turned away, reaching blindly for the lid of a pot on the stove. She touched the handle and yanked her hand away with a hiss. Opening a drawer, she pulled out a pot holder.

Gaby lifted the cover of the huge pot and the delicious aroma of garlic and tomatoes slapped him in the face and made his stomach rumble. It reminded him of the meals their housekeeper Nonna had fixed for him and Theresa. The same comforting scents often greeted them when they got home from school.

Pushing the memories way, he asked, "Are both the girls upstairs?"

The lid to the pot clattered back into place and Gaby spun around. The wooden spoon left a tiny trail of red sauce on the stove. "What's wrong?"

"Nothing." He took the spoon away from her and set it on the spoon rest after running a finger over it and sampling the sauce. The taste stirred long-buried memories.

Pushing them away, he took both Gaby's hands. "Nothing I'm sure about, anyway."

She gripped his hands tightly. "Tell me."

Rubbing his thumb over the silky smooth skin on the back of her hand, he wondered if the rest of her would feel as good. Wondered what she'd taste like if he kissed her cheek. Her neck. Her mouth.

"Alex?" Her chest rose and fell too fast, and pink color crept up her cheeks.

"Sorry." He let her hands go and immediately wanted them back again. Wanted her closer. He cleared his throat. "I have no proof, nothing more than a hunch, but I wondered whether it might have been Abrietto who held up that currency exchange."

She sucked in a breath and her eyes widened. "Julio? How would he get a gun?"

He saw shock but not disbelief in her expression. "Aren't you going to say that Abrietto would never hold up a currency exchange? That he was a horrible husband, but not a thief?"

Gaby shook her head slowly. "No. He *was* a thief. I used to keep some spare cash in the freezer." She rolled her eyes when Alex tried to speak. "Yes. I know. The first place a burglar is going to look. I figured that out when Julio stole it. I don't keep cash in the house anymore.

"I have some money from an insurance settlement I got after Antony's death. It's invested for the girls – their college funds, but I keep a little of it in a checking account in case they need something I can't afford. Julio found the check book and stole a check. Forged my name and cashed it. He got almost all the money in the account."

She stared down at her hands, and Alex wondered if that money wasn't also her escape fund. Money waiting for her to get up the courage to walk away with the girls.

Finally she looked up at him. "I found out when I got the statement. We fought. That was the *girls'* money, money we got because their father was killed. Julio said any money I had was his money, too.

"I closed the checking account and opened another one. And I put the checkbook in a safe deposit box. I had to go to the bank if I needed money from the account, but it was worth it." Her lips pressed together. "Julio kept asking me where it was. When I wouldn't tell him..." She stared at the refrigerator and rubbed her chest, as if remembering pain. "So yes. Julio is a thief."

Alex followed her gaze to the refrigerator, which was covered with pictures of the girls. They looked like the school pictures he remembered when he was a kid, an array that showed both Bella and Cece growing up. Changing. Maturing.

Above the school pictures a painting was stuck to the freezer door with magnets. The paper was yellowed and curling at the edges. It showed stick figures that looked like a mom and a dad and two girls.

Gaby was staring at the painting, her eyes drenched in sadness.

Alex had vowed not to touch her, but he couldn't stop himself from drawing her close. Folding her against his body. Trying to comfort her. "Abrietto's gone," he murmured, rubbing his hand up and down her back. "He's not going to get near you again. Every patrol car has his picture. A lot of people are looking for him."

He bent and pressed his cheek to her hair, breathing in her subtle ginger scent. "You're safe now, and Abrietto won't hurt you or the girls. I'll make sure of it."

Her body relaxed against his, the soft weight of her breasts crushed against his chest. She gripped his shirt on either side of his waist, her fists crushing the material. Her fingernails rasped against the starched cotton, and he closed his eyes as he imagined those nails scraping along his skin. Digging in as she cried his name.

Their embrace was quickly becoming more than mere comfort, and Alex tried to draw away. But Gaby tightened her grip on him.

"I've wanted to hold you for so long," she whispered into his neck. "But I wouldn't let myself go there. You were here as a friend, and that's what I wanted. What I needed. And what the girls needed."

The words were on the tip of his tongue. He tried to hold them back, but they burst out in spite of his efforts.

"And now?"

She sighed, pressing her breasts even more tightly against him. "Now, I just need someone to hold me for a moment. It's been a long time since someone made me feel safe."

"'Someone?'" he asked into her hair. Had he been reading her wrong? Was he just a 'someone' to Gaby?

She stilled against him. Finally raised her head. "No, not someone. You, Alex. You make me feel safe. Strong." She stared at him, her eyes dilated, her chest rising and falling too quickly. Then she let go of his shirt, but her hands lingered as she smoothed the material down his sides, flattening the wrinkles she'd put there.

"No one but you. There's no one else I want." Finally she stepped away from him, letting her hands fall away slowly. "I've got a lot of baggage, though, and it's not fair to burden you with that."

His heart soaring, he said, "Maybe you should let me decide what's fair to me."

He reached for her, but she backed out of his reach. "I don't make good decisions, Alex. They explode in my face. And I don't want you caught in the blowback."

"I'm not asking for a decision. For any kind of committment. I only want to comfort you. To take care of you and the girls. Make sure you're safe," he said. "We'll leave it at that, if it would make you feel better."

She tilted her head as she studied him. "I don't think that's what you want, Alex."

She was right. He wanted far more than a friendship with Gaby. More than a casual, no strings hook-up. But he wasn't going to push her. On countless ops as a SEAL – lying in the undergrowth in the jungle, watching a terrorist compound, hiking up a mountain trail with no idea how far his team would have to go – he'd learned patience.

He'd honed his patience while stalking murderers on the streets of Chicago.

He had all the patience in the world when it came to

Gaby Stefano. So he picked up her hand, kissed her palm, then curled her fingers into it. "That's what I want for now," he said.

He turned to the stove and picked up the lid from the simmering pot. "Are we having spaghetti tonight?"

* * *

In spite of herself, Gaby's heart clenched tight at the sight of him in her kitchen, sniffing her sauce, like he was here every day. As if asking what was for dinner was a habit. Familiar.

As if it was a question he asked every evening when he got home from work.

"Nope." She managed to keep her voice light. "We're having rice and beans with sauce tonight."

Still trembling from Alex's embrace, she smoothed her sweaty palms down the thighs of her jeans. She knew it would be a mistake, knew it would end badly, but she really wanted to fall into the promise in Alex's eyes. She yearned to take him up on his offer of no-strings, no promises.

The footsteps clattering down the stairs reminded her she had more than herself to think about. There was more at risk than her own heart.

So she swallowed the lump of regret lodged in her throat and forced a smile. "Can you stay for dinner?" she asked.

He gave her the smile that made his eyes dance. The one that turned her to mush. "I thought I was being pretty obvious about fishing for an invitation."

"You know you're welcome any time."

He set the lid carefully on the pot, but the scent of tomatoes and spices hung in the air between them. Not just dinner. So much more. "Am I, Gaby?"

She meant to say no. Intended to say no. But before the girls reached the kitchen, she whispered, "Yes, Alex. Any time."

"Thank you, Gaby." He touched her cheek, then

stepped back as the girls neared the kitchen. "What can I do to help get dinner on the table?" he asked, his voice easy and light, as if nothing had shivered in the air between them.

"I have salad ingredients ready in the refrigerator. You can toss them together and put them on the table, please."

As she poured the aready-prepared rice and beans into the sauce, she sneaked a glance at Alex as he carefully emptied glass dishes of lettuce, chopped carrots, celery, tomatoes and cucumbers into the big salad bowl on the counter. He grabbed spoons from the silverware drawer and tossed the ingredients, then set it on the kitchen table.

He looked like he belonged here. Like he was part of the family.

Distracted, Gaby stirred the sauce a little too hard, and a tiny splatter of tomatoes splashed onto the back of her hand. The quick stab of pain reminded her of what could happen with Alex.

She was playing with fire. And she would get burned.

CHAPTER 9

The bowl of rice and beans rattled on the table as Bella set it down a little too hard. Cece's fork clanged against the side of her plate, and Alex shifted in his seat as he watched the Stefanos. Gaby was trying desperately to act as if everything was normal. As if Abrietto hadn't been at Bella's school. As if the currency exchange close by hadn't been robbed.

As if this was a normal dinner on a normal school night. But nothing was even close to normal.

"Gaby, how was your day?" Alex asked, trying to lower the tension swirling around the dinner table.

Throwing him a grateful look, she described a student she'd been working with. Told him and the girls about how she'd written a story, and how good it had made Gaby feel.

Thank you. He mouthed the words to Gaby when the girls weren't looking, and her shoulders relaxed. She'd been feeling the tension as much as he had.

He turned to Bella and Cece. "What did you guys do at school today?"

Bella lifted one shoulder. "Nothing."

He tilted his head as he swallowed a forkful of salad.

84

"Really? You sat in every class, your hands folded, staring at the teacher? No one spoke? Did your teacher stare back?"

Predictably, Bella rolled her eyes. "You want to hear how to solve a quadratic equation? How about the strategies for the battle of Gettysburg in the Civil War? Or what about The Scarlet Letter? Should Hester Prynne have been punished?" At that last one, she glanced from Alex to her mother. Back to Alex. "It takes two to make a baby, right? Should my mom be punished and you get off scot-free if she gets pregnant?"

Gaby sucked in a breath, then began to cough. Her fork dropped to her plate with a bang that echoed too loudly in the suddenly silent kitchen. Alex reached over to pat her on the back, but she waved him off. Gulped iced tea.

Once she set her glass on the table, she swiveled to face Bella. Her eyebrows squinched together and she scowled, her face fierce. Poor Bella. Alex did not *ever* want to be on the receiving end of that look from Gaby.

"I cannot *believe* you said that, Isabella." Gaby glared at her daughter, and Bella seemed to sink into her chair. "To a *guest* in our house. What is the matter with you? Where are your manners?"

Bella stared at her plate. "Sorry," she said, her voice sullen.

"Apologize to Alex," she said, a bite in her voice. "A guest shouldn't be subjected to such rude behavior. Especially from someone who is old enough to know better."

Bella glanced at him, then quickly stared at her plate again. "Sorry, Alex." She shoved some beans and rice around her plate, splattering a dab of sauce onto the table. Her hand shook as she wiped it up with her napkin.

"Apology accepted," he said, trying to keep his voice even. Calm. He glanced at Gaby, but she was staring at her daughter, her eyes narrowed to angry slits. Trying to lighten things up, he added, "I'm a little concerned, though, Bella, that you think women get pregnant by shaking hands with a guy or sitting in the same room with him."

Bella's glare should have frozen him solid. Gaby snapped her gaze to him. Frowned, her mouth a thin line.

Alex took a deep breath. Okay. No lightening. He closed his mouth. Focused on his food and took another bite.

"You and I will talk later, Isabella." Gaby stared at her daughter for a long moment, then turned back to her plate.

"You can talk about sex in front of me," Cece said, her head swiveling from her sister to her mother to Alex. "I had health class this year."

Gaby swung around and shared the same angry glare with Cece. "Cecelia, we do not talk about sex at the dinner table. No matter how much you know about it. Is that clear?"

Cece nodded. Hard. "Yes, Mama."

The next couple of minutes stretched into silent, awkward infinity. This family thing was a lot more complicated than he ever imagined it would be. After his own unhappy, lonely childhood, he'd figured that a happy family like Gaby's would be easy. Lots of love. Smiles. Happiness fluttering around them like a damn flock of twittering bluebirds.

Not a bluebird in sight.

"Bella." Gaby stared at her daughter, and Bella reluctantly lifted her head. "Why were you talking about me having another baby?"

Bella stabbed a bean as if it had been attacking her. "I don't want any more siblings."

Alex flashed on an image of a little girl who looked just like Gaby. Or a little boy with her beautiful grin. He blinked twice as he sat frozen, a pile of beans balanced on his fork.

He wanted that. With Gaby.

Before he could banish the image, Gaby set her fork on the plate. "That's not up to you, Bella."

After what seemed like hours of Bella staring at her plate,

she lifted her head. Narrowed her eyes. "So you're thinking about it?"

Gaby tilted her head. "Why would I be thinking about having another baby?" She frowned as she studied her daughter. "Bella, where did this come from? Alex and I are friends. You have guy friends, too." Her eyes narrowed as her daughter's cheeks turned pink, and Alex flashed back to the kid in the gym. Piotr.

"Oh, my God," Gaby breathed. "You've talked about your friend Piotr a lot lately. Is he your boyfriend?"

"Mooom." Bella scowled at her, but her face was bright red.

"*He is*," Gaby said, feeling her throat close around the words. "I'm not ready for boyfriends."

"We're just friends. Why are you assuming he's my boyfriend?" Bella shoved a bean around the plate with her fork.

"Because you're as red as a ripe tomato."

Bella shrugged. "Whether or not he's my boyfriend isn't up to you, anyway," she said, sticking out her chin as she mimicked her mother's words.

Gaby closed her eyes. Her fingers tightened around the fork until her knuckles turned white. Finally she took a deep breath. "Okay," she managed to say. "I won't make assumptions. And you shouldn't either. Not about Alex and me." She avoided Alex's gaze, and the memory of their heated conversation washed over him.

He and Gaby were more than friends. Not quite anything else. *Not yet.*

His heart thundered at the images *not yet* evoked. They would be, Alex vowed. Soon.

Gaby took a deep breath. Tried to smile. "Let's finish dinner so you girls can do your homework and watch the ball game with Alex."

Bella stared from her mom to Alex, then back to her mom. Alex saw the tiny tremble in the older girl's lower lip, then Bella shoved away from the table. "I have a lot of homework. I need to get started."

"All right." As Bella started to march out of the kitchen, Gaby said, "Clear your plate first, please, Bella. We'll see you after you're done with your homework."

Bella dropped her plate and fork into the sink, along with her salad bowl, then stormed out of the kitchen without answering.

Moments later, Alex heard Gaby's daughter's footsteps pounding up the stairs, then the slam of a door. God! Were all teens this volatile? So difficult to read? He swallowed and set his fork on his plate. How the hell did he think he could handle being a stepfather?

Gaby glanced at him, and he saw her shoulders relax a little. "Welcome to the world of teens," she murmured.

"Could have been worse," Alex sighed, nudging her foot with his.

"Really? Worse than asking if we're sleeping together?" Gaby rolled her eyes, but it seemed like her anger had dissipated. He wondered how she did it – dealing with this stuff by herself. Every day.

Cece glanced from her to Alex, then back again. "*I* don't care if you and Alex are having sex."

"Oh, my God." Gaby looked as if she wanted to bang her head on the table. "Cece, what did I just tell you? Polite people don't talk about having sex at the dinner table," she finally said.

"Why not?"

"Because it's private. Something very special that two people share. They don't discuss their sex life in front of other people."

Cece studied them for a moment. "Okay," she said, standing up and going to the refrigerator to pour herself more milk.

Behind the cover of the open refrigerator door, Alex leaned over to Gaby. "For the record, I wouldn't mind having sex at the dinner table. Or anywhere else, for that matter. You know, long as it's with you."

Gaby shoved him away, her face flaming. "That's not helping."

"What's not helping?" Cece asked as the refrigerator door swung shut.

"Alex was teasing me," Gaby managed to say. "He likes to tease people. Haven't you figured that out yet?"

"He teases me a lot," Cece said, slipping back into her chair.

Alex nudged the girl's shoulder with his. "Why don't you tell us about *your* day, Cece?" Gaby pressed her foot against his in a silent 'thank you.'

"Jeremy Powell said a bad word in French class." Cece took a drink, then grinned beneath a milk mustache. "He said *merde*. Madame Renoir got upset. I tried to look it up in the French dictionary, but it wasn't there." She frowned. "It should have been there. How come it wasn't?"

Alex's lips twitched, but he put his fork down and tried to look stern. "That's not a nice word, Cece," he said, flicking the girl's pony tail off her shoulder. "Of course Madame Renoir was upset. Your mother's going to be upset, too, if you repeat it."

Cece's gaze moved between Gaby and Alex. She nodded. "I won't repeat it. But you can tell me what it means, Alex. You speak French."

Alex tilted his head. "I could, but I'm not going to."

"But I want to *know*," Cece said, her voice close to a whine.

Alex knew Cece. He'd bet big bucks she'd check out Google Translate as soon as she could to find out what *merde* meant. Probably say it to Bella, too. If she was anything like Alex had been at Cece's age, she'd lord it over her sister because she knew a word Bella didn't know.

Watching the calculating look on Cece's face, Alex said, "Okay. I'll tell you."

Cece straightened and shot her mother a triumphant look.

"When you're twenty-five or so," Alex continued.

"Maybe I could tell you then."

Cece scowled. "You're really mean, Alex."

"Mean as a snake," he agreed, taking the last bit of his dinner.

Gaby closed her eyes and stacked the plates on the table. "Can we have a peaceful rest of the evening?" she asked, studying her younger daughter.

Cece frowned. "I don't know. Julio was at the school today. Bella told me. Is he coming over here tonight?"

Gaby whitened. Opened her mouth to say something to Cece. Alex put his hand on hers to stop her. Took it away quickly. Cece was watching.

"I don't think he will, Cece. He'd be really stupid to come over here. He knows that if he shows up, your mom would call the police and they'd come and arrest him. They'd put him back in jail and make sure he doesn't get out again. I don't think you have anything to worry about."

Cece studied him for a long moment, suddenly looking far older than her ten years. "He's angry at Mama."

"I know he is." Alex took her tiny hand in his. Squeezed gently. "That's because your mama was very smart and very brave. She called the police when he came over last time, and Julio didn't like it. I don't think he's coming back."

"Okay," she said, taking the stack of plates from the table and setting them in the sink. Then she ran out of the room and up the stairs. "I'm going to do my homework so we can watch the Bearcats," she called.

"Sounds great," he called back.

Gaby watched him with cautious eyes. It was a little scary that he knew exactly what she was thinking. "I'm still interested, Gaby. You think an awkward scene at dinner is going to scare me away?" He snorted. "We had awkward scenes at dinner every night when I was growing up. I'm immune to them."

The difference? His awkward scenes had no love underlying them.

Dinners for him and Theresa were all about gulping their

food down and escaping to their lonely rooms.

Yeah, he'd trade some awkwardness and some difficult conversations for the close bonds Gaby shared with Bella and Cece. That is, if Gaby would ever let him in.

* * *

Glancing at Gaby out of the corner of his eye, Alex leaned into his corner of the couch. She was tucked into the opposite corner. The cushion was indented where Cece had sat between them five minutes ago, happily munching popcorn and peppering him with questions about the baseball game.

Gaby had finally sent her upstairs to get ready for bed.

Now they were alone. They had a lot to talk about. He didn't know where to begin

Apparently Gaby didn't, either. Neither of them had said a word since Cece trotted up the stairs.

Gaby finally set aside the pillow she'd been hugging to her chest and stood up. "Would you like a beer?"

"I'd love one." He stood as well, relieved to have something to do. He took her hand and tugged her back down to the couch. "Stay here. I'll get them."

Without waiting for an answer, he walked into the kitchen. Opened the refrigerator and pulled out two bottles of Goose 312. The bottles clinked together as he set them down, and after he rummaged in the gadgets drawer and found an opener, the caps plinked onto the counter. "You want a glass?" he called.

"No, thanks," she said from the other room. "Bottle's good."

This was feeling...hopeful. Staying for dinner. Talking about school with the girls. He and Gaby having a beer together after the girls were in bed.

They were still pretending they were merely friends, but he knew they weren't. He was pretty sure Gaby did, as well.

She'd leaned on him tonight, although she'd said only

this morning that she couldn't. That she had to learn to stand on her own.

As far as he could tell, she was doing a damn good job on her own. He wished he could share some of the load with her. He knew from experience that *on your own* was a very lonely place sometimes.

He tried the back door and realized the deadbolt wasn't engaged. "I'm locking the deadbolt and hanging the key on its hook," Alex called.

A long pause. Then, "Okay. Thanks," Gaby replied.

He heard her moving around in the living room as he turned the key and hung it on the wall. When he reached the living room, she was sitting on the edge of the couch, using the coffee table to write a check.

Damn it! The door. He should have just locked the door and kept his mouth shut.

He sat down next to her, claiming the spot at her side that Cece had occupied during the baseball game, set the two bottles on coasters on the coffee table. Watched as she finished the check.

She tore it off, then entered it into her register. He didn't look over her shoulder for her balance. Wouldn't invade her privacy. But no way in hell was he taking that check from her.

She handed him the check. Narrowed her eyes until he reached out and took it. "Thanks again for getting Matt to come out on such short notice to replace the doors and the locks. I really appreciate it, Alex."

Alex studied the check for a moment, then set it on the table between them. Nudged it toward her. "Why don't you keep this and think of it as a loan. You can pay me back a little at a time. Maybe fifty bucks each pay period."

She reared back, her expression stunned. Then swung around to face him. "Are you kidding me? That would take almost six months. Five hundred dollars is a lot of money. For a cop as well as a teacher's aide." She shoved the check in his direction. "If you don't take this check, you can leave right now."

He took a deep breath. Let it out slowly. She had no idea he came from money. That he had a trust fund from his grandparents. Five hundred dollars was nothing for him.

He'd been careful not to let anyone know about his money. He wanted to be just another cop on the force. One of the guys. And if everyone knew he'd grown up in the North Shore suburb of Oakvale, they'd treat him differently. He'd be an outsider.

If Gaby knew, she'd treat him differently, too. Probably think she couldn't be with a rich guy.

That was the last thing he wanted.

So he sighed as he sank back on the couch. "You know I can't leave, Gaby. I'm staying for you and the girls. I'm not going anywhere until Abrietto is caught."

"Then take the check and put it in your wallet."

He studied her for a long moment. Then, seeing the resolve in her expression, he folded it, pulled his wallet out of his front pocket, and slid it inside. "Satisfied?"

"Yes. Thank you." She narrowed her eyes. "And I'll be checking to make sure you cash it. Are you clear on that?"

"Crystal." She could make him take the check, but she couldn't make him cash it. He shifted on the couch until he was right beside her. Her heat warmed him, and her spicy, fresh scent washed over him in a reassuring wave of comfort. "How come, Gaby?"

"How come what?" she asked cautiously.

"Why won't you let me help you?"

"By paying my household expenses?" She stared at him, her expression shocked. "I can't do that."

Alex sighed and leaned a little closer. "This was an emergency," he murmured, touching the back of her hand. Circled her wrist. His fingers drifted over her soft, smooth skin. Her pulse raced beneath his fingers, and goosebumps erupted all the way up her arm. "I'm pretty sure new doors and locks weren't in your budget. I have some money saved. Let me loan it to you."

"I wish I could say yes," she admitted. "But I can't. *Won't.*

"You're far too generous, and I appreciate it so much. But I…" She took a deep breath. "I can't let another man take care of me. Not if I want to have a relationship with him. I want to be a partner next time. Not a dependent."

* * *

"Are you talking in general terms, Gaby?" His deep voice made her stomach flutter, and the touch of his breath on her neck sent prickles of need coursing through her. When had he gotten so close? "Or were you talking about me when you said you want to be a partner in your next relationship?"

She should tell him she was talking in generalities. Not specifics. Not about *him.*

But of course she was talking about him. She couldn't imagine wanting anyone else. Even now, with the chaos that was her life at the moment, she wanted him.

"Only one reason I can think of that you're not answering me," he said. He skimmed his mouth over her neck, and she had to bite her lip to keep from moaning. He paused when he reached the sensitive tendon, and she held her breath while his breath puffed over it.

Finally he put his mouth to her skin and sucked gently. Her moan quivered in the air between them. He moved closer. Searched for her mouth. Kissed her lightly.

He was waiting for her to respond. To push him away, or draw him closer. Her head told her to push him away. *Later*, it whispered. *Not now.*

Her heart urged her to jump in. To take what she wanted. What Alex wanted.

Her eyes fluttered open – when had she closed them? – and found Alex too close. His eyes were dilated, dark with need, the vivid blue barely visible. He held her gaze as he bent his head and covered her lips with his.

CHAPTER 10

Gaby's heart raced in her chest, beating so hard she was sure Alex could hear it. He'd realize how he affected her. How much she wanted him.

But his mouth was gentle on hers. Tender. As if he was afraid to scare her off. Bracing for her to shove him away.

Do it, her head urged. *You know it's wrong to encourage him.*

It was wrong, but she wanted to encourage him. She wouldn't let it get out of hand. She'd stop before she *couldn't* stop. But for just a moment, she wanted to kiss him. Taste his mouth on hers. Drink him in. For just a moment, she wanted to know exactly what she was waiting for.

Alex's kiss was tentative at first. He ran his tongue over her lower lip, as if memorizing her taste. Cataloguing every caught breath, every tremble, every sigh. When he sucked her lip into his mouth, she clutched at his shirt. Drew in a deep, shaky breath and opened to him.

He froze, his hands flexing on her shoulders, as if deciding whether to drag her closer or let her go. She made the decision for him when she leaned closer. His hands gentled on her shoulders. Instead of holding tight, his fingers played with the soft cotton of her shirt. Slid beneath the shirt where it was open at the neck and caressed her collarbones. Drew delicate patterns on her skin. She felt his touch all the way to her core, and she shifted on the couch. Edged closer.

He touched his tongue to hers, moving slowly. Reverently. She wanted more. Wanted to feel his chest against hers. She was on fire, and she wanted to make him burn, as well.

She draped one leg over his thighs and slid onto his lap. He groaned, his hands gripping her harder, then he wrapped his arms around her and pulled her against his chest.

His erection pressed into her at exactly the right place. Even through layers of clothing, she felt his heat. His size. She moved against him, unable to contain the tiny whimper at the hard pressure.

Slipping his hands beneath her shirt, he pressed his palms to her back. She felt the imprint of each of his fingers, ten tiny brands burning into her skin. She flexed her hips without thinking, arching into him, and he pressed closer. Murmured her name into the skin of her neck.

She needed to touch him. To feel his muscles against her palms. Press her bare chest against his. Fumbling at his waist, she tugged his shirt free of his jeans. She played with the button at the waistband, starting to push it through the buttonhole. Let it go. Traced the cold metal bumps of the zipper down, feeling him twitch beneath her fingers. Hearing him gasp against her neck.

"Gaby," he said into her skin, his voice rough and breathy. He moved his hands away from her back and cupped both her breasts. Traced the top edge with one shaking finger. "I've been dreaming about this. About you. Every night."

He hooked one finger beneath the bottom band of her bra, between her breasts. Then he stopped. As if waiting for her permission.

Her breasts swelled beneath the soft cotton, aching for his touch. For his mouth. She'd wanted this for so long.

Wanted *Alex* for so long. A haze of lust and need washed over her in a huge wave, dissolving every rational thought. Demolishing every barrier she'd put up against Alex.

"Yes," she murmured, seeking his mouth with hers. When she found it, she opened to him, let her tongue dance with his. Shuddered when he moved his hips in time with his tongue.

Then he opened the front clasp of her bra, and her breasts fell into his hands. He stilled for a long moment, cupping them tenderly, then he smoothed his thumbs over her nipples. His touch was light, but she felt it deep inside.

She pressed her mouth more tightly against his to keep her long, low moan from escaping.

"*God*, Gaby," he panted into her neck. "I barely touched you." He did the swirly thing with his thumbs again, and she surged into him. She needed him now. Inside her. Thrusting for real.

Her hands fumbled with his waistband, shoving the metal disc all the way through the buttonhole. But as she started to lower the zipper, one tooth at a time, he set his hands over hers.

"Cece," he murmured. "She's calling you."

Gaby shot upright, fumbling with the clasp of her bra, her hands shaking too much to close it. Alex pushed her hands away and fastened it.

"Mom?" Cece called "You gonna tuck me in?"

"Coming, baby," Gaby said, her voice shaking. She slid off Alex's lap, straightening her shirt. Smoothing her hair. Tucking the strands that had escaped her braid behind her ears.

She couldn't look at Alex. Instead, she hurried up the stairs and found Cece in her bed. "I wasn't sure you were ready for bed yet, honey."

"That's why I called you," her younger daughter said, smiling at her in the moonlight that spilled between the blinds over her window. "In case you forgot."

"I'd never forget that," Gaby said. But she had. She

hadn't even thought about her girls as she kissed Alex. Touched him. Wanted him.

She sat on the edge of Cece's bed, tucking the blankets under her chin. She pressed a kiss to her daughter's cheek, inhaling Cece's distinctive smell. "Sleep well, baby. I'll see you in the morning."

Gaby kissed Cece one last time, murmured, "I love you," and stood up. Left the bedroom door open a crack.

In a couple of years, Cece's door would be firmly closed like Bella's was. But for now, she wanted it open. As she fell asleep, Cece liked to listen to her mother moving around downstairs. To make sure she was there. Safe.

Another of Julio's legacies.

God! Another reason to be careful with Alex. She'd damaged her children enough. She needed to remember that the next time she thought about making out with Alex on the couch. While her girls were upstairs.

Gaby slipped into the bathroom and plucked one of the tiny disposable paper cups out of the holder. Gulped down three glasses of cold water. Finally, when her breathing had steadied and her hands stopped shaking, she turned and touched her hand to Bella's door. "Good night, Bella bug," she murmured.

There was no answer. After waiting for a long moment, she walked down the stairs.

* * *

Alex watched Gaby flee up the stairs without looking back. He took a deep breath. Then another one. Eventually, the pressure in his jeans eased a little. Enough to walk around.

He paced the living room, wondering if Gaby was coming back down. Would she simply go into her room, close the door and pretend that the last fifteen minutes on her couch had never happened?

No. Gaby wouldn't take the easy way out. She was one

of the strongest women he knew. One of the bravest, too. She wouldn't shy away from an awkward conversation.

And one of those was coming. He'd violated their unspoken agreement. *Friends. No more than that.*

They'd been more than friends for a while. Gaby just wouldn't admit it.

Until tonight.

She'd been as into that kiss as he'd been. The tiny sounds she'd made in her throat, the way she'd touched him, had driven him wild. Made him forget all about his vows to take things slow with Gaby.

She hadn't even heard her daughter calling for her. If *he* hadn't heard Cece, they might have been naked on the couch by now.

He stopped pacing and closed his eyes, dread sweeping over him. If Gaby hadn't gone to her, Cece would have walked downstairs. Maybe caught them having sex. Right after their conversation about sex being private.

He swallowed hard. He'd never dated a woman with kids. It was…different. More than just another adult to think about. Spontaneous lovemaking was probably not on the agenda. Especially not the 'on the kitchen table' kind of sex he'd whispered to Gaby at dinner.

He was about to drag the cushions off the couch and lie on the floor when he heard a floorboard creak above him. Gaby appeared on the stairs, walking slowly. Deliberately. Not looking his way.

He stood up to meet her at the foot of the staircase. "Hey," he whispered. "Everything okay upstairs?"

"Yeah." She took a deep breath and blew it out, fluttering the strands of hair that curled over the sides of her face. He was pretty sure they'd come out earlier. On the couch. "Cece wanted me to tuck her in." She closed her eyes and leaned against the newel post. "I do that every evening. Tonight I forgot."

A faint blush colored her cheeks, and she finally glanced at him. "I wasn't thinking about the girls at all," she confessed, the color in her face deepening.

"Neither was I." He tucked the strands of hair behind her ears. He'd rather tug out the band holding her braid together and comb his fingers through her silky hair, but he'd save that pleasure for another time.

He took her hand, twining their fingers together as he tugged her toward the couch. He sat first, then drew her down beside him. Wrapped his arm around her shoulder, and felt her relax into him. Her chest rose and fell as she exhaled.

Had she been afraid he would want to pick up where they'd left off?

"I got a little carried away earlier," he said quietly. "Forgot about the girls upstairs. I'm sorry."

A tiny laugh huffed out of her mouth. "Nothing to apologize for. *I* forgot about them, too. And they're *my* kids."

"Want to hear my takeaway?" Her braid had draped over her shoulder, and he played with the soft ends of her hair.

"Yeah." She shifted so she was facing him, displacing his hand and tugging her braid out of his fingers. "Can't wait to hear your spin on this disaster."

"*Not* a disaster." He curled his fingers into her shoulder. "I hated being interrupted." Sliding away from her shoulder, he cupped the back of her neck, drew her closer and pressed a soft kiss to her mouth. Backed away, but let his hand linger on her nape. He needed to touch her silky skin. Savor the tiny tremor he felt every time he smoothed a finger down the bumps of her neck .

"But I shouldn't have started anything with the girls upstairs. I'll be more careful next time." He wanted to kiss her again, but he wouldn't do it. "Delayed gratification. We can both think about that next kiss. What might come after a kiss."

"You're not the only one at fault," she murmured, holding her gaze. Her hazel eyes glowed, tiny flecks of gold shining in the green and brown. "In case you didn't notice, I was as much into it as you were."

"Oh, I noticed." His glance dropped from her mouth to her chest. She was breathing too quickly.

He closed his eyes. Breathed deeply as he struggled for control.

When he finally opened his eyes, she was watching him. Her mouth was slightly open, and she swallowed when he stared at it.

He wanted to press his mouth to hers again. Instead, he stood and moved away from the couch. Eased the shade covering the front window to the side and studied the street. He needed to take his mind off Gaby and what they'd done on her couch.

Abrietto was out there somewhere. Was he watching Gaby's house? The thought of Abrietto stalking Gaby or the girls was a splash of ice water to his libido. Exactly what he needed to remind himself to focus.

Moving back to the couch, he sat at the other end. Far enough away from Gaby that he couldn't touch her. "Can we talk about Abrietto for a little bit?"

Gaby frowned and raised an eyebrow at him. "That's a mood killer."

"Supposed to be. I'm trying to distract myself from what I really want to talk about. Want to do. So humor me."

"Okay." She sat back into the corner of the blue and yellow plaid couch. "What do you want to know?"

Alex stretched his legs out and picked up his now-warm beer. "Where did you work when you were married to him?"

"That's an odd question."

"I have a good reason."

"Okay." She shifted on the cushion to face him, tucking one leg beneath her. "I worked at Illinois Masonic Hospital. As a nurse's aide." She sighed. "I cleaned bed pans. Helped patients to the bathroom. Cleaned up messes. Changed bed linens if a patient got sick or sweaty."

"Did you ever bring things home from the hospital?"

She reared back as if he'd struck her. "Are you asking me if I brought drugs home to Julio?"

He was an idiot. "Of course not, Gaby." He leaned toward her and took her hand. Kissed her palm. "I know you wouldn't do that. I meant accidentally. Stuff that might be in your pocket when you walked out the door."

She scrunched her forehead as she thought. "I guess I did," she finally said. "I always had a pair of gloves, so they were handy if I needed them. Never syringes or things like that, things that needed to be disposed of properly. But bandages, maybe. I'd stick a roll of tape in my pocket and forget it was there. Gauze pads. Stuff like that. Scissors sometimes. I always took those back. Not the bandages or the gauze or the gloves. I'd just throw them away when I found them in my pocket at home."

Alex nodded, but he sat up straighter. His heart began to thud, and his hands tingled. "What did the gloves look like?"

She shrugged. "They were latex gloves. The kind that are in every doctor's office."

"What color?" *He'd asked too sharply.* He needed to dial it down.

"Why is that important?"

"It just is."

"Blue. Blue latex."

A bolt of electricity shot through him at the world 'blue'. He leaned over and pressed another kiss to her mouth. "Thank you, Gaby. I can't tell you why, but that's a huge help." He didn't want to ask Gaby about Julio's finger – he didn't want to alarm her about the possibility Julio had robbed the currency exchange until he was more certain.

First thing he'd do tomorrow, though? Check Julio's record for identifying marks. See if part of the little finger on his left hand was missing.

He edged back to his corner of the couch before he could touch her again. She watched him move away, a smile playing on her mouth. "Have we been sent to opposite corners of the couch for being naughty?"

"Not nearly as naughty as I'd like to be," he said without thinking.

"Me, either," she whispered, her smile fading.

"May I ask you a more personal question?"

"Sure. Go ahead," she said, eyeing him speculatively. "I can't wait to hear what comes after 'what color latex gloves did you use'."

"Why did you quit that job and become a teacher's aide? Since you want to be a nurse. Wouldn't working in a hospital have been better for you?"

She flopped back into the couch, regret in her eyes. "Yeah. It would have been. The hospital would have helped pay for my nursing classes, too. But the hours were too unpredictable. I didn't know until a week before what days I'd be working. Or which shift. And after Julio was...gone, I needed a job that meshed with the girls' hours. So that I could be here after school, then go to my own classes at night."

"You're a good mother, Gaby," Alex said, remembering how his own mother had handed him and his sister off to nannies. "Your girls are lucky."

"Not as good as you think." She stood, Alex's words reminding her of what she'd done to Bella a year ago. The way she'd put her daughter in danger. No, she wasn't a candidate for mother of the year. "I need to go to bed. I'll lock up behind you."

He stood, as well. "I'm not going anywhere, Gaby. Until Julio is safely behind bars again, I'm spending my nights here."

"You don't have to do that. I have solid doors. New locks. We'll be fine."

"Probably. But I'm still staying. All I need is the pillow and blankets I used last night."

She stared at him for a long moment. Finally she nodded. "All right. And thank you. I feel better, knowing you're down here."

"That's why I'm staying."

* * *

The next afternoon, Alex was sitting in his car, writing up the notes from a witness interview he'd just done, when his cell phone rang. He pulled it from his pocket and glanced at it. Gaby.

Smiling, he pushed the call button. "Hey, babe. What's going on?"

"He's here," Gaby said, her whisper taut with fear. "Julio. He broke one of the windows in the back door. He's trying to get into the house."

CHAPTER 11

Clutching the phone, Gaby backed away from the kitchen door. Julio stared at her through the small broken pane of glass, his face contorted in a snarl of anger and hatred. She couldn't tear her gaze away from him as she fumbled on her counter, searching for her knife block.

"Gaby!" Alex's voice. "Take a deep breath. I'm calling 911. I'm on my way."

"I...I already did that." Her teeth chattered together as she spoke.

"Good. That's good. An officer will be there in..." Gaby heard him murmuring through the phone. "Two minutes," he said. "I'll try to get some squads there sooner."

Gaby gripped the phone tightly. Pressed it against her ear so hard that it hurt. Watched Julio, his hand twisted inside the door, blood dripping down his hand. He'd cut it when he reached through the broken glass to try and open the door.

"Follando perra," he shouted. "I want what is mine. *Abra la puerta de mierda."*

Open the door. Yeah. She'd do that right away.

Gaby sucked in a deep breath as Julio's fingers found the

doorknob. He curled them around it, shaking it violently. Blood spattered onto the door. The glass. The wall.

He searched for the knob to unlock the deadbolt, leaving smears of blood on the wood and the metal doorknob. When he didn't find it, he lunged, banging into the door. Cutting his arm as he reached for her.

Alex's voice murmured in her ear, but she couldn't understand what he said. He was talking to someone else. But the sound of his voice steadied her. He was on his way. So were other police officers.

Julio couldn't get into the house. The door was locked. Thank God Alex made sure Matt got the strongest door available. The strips of wood separating the panes of glass were solid. Julio could pound on them all he wanted, but they weren't going to break. He couldn't kick the door down. But her heart pounded so hard that she heard the blood rushing through her ears.

Her searching fingers found the wooden knife block. Scrabbled at it, her shaking, sweating hands slipping off the smooth knife handles. Finally she got hold of a knife and pulled it out. Curled her fist around it and extended it toward Julio.

"Get your hand out of the window," she said, surprised that she could even speak. "Or I'll cut you."

He lunged at her again, his body barely rattling the solid new door. Thank God Alex had made sure it was installed yesterday.

He slid his hand away from the shards of broken glass, and she took a shaky breath. Maybe he was leaving. But she gripped the knife more tightly. In case he wasn't.

He fumbled in his pocket. When he brought his hand up again, he was holding a gun. Black. Enormous.

Fear swept over her in a black wave. She stared at the gun as Julio aimed it at her. His hand steadied. Blood from his cuts dripped onto the floor. Ran in rivulets down the door.

Feeling as if she was moving in slow motion, she stabbed

at his hand with the knife, gagging when it hit resistance, then sliced into flesh. Julio jerked back, swearing at her in Spanish. Words she'd never heard before.

He lifted the gun again, leaving fresh splatters of blood, then froze. Turned and ran down the steps and into the alley. The gun bounced against his right leg as he ran.

He turned right. Stumbled over the pothole in the cement in front of her neighbor's garage. Then he disappeared.

A siren wailed. Close by. Julio must have heard it. That's why'd he'd run.

Moments later, someone pounded at the door in the front of the house. Gaby hurried to answer it, hoping it was Alex.

A uniformed officer stood at the door, her hand on her gun. "Ms. Stefano?"

"Yes." Gaby's teeth chattered. "He has a gun. He ran down the alley. That way." She waved her hand toward the left. Frowned when the officer flinched. Stepped back.

The officer touched her radio. "Suspect ran toward Keeler. In the alley behind the house. He has a gun. I repeat, he has a gun." Then she looked at Gaby again. "You need to put down the knife, Ms. Stefano. Now."

Gaby looked at her hand, saw the long, serrated bread knife. Huh. She'd tried to stab Julio with a bread knife?

"Put it on the table, Ms. Stefano. Okay?" The officer pointed toward the table next to the door, the one that held the vase she'd used to hit Julio the last time he'd attacked her.

A bubble of hysteria rose in her throat as she gently set the knife on the table. Forced her fingers to relax so she could let it go.

Now the table held both of her weapons.

She took a step back and collapsed heavily on the stairs to the second floor. Studied her hands as they shook. How had she gotten Julio's blood on her hands? Had he touched her? She didn't remember.

"May I come in, Ms. Stefano?"

Gaby nodded. "Yes," she said, her voice a hoarse croak. "Of course." She waved toward the kitchen. "He was back there. Broke a window on the door."

Instead of running toward the kitchen, the police officer crouched on the floor in front of Gaby. "Are you hurt, ma'am? Did the intruder cut you?"

"I don't know," Gaby glanced at the woman's name badge, "Officer Kramer. I don't think so."

The officer pulled gloves out of her pocket as another car pulled up. Turning, she opened the door and called out, "He ran toward Keeler." Then she gloved up and took Gaby's hand.

"You have a cut on your palm," she said. "It might need a couple of stitches." She touched her radio, said, "We need a bus." She rattled off Gaby's address, then let go of her hand. "Where can I find a clean towel?"

"In the..." Gaby swallowed, the mental images making her heart crash against her chest. "In the kitchen. The drawer on the left side of the stove."

"Got it." The woman rose to her feet. "You stay here. I'll be right back."

Two more doors slammed, and another uniformed cop ran up the stairs to the front door. "All right if I come in?" he asked.

"Yes." *Where was Alex?* "The other officer is in the kitchen. Back there." Blood trickling down her arm, she waved toward the back of the house.

Another officer ran up the stairs, and Gaby waved him toward the back of the house, too. The officers already there were talking, but Gaby felt as if she was floating, wrapped in a thick layer of cotton that blocked out everything. She heard voices, but couldn't make out the words. She saw the blood on her arm, but nothing hurt.

The first officer returned with a dishtowel and pressed it to Gaby's palm. "Lots of blood in the kitchen," she said. "Are you injured anywhere else?"

Gaby frowned. "I don't think so. I don't feel any cuts." She looked down at herself, saw only drops of blood on her khaki pants, on her green sweater. "I don't think that's my blood." Her voice began to shake. "He was bleeding a lot. Trying to grab me. It's probably his blood."

"Who was this?"

"Julio Abrietto. My ex-husband. He...he escaped from Cook County jail a couple of days ago."

The woman scowled. "The idiots at the jail let him go, you mean."

"Doesn't matter how it happened. He got out of jail." Gaby wrapped her arms around herself, suddenly freezing cold.

"Looks like he lost a lot of blood. I doubt he'll get far." The woman was trying to reassure her. But all Gaby could see was Julio's face. The rage in his eyes. The murder in his expression. The gun in his hand.

Another door slammed outside. More footsteps pounded up the stairs. The cop kneeling in front of Gaby turned around. "Jennings? What are you doing here? This wasn't a..." She glanced at Gaby. Cleared her throat. "This was an attempted home invasion."

Gaby knew what the cop had started to say – Alex was a homicide detective. And this wasn't a murder.

It would have been, though. If Julio had gotten into her house, he would have killed her. If he hadn't heard the sirens and run, she would be dead.

What would happen to her girls if she died? Where would they go? Who would take care of them?

A sob rose in her throat. Burst free, in spite of her efforts to stop it. Then another. My God! Her girls would be left with no one if Julio killed her.

"Gaby?" Alex's voice. His hands settled on her shoulders. Lightly, as if afraid he might hurt her. "God, Gaby! Are you all right? Did that bastard hurt you?"

Gaby stumbled to her feet and reached for him. He pulled her into his arms and held her so tightly she could barely breathe.

He pressed his face to her head, and his whiskers caught in her hair. She spread her palms on his back, pressing her fingers into his muscles, holding him against her. She couldn't bear to let him go, but he didn't seem to want to let her go, either.

"Promise me," she said into his chest. "If Julio kills me, will you take care of the girls?"

"Gaby." He eased away from her and cupped her face, wiping tears from her cheeks. "Abrietto isn't going to kill you. I'm not going to let him. That's what I'll promise you."

"No!" she cried. "You can't promise that. Tell me you'll take care of them."

She felt his mouth brush her hair. "Of course I will, sweetheart." He caressed her back, slow circles that calmed her. "I'll take care of Bella and Cece as if they were my own kids. Okay?"

Gaby drew a shuddering breath and nodded against his chest. "Thank you, Alex."

"I'll do anything for you, Gaby."

She let the reassuring beat of his heart calm her. Settle her. Alex was here, and she was alive. She was alive, and the girls were safe. They would be safe if she…if she wasn't around. That was all that mattered.

She had no idea how long she'd held onto Alex when he eased away from her. "The ambulance is here," he said, kissing the palm of her uninjured hand. "Let's have them take a look at you."

"I'm okay," she said. She moved the hand clutching the kitchen towel. "It's just a small cut."

He cradled her injured hand in his, then wrapped an arm around her shoulders. "We'll let the paramedics confirm that for both of us. Okay?"

Opening the door, he held her close as they walked down her front steps. He helped her into the back of the ambulance, then sat beside her on the gurney as one of the paramedics unwrapped the blood-spattered towel from her palm.

"I'm Suzie Chapman," the paramedic said as she cleaned away the blood and cleaned the wound with a yellow-brown liquid. After spending some time examining the inch-long cut with a magnifying glass, she finally set the magnifier aside.

"I don't see any glass, and it's a small cut. It needs a few sutures, though. I could suture it for you here, or we can take you to the ER if you'd prefer that."

"You do it, please," Gaby said immediately. She turned to Alex. "The girls." She heard the panic in her voice and tried to tamp it down. "Julio might be going to the school. I need to get over there and pick them up."

"Already covered. I talked to Raine and Connor. Connor's on his way. He's picking the girls up when he gets Raine. He'll bring them home."

Remembering what the kitchen looked like, Gaby shuddered. "They can't see what happened." She grabbed Alex's arm with her uninjured hand. "It's...there's a lot of blood in the kitchen. He cut himself when he was trying to get into the house. The girls are going to be scared enough. I don't want them to see all that blood. They'll have nightmares."

The girls weren't the only ones who'd have nightmares.

Alex took out his phone and typed in a text. Slid the phone back into his pocket. "I just asked Connor to take them to his place. We'll pick them up there." He rubbed her back with his free hand, and it soothed her. Made her feel less alone. "Then I'll take you to a hotel for the night. Okay?"

After paying for the new door and locks, she couldn't afford a hotel. She'd have to suck it up and stay here. She shuddered, remembering the broken glass. The blood. The knife on the table next to her front door.

So many things to remind the girls of what had happened at their home.

"No, we'll stay here," she said, swallowing hard. "We'll

go out to eat, and afterward I'll send the girls right up to their rooms so they don't see the mess. I'll clean the kitchen after they're in bed."

"Listen to what you're saying, Gaby." His hand tightened on hers. "If the girls come back here, they'll see the kitchen. So let's do this. If you don't want to stay at a hotel, you and the girls can stay at my place tonight. I have a guest bedroom, and a small room I use as an office that has a pull-out couch. The girls can sleep in the guest room. You'll sleep in my room, and I'll sleep on the pull-out in my office."

"Alex…" She swiveled to face him as the paramedic was setting a purple packet of suture material on a tiny table. "I don't want to intrude on your space. You've done so much for us. I can't let you give up your bed for us. It's…it's…"

"It's what, Gaby?" He continued to rub her back. "What if something happened at my apartment? Would you let me stay with you?"

"Of course I would." She didn't even have to think about it.

"Then why won't you stay with me?" Without giving her a chance to answer, he continued, "I'll get Matt out tomorrow to replace the broken glass. I've got the names of several companies that clean up after this kind of…of attack. By the time you and the girls get home tomorrow, everything will be back to normal."

Nothing would be normal until Julio was back in jail. But Gaby sighed. Nodded. She didn't really have a choice. She didn't want the girls anywhere near this house until every trace of Julio's presence had been scrubbed away.

"I'm going to give you a shot to numb the area," the paramedic said, swabbing the area with alcohol. "Are you allergic to any local anesthetics?"

"No." Gaby shook her head. "I'm not."

Alex held her hand when she winced at the prick of the needle, but in moments, she couldn't feel a thing. As the paramedic tore open the suture packet, Alex twined his fingers with hers. "After she's done, I'll help you put bags together for yourself and the girls. I want to take a quick look at your kitchen, then we can go."

The paramedic was bent over her palm, but Gaby couldn't feel a thing. "Go ahead and check out the kitchen while I'm getting sewn up. I'll come in the house when Ms. Chapman's finished and get the girls' things together. You can help me pack their old backpacks."

Alex held her hand a little more tightly. "You sure you don't want me to stay here with you?"

She wanted him to stay. She wanted to hold onto his hand and never let go. But she *needed* to see her girls. The sooner they finished here, the sooner they could pick up Bella and Cece. "I'm training to be a nurse," she said. "I think I can handle seeing my hand get sutured. Go." She untangled her hand from his and waved him toward the house. "I'll come in when we're done here."

The paramedic looked up with a tiny grin. "I think she's telling you to quit hovering, Jennings. She's got this. Steady as a rock."

"You're sure, Gaby?"

"Positive." She leaned toward him impulsively and pressed a quick kiss to his mouth. "Thank you for coming when I called you."

"Any time, Gaby." He kissed her back, lingered long enough for Gaby to rethink her effort to get him to leave, then he was gone.

The paramedic resumed suturing. "Jennings has it bad," she said, her eyes twinkling. "Good thing it looks as if you do, too."

Gaby swallowed, embarrassed heat flooding her face. She stared out the door as the paramedic suturing her hand, smiling wanly at her neighbors as they gawked at her in the back of the ambulance.

Finally she said, "Alex is a friend. That's all."

The paramedic looked down at Gaby's hand, but Gaby knew she was rolling her eyes. "Right. Just a friend. Sorry

I misunderstood."

She placed the last two stitches, then gently bandaged her hand. "Leave that on for twenty-four hours," she said. "Then start changing the bandage every day. Wear gloves if you're putting your hands in water, and try not to get it wet. If you notice any puffiness, or if there's any discharge, call your doctor for an antibiotic prescription."

She swiveled her stool around and put her instruments into a rectangular metal pan, then set it in a cabinet. "Don't try to do too much with that hand," she said. "Take it easy for a few days."

"Thank you," Gaby said, standing up. Dizzy, she swayed for a moment, and the paramedic grabbed her arm.

"I'll walk you into the house. Your adrenaline rush is burning off."

"I'm fine," Gaby protested.

Instead of answering, the paramedic held her with a firm grip and helped her down the step onto the street. Once past her front door, Ms. Chapman called, "Jennings?"

"In the kitchen," he answered.

"Ms. Stefano's a little…"

Gaby interrupted. "I'm a little what?" Gaby turned her head to stare at the paramedic.

"I was going to say wobbly," the woman said after a long moment.

"You're not telling Alex that I'm wobbly." She narrowed her eyes until Suzi Chapman nodded reluctantly. "Thank you. I'm fine."

"You're not fine," Suzi said calmly. "If I'd taken you to a hospital, they wouldn't let you walk out the door. You'd have ridden in a wheelchair."

"Yes, well, we're not at the hospital, are we?"

A flicker of admiration came and went in Suzi's eyes. "I was going to tell Jennings to take care of you. But you can take care of yourself, can't you?"

"Yes, I can." She'd been taking care of herself for a very long time. Long before she met Alex.

He was walking toward them, his expression filled with concern. Caring. Something else she refused to name.

What would it be like to have someone take care of her once in a while?

She couldn't let herself think like that. Couldn't allow herself to *want*.

The paramedic studied Gaby, then nodded, apparently happy with what she saw. "Take care of that hand." She glanced at Alex and smiled. "Take care of Jennings, too. He's a good guy."

Alex stared after Suzi for a moment, then wound his arm around Gaby's waist. She wanted to lean on him. Wanted to forget about Julio. Just for a few minutes.

Instead, she kept herself rigidly erect as Ms. Chapman repeated her instructions to him. Having two people know what to do was smart. Careful. But she hated feeling like Alex's responsibility.

She didn't want to be anyone's *responsibility*. She wanted to be a partner.

Gaby stared at the bulky bandage on her hand. What was she going to tell Bella and Cece? That Julio had tried to break into the house? That he'd tried to shoot her?

They would be terrified. But not telling them would be worse. They had a right to know what was going on. They wouldn't be safe if they didn't know what had happened.

Bella could no longer walk the few blocks from the bus stop to Spencer. Gaby didn't have the money to pay for a cab or an Uber, so Bella would have to stop helping with the tae kwon do club, at least until Julio was caught.

Her heart twisted for her daughter. She knew how much Bella enjoyed her role on her former team. How much she loved working with Raine and her former teammates.

Her involvement with Julio had put her girls at risk. Now, with Julio out of jail and apparently bent on revenge, that risk was amplified.

She glanced at Alex as he listened to Suzi. Asked questions. Nodded. The paramedic was right – he *was* a good guy.

He and Julio were as different as two men could be. Polar opposites.

The memory of that kiss they'd shared last night burned in her memory. She'd spent a lot of time today thinking about it. Wondering when they could do it again.

She hadn't lied to Suzi Chapman – she hadn't been wobbly when she walked into the house.

A few minutes ago, though? Watching Alex walk toward her? *That* had made her wobbly.

She could no longer deny she wanted him. Badly. And he clearly wanted her.

But that desire had to go on the back burner. She needed to focus on other things – making sure her girls were safe. Figuring out where Julio might go. How best to catch him.

She could do that. *Would* do that.

Alex took his arm away from her waist and pulled out a chair for her, and as she sank onto it, he took his hand away.

She wanted to ask him to put it back. To let her feel his calm strength. His concern.

She wanted to rewind the last few moments and let herself lean against him. Allow him to comfort her.

Comfort him in return.

Once seated, she glanced around her kitchen and awareness swept over her. Blood-spattered walls. The door. Glass crunched beneath the technician's feet.

What she wanted with Alex? That was a dream.

This was her reality.

CHAPTER 12

The ambulance light flashed rhythmically, sending bursts of red light through the living room window and into the kitchen. Alex watched it spin for a moment, clenching his fists.

Gaby was in that bus, getting the cut on her hand sewn up.

A picture of her, blood-soaked towel wrapped around her left hand, was permanently engraved on his brain. Every flash of red light amped up his anger. His rage and hatred for Abrietto.

His fear for Gaby and her girls.

He could have lost her today.

He needed to be in that bus with Gaby. Holding her hand. Distracting her.

Reassuring himself she was safe.

Letting his fear and concern control him wasn't going to help Gaby, though. Neither was hand-holding. She could handle getting her palm sutured. She was one of the toughest women he knew.

But even a tough woman would be shaken by what had happened in her kitchen. Gaby must be terrified. And based on what Gaby had asked him, she was more scared for the girls than for herself.

If Julio kills me, will you take care of the girls?

He wanted to wrap his arms around Gaby and never let her go. Of course he'd take care of the girls. But there was no way he'd be doing it himself. He'd die himself before he let Abrietto hurt a hair on Gaby's head.

As the ambulance light washed over him, he took a step toward the bus, then stopped. Gaby hadn't wanted him to hover. So as much as he wanted to sit next to her, to hold her hand and comfort her, he'd give her time to collect herself. To put her game face on.

The best thing he could do for her right now was figure out how to catch Abrietto. Give Gaby her life back.

Rolling his shoulders, he retreated back to the kitchen. Forced himself to focus on what had happened in this room.

He watched the evidence tech take samples of the blood, lift fingerprints and photograph the crime scene. The room looked like a slaughterhouse, with blood spatters sprayed across the floor, the walls, even the counter. Abrietto must have punched his bare fist through the window, then stuck his hand through the opening. Judging by the amount of blood, he'd ignored the tooth-like shards of glass lining the wood lattice in his eagerness to get to Gaby.

Blood smears stained the glass red, and blood had congealed in the seam between the wood and the glass. Abrietto had been desperate to get inside.

Desperate to get at Gaby.

The hard knot in Alex's gut hadn't eased since he'd gotten Gaby's call. Now, seeing the damage in her kitchen, knowing it was the result of Abrietto's obsession with Gaby, his dread torqued even tighter.

He reached for his training and forced himself to study the room objectively. His gaze moved from the door to the counter to the floor. Why had Abrietto come back here?

He had money from the currency exchange robbery. He

could have left Illinois and disappeared. Instead, he'd stayed in Chicago.

Why? To kill Gaby?

Why kill her? Revenge? Anger that she hadn't bailed him out, like she'd done in the past?

Rage because she'd managed to escape his control?

All of those reasons were irrational when weighed against freedom. Abrietto had been released by mistake. Why not take advantage of it and get out of town?

There was only one reason Alex could think of. Hatred and anger had made Abrietto irrational.

He swallowed, and a lump of ice slithered down his throat. Irrational men were dangerous. They didn't think logically. Didn't behave the way you expected them to behave.

"Jennings?" Suzi Chapman called from the other room.

"In the kitchen," he called as he turned around.

Suzie held Gaby by the elbow, although it looked as if Gaby was trying to shake her off. Alex hurried over and wrapped an arm around Gaby's waist, guiding her toward the kitchen.

She turned her head and glared at him. "It was five stitches, Alex. With a local anesthetic. I think I can manage to walk into the kitchen."

"Who said I was trying to help you?" he said, tightening his arm around her waist. "You scared the crap out of me, Gaby. Maybe *I'm* feeling a little wobbly."

Gaby's snort echoed the sound Suzie Chapman made. At least Chapman tried to disguise it as a cough.

He pulled out a chair for Gaby, then stopped. Pressed his fingers into the muscles over her hip. "Wait. Are you sure you want to be in here? We can go into the other room."

Gaby didn't roll her eyes at him, but her expression told him she wanted to. "I want to be in here," she said. "I need to see what Julio did."

He eased her onto a chair, then sat beside her. Her

bandaged left hand rested in her lap. He reached for her right hand, then hesitated.

One of her nails was ragged and torn off. A dark red crescent of dried blood lined her cuticle. It looked as if she hadn't even noticed.

He curled his hand into a fist as he stared at Gaby's hands. Those small, delicate fingers shouldn't have to know how to stab at someone with a knife. How to grip a wall or a counter to avoid being grabbed through a pane of glass.

Gaby tucked her girls into bed with those hands. Made her daughters meals.

Touched him.

No. He wasn't thinking about that. Right now, he needed to focus on catching Abrietto. On making sure Gaby and Bella and Cece were safe.

"Hey, Jennings," the tech called. He crouched on the porch in front of the open door. "You want to take a look at this?"

Alex glanced at Gaby. She made a shooing motion, and he walked into the chilly sunshine. "What've you got?"

The tech tapped at the keyhole. "Do you have any idea how old these locks are?"

Alex frowned. "About twenty-four hours, give or take."

"Brand new?" The tech glanced up sharply. Alex nodded.

"Take a look here." He circled the lock with a pencil. "Something's jammed into the keyhole. Can't tell what it is, but it's shiny. A gum wrapper, maybe?" He shrugged. "Who knows?"

Alex crouched in front of the door and stared at the lock. Something bulged out of the keyhole, but he couldn't grasp it. "Think you can pull it out?"

"I tried. It's stuck in there good. Couldn't budge it."

Alex stood. "Damn it," he said softly. "Abrietto wedged something in there so the key wouldn't work."

The tech's eyes narrowed. "You think he planned to hide somewhere and watch the place? Grab her when she couldn't get the door unlocked?"

"Maybe." Alex clenched his hand into a fist. Released. Imagined that hand was around Abrietto's neck. Clenched again. "Whatever that is, it didn't get there by itself."

He pulled the door wide to go back into the kitchen and found Gaby on the other side of it. "What's wrong with the door?" she asked.

He hesitated for a long moment, trying to protect her. Realized quickly that trying to protect her would be worse than telling her. She needed to know. "Come outside," he said, taking her good hand, being careful with the broken nail.

"Take a look there," he said, pointing toward the keyhole without touching it.

Gaby crouched, just as he had, and frowned. "Something's in the lock."

"Yeah. I think Abrietto shoved something in there."

She stood up, glancing from him to the tech. "Why would he do that?"

The tech nodded at him. *This one's all yours.*

Taking a deep breath, Alex said, "You won't be able to unlock your door. It makes you a sitting duck."

Gaby paled. Glanced toward the alley. The garage. "He'd wait for me," she said in a low voice. "In the afternoon. I go in the front door when I get home from work, but when I pick up the girls, I park in the garage. I'd be trapped back here. With the girls."

God! Alex hated to do this to her. Hated seeing that knowledge on her face. "Matt will replace the lock when he fixes the glass."

Gaby wrapped her arms around herself and stepped back into the kitchen. Sank down in her chair.

The tech waited for Alex to enter, then followed, closing the door behind them. "You've got kids?" he asked Gaby.

"Two girls," she answered.

"I'd get them out of town. A whack job like this?" He waved his hand toward the broken window, the smears of blood. "Who knows what else he'd do?"

Gaby nodded and bowed her head. Her throat rippled as she swallowed. She had both hands in her lap where he couldn't see them.

Alex wanted to punch the tech for scaring her, but he was right.

"The whack job have a car?" the tech asked Alex.

"Not sure. I pulled all the reports of vehicles stolen from this neighborhood, but I haven't looked at them yet." He'd gotten the call from Gaby and run out of the station.

"Good thinking." The tech put a flat silver tin back into a large tackle box. "You should get her and her kids into protective custody."

Alex glanced at Gaby. Her face was ashen, but she glanced from him to the tech. Listening.

"He'll come back," the tech said.

"Yeah, I figure he will," Alex replied. "He's failed twice now. But failure doesn't stop an irrational man."

He dropped into the chair beside Gaby. She'd clenched her hands together so tightly that the tips of her fingers were white. God! She was trying so hard to be strong. To keep it together. It made him want to sweep her into his arms and promise that he'd always keep her safe.

He couldn't promise that, though. No one could promise that. He'd told his sister he'd take care of her, and...

Swallowing hard, he gently pulled Gaby's hands apart. "Hey. You're gonna pull out your stitches if you keep that up."

She glanced at her hands. Flattened them on her thighs. "Yeah. You're right."

Lifting her bandaged hand, she cupped it in the good one.

"Anesthetic wearing off? Hand starting to hurt?"

She lifted one shoulder. "A little. Not too bad." Staring at her bandaged hand, she whispered, "Julio was like...like a mad man. Why would he come here again? Why wouldn't he try to get away?"

She sat so straight in the chair. Looked around the room so calmly. If Alex didn't know her so well, he'd think she was handling it just fine.

But the tiny tic beneath her eye, the tremble of her hands she tried to hide, told him how terrified she was. How frightened she was for her girls. Alex took her good hand and held it in both of his.

"I have no idea why he'd come back here. A smart man would leave town. Get as far away as possible." His hand tightened on hers. When he realized he was gripping her too hard, he relaxed his fingers. "I'm pretty sure he was the guy who robbed that currency exchange. If he was, he has plenty of cash."

Gaby froze. "How do you know that was him?"

"Julio is missing part of the little finger of his left hand, right?" He'd checked Abrietto's file today.

She nodded. "It happened at work." Her lips flattened. "He told me he was talking to the guy next to him, not paying attention to the saw he was using, and he cut his finger off."

Dangerous and *stupid. A bad combination.* "The man who robbed the currency exchange wore blue gloves." She tensed against his arm at 'blue gloves'. "And the little finger of his left hand was missing. The clerk noticed the floppy glove on that finger."

"Had to be Julio," she whispered.

"Yeah."

Alex didn't say anything else. He merely held her hand, let her work through it on her own.

Gaby finally took a deep, shuddering breath. She glanced around the kitchen one more time, then used her good hand to steady herself as she stood. "Let's go upstairs. Get the girls' stuff."

As they walked up the stairs, Alex said quietly, "You know you have to be careful at work. If Abrietto has a car, and I'm betting he does, he could follow you there. Attack you when you're walking from your car to your building."

They'd reached the top, and Gaby stopped. Shuddered. "I won't be safe anywhere. Neither will Bella and Cece."

"You'll be safe at my place," he assured her. "Lots of locked doors. A doorman."

"We can't hide in your apartment until they catch Julio," she said, lifting her chin. Her hazel eyes were troubled, the green mixed with flecks of gold that made them glitter. As if she was crying.

She wasn't, though. Alex wondered if she ever cried.

"Yes, you can," Alex replied. "I have plenty of room. Or we could arrange for protective custody, like Frank downstairs suggested. Abrietto's angry. Acting out. Angry men make mistakes. We'll catch him soon," he said, trying to reassure Gaby. "And this time, I'll personally load his ass onto the prison bus to Joliet."

She put her hand on his arm. "I don't want you to get into trouble," she said, her voice low. "Julio is my problem. Not yours."

"Gaby, your problems are mine." He stroked his hand down her head, his fingers tangling for a moment in the smooth silk of her braid. "Don't you know that?"

"That doesn't seem fair." She gripped both his arms. "You never tell me your problems. So I can't help *you*."

"Okay. I'll make you a deal." The heat from her fingers burned through his suit jacket and dress shirt. All he could concentrate on was the grip of her strong fingers. The want in her eyes.

"What deal?" she finally asked.

Not the time, Jennings. He cleared his throat. "The next time I have a problem, you can help me work it out."

A tiny smile flickered over her mouth and disappeared. "I'll hold you to that."

"I hope so."

He stared at her for a long moment. She stared back. Finally, seeing the fear she was trying so hard to hide, he wrapped his arms around her and drew her close.

She resisted for a long moment. Finally, with a sigh, she relaxed into him. Burrowed her hands beneath his jacket and flattened her palms against his back.

Heat roared through him, wiping away every thought. Leaving only sensation behind. The heat of her hands. The scent of her hair, that orangey ginger he was becoming addicted to. The pressure of her chest against his.

He closed his eyes and rubbed his cheek against her hair. *Her nipples were hard.*

As hard as a certain part of his anatomy.

This was insane. They didn't have time for this. They had to pick up the girls. Get some food. Settle into his place.

But Gaby didn't seem in any hurry to let him go. And he was thrilled to hold onto her. Breathe her in. Run his hands up and down her back, soothing. Telling her that she wasn't alone in this.

He had no idea how long they stood there, clinging to one another. He wanted to push her against that pale yellow wall behind her. Feel her body form itself to his, from their chests to their thighs. Kiss her until she was trembling in his arms.

And he was trembling in hers.

He lowered his mouth to hers and tasted. She opened to him immediately, and he groaned into her mouth. Let his tongue tangle with hers. He didn't remember moving, but somehow she was against the wall, one leg curled around his.

"Jennings?"

The tech. In the living room.

Gaby slid sideways, putting some distance between them. She tucked a strand of hair behind her ear. Her hand trembled, and she sucked in a shuddering breath.

"Yeah?" he said as the tech moved into view at the bottom of the stairs. Desire hummed like a living thing between him and Gaby. He ached to feel her skin against his. Needed to taste her. To listen to the sounds she'd make as he explored her body. He had to shove his hands into his pockets to keep from reaching for her.

"I'm done here. You have any lumber in the garage? Want me to nail that door shut for you?"

Alex glanced at Gaby. She nodded.

"That would be great, Frank. I'd do it myself, but we have to pick up Gaby's kids."

"No problem. Catch you later."

He listened to the evidence tech pound down the porch stairs in the back of the house.

When he turned back to Gaby, she'd moved to the door of a bedroom. Far enough away that he couldn't reach out and touch her. Their eyes met and held for a long moment, and desire arced between them. Urgent. Powerful. Overwhelming.

Finally, retreating into the room, Gaby said, "I should pack."

She hesitated. Glanced over her shoulder. "I shouldn't let you come in here right now." Her low voice was raspy. Too breathy. "But I need help getting my duffel bag from the closet."

It wasn't a huge bedroom, like the one at his apartment, but it told him a lot about Gaby. A queen-sized bed stood against one wall. The brass headboard and footboard looked old, as if she'd had them for a long time. The bed was covered by a gorgeous handmade quilt in soothing blues, greens and yellows. Gauzy green drapes covered windows on either side of the bed, thin enough to let in light but still provide privacy.

His gaze swung back to the headboard. When they finally made love, would Gaby grip the bars? Or would she hold onto him instead? Wrap herself around him and let go.

He closed his eyes at the vivid mental picture. Shifted to ease the pressure in his suit pants.

Swallowing hard, he forced his gaze away from the bed. An old dresser stood against the wall at the end of the bed, and a rocking chair sat in the corner. A pile of three or four books sat on the nightstand beside her bed, along with a lamp.

Clearing her throat, Gaby said, "The duffel bag is on the top shelf in the closet."

Alex opened the door, and the spicy, gingery scent he associated with Gaby drifted out. Tightening his hand on the doorknob, he struggled to control his body's reaction.

After a long moment, he looked up at the shelf, saw a red duffel in the corner and pulled it down. He glanced at Gaby's clothes, the shoes standing in neat rows on the floor. A pair of heels in bright blue suede caught his eye. He wanted to see her wearing those shoes.

Carefully closing the door, he set the bag on the bed, next to a pile of folded clothes. The black strap of a bra peeked out from the bottom of the pile, and he stared at it. Wondered what the rest of the bra looked like. Would it be lacy? Silky? Or practical black cotton?

He looked up to find Gaby watching him. Another jolt of electricity flashed between them. Alex swallowed. "How about I wait in the hall while you finish here? Then I can help you with the girls' things."

Gaby tucked the bra strap beneath the small pile of clothes. Her hand shook a little as she smoothed her finger over the neat stack of clothing. "That would be great. Bella and Cece both have old backpacks in their closets I can use for their things. If you could find them, that would help."

"Will do."

He hadn't been in a kid's bedroom in a while, but Cece's was about what he'd expect from a ten-year-old. She had two stuffed animals on her bed, and he'd bet Cece had had them for a long time. The black bear's tail was partially torn. The white dog with black spots had become a gray dog with black spots.

A low bookcase full of colorful books stood in the corner. He spotted the Harry Potter books he and his sister had read together and swallowed hard.

Cece's twin bed had a floral quilt, and pictures of teens with guitars hung on the wall. Probably from some boy band. There was also a picture of the red-haired heroine of the Disney film 'Brave'. He opened her closet door, spotted the worn backpack in the corner, and took it out.

Bella's room belonged to an older girl. 5 Seconds of Summer and Taylor Swift decorated her walls, reminding him of Theresa's posters of Blink 182. His sister had adored that band.

Swallowing the lump in his throat, he spotted a team picture of the Chicago Bearcats. He drew in a deep breath and willed the emotion away. Tapped the picture lightly. "That's my girl."

Bella had a bookcase, too, as stuffed with books as Cece's was. The night table beside her bed held two books and an iPod. He was heading to her closet when he saw a hint of brown peeking out from beneath her pillow.

He hesitated, but curiosity got the better of him and he lifted the pillow. A long, ragged monkey stared up at him with beady black eyes. It looked like a piece of cloth with a monkey's face, until he realized it was a hand puppet.

Alex carefully replaced the pillow, making sure he arranged it exactly as it had been before. Bella would be completely mortified if she knew he'd seen the monkey.

It was no wonder the kid needed her old puppet. Bella had been having a rough few days, with Julio showing up at her house, then appearing at her school. And Alex's constant presence in the house was obviously unsettling for her, based on the way she'd acted at dinner last night.

He found her old backpack on the floor of her closet, and set it on the bed. Then he walked out of the room.

Gaby was walking out of her room, clutching the red duffel bag in her right hand. She had her left cradled against her chest. The local anesthetic must be wearing off

"Let me take that," he said, sliding the bag out of her hand. He set it in the hall. "If you want to set out things for the girls, I can pack them in their bags. Looks like that hand is aching."

She glanced at her left hand with a frown, as if she hadn't realized she'd pressed it against her chest. Staring at it for a long moment, she sighed. "It's starting to throb."

"Amazing how much a little cut can hurt, isn't it?" He cupped her elbow and steered her toward Cece's room.

He headed into the younger girl's room, then realized Gaby wasn't with him. Turning, he found her staring at him, her forehead wrinkled.

"Does it hurt that bad?" he asked, cradling her bandaged hand in both of his.

She shook her head slowly. "No. I mean yes, it hurts, but not that much. I was just surprised."

"At what?" he asked, trying to remember why she might be surprised.

She took a deep breath. Let it out slowly. Finally, in a low voice, she said, "It *was* a little cut. I expected you to say it couldn't hurt that much."

Fury rose in him like a tsunami, making him clench the door jamb to steady himself. If that was the reaction she expected from a man who lo...was crazy about her, no wonder she was so reluctant to get involved.

"Is that what Abrietto would have said?" He kept his voice low. Even. But he curled his hand so hard around the door jamb he was afraid he'd left nail marks in the wood.

"I'm sorry, Alex," she said, moving closer to him. She wrapped her arms around him and held him tightly. "I know you're nothing like Julio." She leaned back and looked at him, tried to smile, but it wobbled on her mouth. "If anything, you're the anti-Julio. As different from him as night to day. I...I guess I have a new normal to figure out."

"We'll figure it out together," he whispered. "Because I have a new normal, too."

Gaby leaned back and frowned at him. "What are you talking about?"

"You're my new normal, Gaby. I want you in my life — you and Bella and Cece. It's been a very long time since I thought about sharing my life with anyone."

Fear flashed momentarily in her eyes, quickly replaced by caution. "I'm not...I can't ask the girls to accept another man into our family, Alex. They're still getting over having Julio in our lives."

"I know that." He stroked wisps of hair away from her face. "I'm not asking you to marry me, Gaby. But how about dating? Can we date?" His heart beat faster just saying the words, and he had to hold back a wince. Man, when had he become such a sap? He glanced at Gaby. He was pretty sure it was the day he met her.

"I want to do things with the girls. Go out by ourselves once in a while."

Gaby took a deep breath. Let it out slowly. "I can't think about this until Julio has been caught."

It was time to lighten this up. "I know." He brushed a kiss to her head and stepped away from her. Away from the need to kiss her mouth. "So I'll put it on my calendar." Giving into temptation, he pressed his mouth to hers. Lingered a beat too long. "But I'm warning you, I'm gonna nag until you say yes."

Gaby stared at him, her eyes dilated with desire, her cheeks flushed. "I'll want to say yes, Alex. So much. But I'm not sure I can."

CHAPTER 13

Gaby took a deep, shuddering breath. She had to be scrupulously honest with Alex. It wouldn't be fair to him otherwise.

She unwound her arms from him and took a step backward. Brushed her hands down her black pants. How could she explain so Alex would understand?

"I'm pretty sure we come from very different worlds," she began. "You were shocked because I was surprised you were concerned about my pain. But that's the way I was raised.

"My parents were second-generation immigrants." She lifted her head to meet Alex's gaze. "My grandparents didn't have much education, but they worked very hard and raised five children. They didn't have time to coddle their kids. Neither did my parents." She shrugged. "It sounds cold and unfeeling, but my parents were very loving. Just...more matter of fact, I guess.

"I think that's one of the reasons I'm so...hesitant about getting more involved with you. You haven't lived my life. And I haven't lived yours."

Alex stared down at her, and she couldn't read his

expression. Was he angry? Offended? Hurt? She had no idea.

Finally he sighed. "You're right, Gaby. We were raised very differently. Our families were night and day." He took her hands, so careful with the injured one that Gaby wanted to weep.

"But it doesn't matter to me, and I hope it doesn't matter to you. A lot of couples come from different backgrounds," he said carefully. "That's what makes life interesting – learning from each other. Sharing your experiences and blending your traditions. It would be pretty boring if everyone fell...got involved with someone exactly like themselves. So please don't make our differences a barrier."

She wanted to give in. Go where her heart was trying to lead her. But she couldn't dismiss their differences as easily as Alex.

And she had to think of her girls first. Think of how they would react to her and Alex dating. Cece seemed to adore Alex. Bella...Bella liked him, too. But she was jealous. Prickly and difficult, as only a teen could be.

It had been a year since Julio was arrested. A year since Gaby had send Bella away. Gaby still hadn't completely repaired her relationship with her older daughter

Gaby would have to navigate those waters carefully. And she couldn't promise anything to Alex until she was certain there was nothing hidden in the depths that could blow up and destroy them.

He stood waiting patiently, watching her. Alex had eased himself into her family slowly and carefully. Now, it felt as if he belonged. As if the three of them were incomplete without him.

Gaby sighed. "I want to, Alex. So much. But right now, I need to see my girls." She laid her hand on his arm. "Later, okay?"

He covered her hand with his. "Of course, Gaby." He brought her hand to his mouth and pressed a kiss to her palm. "Let's go get them."

She blew out a breath, both relieved and disappointed that their conversation was over. Tugging her hand gently from his, she said, "If you'll take my bag to the car, I'll pack the girls' things. They're probably wondering why they had to go home with Raine and Connor."

"I need to see them, too," he said, picking up her bag. "I'll be right back to get the girls' bags."

Gaby drew a deep, ragged breath. "Thanks, Alex."

He paused halfway down the stairs. Glanced over his shoulder. "Of course, Gaby."

* * *

Fifteen minutes later, Gaby stood beside Alex at the door to Connor and Raine's apartment. Alex had held her hand as they walked into the building and up the stairs. Now he squeezed her fingers and let her go. "You've got this," he said softly.

Yeah. She did. Gaby took a deep breath. Let it go. The girls were here. Safe. From here, they were going to Alex's apartment. He'd assured her it was in a secure building.

She rapped on the door, and Raine opened it almost immediately. "Gaby. Alex. Come in," Raine said, stepping to the side. She nodded toward the kitchen. "They're working on their homework. Connor's in the office, Alex. You probably want to catch him up?"

"Yeah, thanks, Raine." He disappeared into a tiny room and closed the door behind him.

"Mom?" Bella pushed away from the table and hurried toward her. "What's going on? How come we had to go home with Ms. Taylor?"

"A little situation at the house," Gaby answered, trying to hide her hand in her pocket. But Bella had seen the flash of white.

"What's wrong with your hand?" the teen demanded, grabbing her wrist and pulling it out of hiding.

"Something's wrong with Mom?" A chair scraped

against the floor in the kitchen, and Cece ran into the living room.

In the soft light, the white bandage almost glowed. And now that she was looking at it as if through the girl's eyes, it looked enormous.

"Mom!" Bella's voice was panicked. "What happened?"

"Mommy," Cece cried at the same time. "You're hurt!"

Gaby wrapped her arm around Bella's shoulders and hugged her. Hard. She drew Cece against her and kissed the top of her head. "I'm fine, girls. It's just a tiny cut. But I needed a few stitches."

Bella touched the bandage with a tentative finger. "Is that why Mr. Donovan picked us up?"

"That's part of it." She sat on the couch and drew both girls down, one on either side of her. She clutched Bella's hand and wrapped her injured arm around Cece's shoulders.

"I'll be in the other room," Raine murmured. She opened the door to the office, stepped inside and closed it behind her.

"What's going on, Mom?" Bella demanded.

Gaby sighed. She'd hoped to put off this discussion until the four of them were alone. Until she and Alex could explain it to the girls together.

She froze. She was already thinking of herself and Alex as a unit. A team.

As if he was already part of their family.

Trying to ignore the way her heart begun to race, Gaby took a deep breath and said, "Julio came to the house again this afternoon." The words brought all the horror crashing over her again, but she struggled to keep her voice steady. Swallowing, she continued, "He tried to get in, but the door was too strong. He broke a couple of the glass panes in the door, and I cut myself on one of the pieces."

She couldn't tell her daughters that Julio had been trying to shoot her and she'd been forced to stab him. That would be far too frightening for them. "The police scared him away, I have a few stitches in my hand, but everything is okay. The bandage is so thick because I'm not supposed to use this hand, or bend it. That's all."

Bella's gaze slid to Gaby's hand where it rested on Cece's shoulder, and the girl frowned. "Are you sure you didn't have to, like, have your hand sewn back on?"

Gaby pulled her older daughter close and kissed the side of her head. "Nothing like that, baby. Just a very small cut. I promise you. I'll show you when I change the bandage tomorrow."

She took another deep breath. But before she could tell them they'd be staying with Alex tonight, the door to Raine and Connor's office opened and Alex stepped out.

He came around the couch and sat on the edge of the coffee table. "Your mom filling you in about what happened today?"

"Yeah." Bella glanced from Alex to Gaby, then back again. "Why did you have to come with her to pick us up?"

Gaby was surprised at Bella's question, but Alex smiled at her easily. "She shouldn't drive for a day or two – she's not supposed to bend her hand. And you guys and your mom are staying at my place tonight. I have plenty of room for all of you, and Matt's going to come tomorrow and fix the broken glass in your kitchen door. We'll do something fun in the morning, and by the time you get home, everything will be as good as new."

Bella watched Alex for a long moment, then glanced at Gaby and nodded, apparently satisfied. "Okay." She scowled. "Julio is an idiot. Why did he come back?"

"He's out of control," Alex said, his voice neutral. "Which means you girls are going to have to be more careful. Bella, I'm going to send a squad car to pick you up every day and drive you to Spencer, then your mother or I will pick you and Cece up."

"No way," Bella said immediately. "I'll take the bus."

"Why not let someone Alex knows drive you to Spencer?" Gaby furrowed her forehead as she stared at her daughter. After seeing Julio outside the school yesterday,

Bella had to understand the danger of walking the three blocks by herself. "I know you can take care of yourself, but we're both worried about you and want you to be safe."

Bella scowled. "If a cop car picks me up, everyone's going to think I've been arrested. The whole school will know."

"You can just explain to your friends…"

Before Gaby could finish, Bella rolled her eyes. "*Really*, Mom? You think I should tell all my friends about that freak-show Julio? Tell them that my *stepfather* escaped from prison?"

"He's not your stepfather." It was the first thing Gaby could think of to say. "Not anymore."

"He was. That's why he's being such an asshole."

"Bella," Gaby said sharply. "What have I told you about swearing?"

"That's what he is," Bella muttered.

Cece watched, rapt. *Like she was watching a play*, Gaby thought, exasperated.

Gaby stifled a sigh and turned back to Bella. "Whether he is or not doesn't matter – I don't want to hear you using language like that. Especially not in front of your sister." God, all she wanted was to curl up in a ball and forget about today. The *last* thing she wanted to do was argue about swearing with her fourteen-year-old.

"I've heard that word before," Cece volunteered.

"I'm sure you have, honey, but it's not a nice word and we don't use it." Gaby tightened her grip on both girls, then let them go. Stood up. "Let's get going, okay? Get your homework together, girls, and I'll thank Ms. Taylor and Detective Donovan."

As the girls hurried into the kitchen, Alex took her hand. "I think that went okay," he said. "Let's go home."

Home. Like she and Alex returned to the same house every night. As if going home together was normal.

It was way too appealing. Too tempting. She slid her fingers away from Alex's and stood up. "I need to thank

Raine and Connor."

She rapped lightly on the office door, and Raine opened it immediately. "Thank you so much for bringing the girls home," Gaby said to the slender young woman. "I really appreciate it."

"Not a problem." Raine smiled as she glanced at the two dark heads shoving books and papers into backpacks in the kitchen. "Any time. I loved having them here." She hesitated, then lowered her voice. "You're welcome to leave them with us anytime. This is a secure building, and we have good locks on our doors. Connor's usually home on weekends, unless he's on call, so they'd be safe here."

Connor came out and put his hand on his fiancé's shoulder. "Absolutely, Gaby. Whatever you need."

"Thanks. Both of you." Gaby's stomach clenched. If she needed to bring the girls back here, it would mean something bad had happened. "I hope we don't have to take you up on your offer, but I appreciate it."

She turned as the girls hurried into the room, their packs slung over their shoulders. "Thanks, Raine," Alex said, hugging her. "You too, Con." He gave the other detective an awkward man hug, consisting mostly of pounding Connor's back.

Ten minutes later, they were driving away from the apartment. "Hey, you two," Alex began, "I know you're sick of pizza, since we had it the other night, but is anyone interested in getting *pizza* again?"

"Yes!" The girls spoke immediately, in chorus. Vehemently.

"Pizza! Yay!" Cece cried.

"Okay. I'll have them delivered to my place."

He turned to Gaby, frowning. "Wait. Don't you have school tonight?"

"Nope. Today is the first day of Spring break. No classes until a week from Monday."

Alex's eyes caught hers and held for a long moment. Gaby saw hope and reassurance there – in ten days, he was telling her, Julio would be behind bars again. They would all be safe.

That was exactly what she wanted.

She glanced over at him again. Once Julio was caught, would everything change between her and Alex? Would they go from being casual friends to...to something more?

Say it, Gaby. Would they be in a relationship?

He'd still watch the ball games with Bella. He'd still speak French with Cece in an exaggerated, funny accent.

He'd still look at her with longing. But maybe, after Julio was caught and they resumed their normal life, she and Alex could act on that longing.

Gaby studied the bulky white bandage around her hand. If Julio had gotten into the house today, she'd have more than a tiny cut on her palm. She might even be dead.

Did she really want to keep Alex at a distance? Wait until she was 'ready', whatever that meant?

Or did she want to take a chance and risk everything?

* * *

Twenty minutes later, Gaby looked around uneasily on the sixth floor of Alex's apartment building as he unlocked his door. There were only two doors on the floor, and the long hallway was lit with golden light from ornate fixtures. Alex lived in a beautiful building – old and elegant. Well-maintained. Right on Lake Shore Drive. There was a doorman who'd greeted him by name.

The kind of place where people with serious money lived.

Apparently, she didn't know Alex as well as she thought she did.

The lock clicked open, and Alex reached inside to flip a light switch. Then he stood back and waved them in.

Cece stood in the foyer and gazed around, her mouth slightly open. "Wow!" she finally said.

Wow, indeed. Gaby managed to keep her mouth shut as

she glanced around. The huge living room on their left held a couch and two matching chairs, all covered in a deep green fabric. An afghan lay over the back of the couch, crocheted in a vivid rainbow of colors.

The furniture sat on an Oriental rug that shimmered with blues, reds and greens. It didn't look like one of the cheap ones she'd seen at department stores, either. The room looked as if it had been lifted from a design magazine. The décor was subdued. Stylish. Elegant.

Gaby's gaze returned to the afghan. It seemed out of place in the tasteful, refined room.

A fireplace was tucked into one wall, flanked by built-in bookcases. A huge flat-screen television filled another wall. Artwork had been hung carefully in the room, and they weren't paintings by young artists he'd picked up at local art fairs – the kind Gaby had on her walls

Bella gazed around the room. "Awesome TV," she said, her gaze drifting from the art to the television to the fireplace.

"If your homework is done, we can watch the 'Cats later," Alex offered.

One of his feet jiggled, tapping the golden hardwood softly. He dropped his keys into a deep blue glass bowl on a table, then closed the doors. "Come on in and make yourself comfortable." He had a backpack slung over each shoulder and Gaby's duffel in one hand. "Let me show you where you'll be sleeping."

The two bedrooms in the back of the apartment were both huge. One held a king-sized bed, and Alex set Gaby's bag on the floor in that room. The other bedroom held a double bed covered with a floral quilt that looked homemade, a dresser, and a bookcase filled with books. A smaller flat screen television sat on the dresser, as well as a basket filled with travel-sized bottles of toiletries.

Bella studied the room, her gaze lingering on the toiletries that all had French names. "This room looks like a hotel. Do you rent it out on Airbnb?"

"No." Alex bit his lip, but Gaby saw the smile he was hiding. "I have those because someone told me it was a nice touch for a guest room."

"Quite the guest room," Bella muttered under her breath, but Gaby had no problem hearing her. She was sure Alex had heard her, too.

Alex set the girls' backpacks on the floor. "The pizza should be here in about five minutes. Let me show you the rest of the apartment."

All three of them followed Alex through a dining room that held an old cherry table and eight chairs, resting on another Oriental rug. The reddish wood gleamed, clearly polished with loving care. A breakfront against the wall, in the same wood, held what looked like Fiestaware dishes in a rainbow of colors.

Gaby smiled as she studied them. The dishes were a humble touch in an otherwise elegant home. That was the Alex she knew and…and appreciated.

They walked through a long hall, and just before they entered the kitchen, Alex nodded to a small room that held a computer, some filing cabinets and a big couch in a red plaid pattern. "I'll be sleeping in here. In case you guys need anything during the night."

As they stepped into his kitchen, Gaby glanced around the room. Cabinets that she suspected were also cherry lined the walls, and light green granite made up the counters. A giant refrigerator and stove stood against one wall. Alex reached into a large pantry and pulled out a couple of packets of microwave popcorn.

Finally something that looked familiar. He bought the same brand as she did.

"For the game," he said to the girls. "After our pizza."

Just then his phone buzzed, and Alex pressed the green button. Listened for a moment. "Thanks, Tim," he finally said. "I'll be right down."

"The pizzas are here," he said as he slid the phone into his pocket. "I have to run down and pick them up."

He was gone before Gaby could reach for her wallet to give him some cash.

As the door closed softly behind him, Gaby and the girls all looked at each other.

Bella spoke first. "Who *is* he, Mom?"

CHAPTER 14

"Alex is our friend, Bella," Gaby said, her gaze touching on every detail of the beautiful, spacious kitchen. "No matter where he lives."

"But he's, like, rich." Bella turned in a circle, her gaze touching everything. "He'd have to be, to live in a place like this."

"That doesn't matter," Gaby replied, but a tiny voice in the back of her mind wondered what *else* she didn't know about Alex. "Being rich doesn't change the kind of person you are."

Bella spun back to face her, rolling her eyes so hard Gaby was afraid they might fall out. "Get real, Mom. Rich people are different. Trust me. I know."

Gaby tilted her head and studied her daughter. "How would you know, baby? None of our friends are rich. Or if they are, we don't know it, because they don't live like this."

"There are rich kids at my high school," Bella muttered, touching a blue and gray ceramic bowl on the counter that held pears and apples. "And they're all assholes."

"Bella…" Gaby sighed, glancing around, but Cece

wasn't in the kitchen any longer. "What do you mean by 'assholes'?"

"They think they're better than everyone else." Bella picked up a red pear and tossed it into the air. Caught it. Tossed it again. "That they're *entitled* to stuff. Like the best tables in the cafeteria. They make people leave if someone else gets the table first." She threw the pear high and wasn't able to catch it before it landed on the floor. Seeds and juice and red pear splattered everywhere.

Gaby's stomach churned as she frowned at the mess on Alex's perfect hardwood floor. It reminded her of the mess left behind in *her* kitchen.

Bella stared at the smashed pear for a long moment. "Sorry, Mom," she finally muttered, grabbing a handful of paper towels from the holder on the counter.

After scraping most of the mess off the floor, she looked around for a wastebasket. Gaby let her gaze drift over the room, but they didn't see the trash bin.

"It must be in a cabinet," Gaby said, staring at the doors. She hated opening them at random – it felt like snooping.

Bella began to yank handles until a door rolled open, revealing two bins. One held bottles and cans. Bella dumped the soggy paper towels in the other bin.

Gaby grabbed another paper towel, held it under the faucet for a moment, then wiped the remaining bits off the floor. She opened the door beneath the sink, looking for a cleaning product, but couldn't find one. Before she could check the pantry, the door of the condo opened. "Pizza's here," Alex called.

Bella and Gaby glanced at each other, and Gaby touched her daughter's arm, trying to soothe the panic she saw in Bella's eyes. "It was only a pear. No big deal. I'll tell him," Gaby told her daughter. "But remember, you *know* Alex. Nothing about him has changed."

Bella lifted one shoulder, her universal 'Yeah, right'.

By the time they emerged from the kitchen, Alex had set the pizza boxes on the table in the dining room and was pulling plates from the breakfront. Gaby leaped for the boxes and lifted them off the beautiful old table. The boxes were hot enough to be uncomfortable. They didn't belong on the bare wood.

"Do you have hot pads or something for these pizza boxes?" Gaby asked. "So they don't mark the table?"

"Don't worry about it," Alex said. "The table can take a couple of pizza boxes."

"You're not going to get grease and heat marks on this gorgeous table." Gaby juggled the hot boxes. "Bella, go find something to put these on."

Bella hurried toward the kitchen as Alex snatched the boxes out of her hands. "You shouldn't be holding that with your injured hand." He reached to set them back on the table, and Gaby grabbed his wrist. "Wait."

Moments later, Bella came out of the kitchen with two oven mitts. She set them on the table, and Gaby nodded to Alex to set the boxes down.

Cece had been reading a book in the living room, and she hurried into the dining room and slid into a chair. As if she'd lived here forever. "What kind did you get, Alex?"

"I got one with anchovy and olives, and one with mushrooms and spinach," he said, his mouth twitching. "Your favorites, right?"

Cece frowned at him. "Eww! That's gross. I hate olives and mushrooms and spinach. I don't even know what anchovies are."

"They're little fish," Alex said. "Here, try some."

He opened a box and set a slice of pizza on a plate, then passed it to Cece. She scrutinized the slice of cheese pizza, the cheese brown and bubbly, red sauce smeared on the crust. "I don't see any fish."

"I was teasing you, Cece," Alex said gently. "I know what your favorite pizza is."

"Thanks, Alex," she said, spinning back to the table. "I was worried."

She spun a little too hard and the slice of cheese pizza

flew off her plate and landed on the Oriental rug. Cheese side down.

Oh, my God.

Gaby rushed over and picked up the piece of pizza. Set it on the plate and stared at the carpet in horror. Greasy cheese and red sauce on that gorgeous rug.

"Where's your carpet cleaner, Alex?" she said, her voice too high.

"Don't worry about it, Gaby. It'll come out."

"Only if we clean it right now."

"I'll get it later," he said, waving her into a chair and passing her a piece of *her* favorite pizza. Pepperoni and mushrooms. He'd already served Bella a slice of the cheese. "What does everyone want to drink?"

No way was Gaby going to sit and eat pizza while that stain darkened the rug beneath them. So instead of eating, she stood up and hurried into the kitchen for a handful of paper towels. She moistened half of them, returned to the dining room and tried to clean up the carpet.

She bit her lip as she blotted up the stain. She and the girls hadn't been here for an hour and they'd splattered a pear across his kitchen floor and dropped a slice of pizza on his expensive carpet.

Heat washed over her cheeks when she stood up and headed back to the kitchen. Was it possible to die of embarrassment?

Alex followed her into the kitchen, took the paper towels and dropped them into the garbage. "Gaby, it's okay," he said, taking her hands after she finished washing them. "I had the carpets Scotchguarded. In case there were ever kids in the apartment."

He glanced toward the dining room, and Gaby suddenly got it. He'd been planning on having her kids in his apartment. "You did it for my kids. You figured we'd be here." She swallowed, knowing what that meant. Alex had been…interested for a long time. "You knew my kids could be careless."

"No. I knew *all* kids can be careless," he corrected. "Adults, too, sometimes. I didn't want anyone to be worried about the furniture or the rugs." A hint of sadness filled his eyes, then disappeared. "Much better to be a little careless and have fun, than always worrying about ruining something. Trust me. That's a real fun-killer."

"Full disclosure," she said, taking a deep breath. "Bella dropped a pear on the floor in here earlier. We wiped it up, but I couldn't find any cleaning supplies and didn't want to poke around."

"You can poke around in here any time, Gaby," he said, curling his hand around hers. In spite of her embarrassment, she slid her fingers between his. "I want you to make yourself at home. Cece and Bella, too."

"Yeah, well, looks like they've already done that," she muttered.

"Let's eat," Alex said, gripping her uninjured hand more tightly and tugging her toward the dining room. "We'll worry about the clean-up later."

Gaby clung to his hand as they walked down the hallway. His fingers were warm and strong around hers. A refuge she wanted to hold close. Instead, she straightened her shoulders and let him go before the girls could see them.

Her daughters had been chased out of their own home by Julio, and were staying in Alex's apartment. They'd realized he was rich. That was enough change for one day.

They didn't need to see their mother holding hands with him.

* * *

An hour later, Alex and the girls were sprawled on the couch, watching the 'Cats game. Gaby had collapsed into one of the big, comfortable chairs, the long, scary, emotional day finally catching up with her.

She hadn't stopped shaking until they were safely in Alex's apartment. Now, the rush of adrenaline finally gone, all she wanted was to curl up and sleep in this cozy chair. Her eyelids tried to flutter closed as she watched Alex and her girls.

Bella seemed to have forgotten her reservations about Alex's apparent wealth. She was having what looked like a serious discussion with him about the wisdom of the last play. Something about whether a bunt had been smart in that particular situation.

Cece kept an eye on the game, but her French book was open on her lap. Gaby watched her studying it during the commercials.

Gaby knew Cece had already finished her homework. She must be reading ahead. Pride fluttered in Gaby's chest. Cece was so excited about learning French. And she was doing so well. The city had a specialty school for languages. Maybe Cece should apply for it.

Gaby sighed. That belonged on the back burner. She had more urgent things to worry about right now. Julio, the house, their safety…scenarios circled her brain, ramping up her anxiety. What should she do next?

Alex could have Matt fix the new door. He could have some special cleaning company get rid of the mess in her kitchen. But he couldn't prevent Julio from coming back.

A phone rang, startling her out of her daze. Alex pulled his cell out of his pocket. Frowned. "I need to take this. Bella, take notes on the game so you can tell me what I missed."

He stabbed hard at the icon. As if he wanted to silence it. "Hello, Mother. What can I do for you?"

His voice sounded…hard. Frigid. Not the way Gaby answered the phone when *her* mother called from Florida.

Alex stepped into the dining room and disappeared down the hall to the kitchen. Gaby could hear his voice, but couldn't make out his words. They sounded cold, though. Even irritated. When she realized she was trying to overhear, she forced her focus onto the television.

Alex's mouth was tight and pinched when he returned a

few minutes later. Gaby began to rise, then sank back down. She couldn't reach for Alex in front of the girls.

"Everything okay?" she asked.

"Fine," he bit off.

Then he looked at her and his eyes softened. *Later*, he mouthed.

She nodded, hoping no one was sick. Hurt.

Alex sat on the arm of her chair and leaned close. His clean, fresh air scent washed over her, and she had to stop herself from reaching for him.

"Nothing's wrong," he murmured, softly enough that the girls wouldn't hear. "I'll fill you in after the girls are in bed."

Had she been that transparent? Or did he simply know her so well?

That was...thrilling.

And scary.

By nine o'clock, the 'Cats were winning handily and Cece was nodding off. Bella was watching the game, but her eyes were wide open, as if she was forcing herself to stay awake.

"I think you girls need to go to bed," Gaby finally said. "It's been a long day." For all of them.

Bella frowned at her. "Tomorrow is Saturday. No school. I want to finish the game."

"You can watch the game on the television in the bedroom," Alex suggested. "I'll put it on mute so Cece can fall asleep."

"I won't fall asleep," Cece said immediately. "I want to watch the game, too."

"You can watch it as long as you want," Alex assured her, rising from the couch. "C'mon. I'll show you the bathroom and make sure it has fresh towels."

Ten minutes later, Gaby bent over the bed and kissed Cece. Went around to the other side and kissed Bella. Then she crouched next to the bed, reaching for both Bella's hand and placing her throbbing, bandaged one over Cece's hand. "I know this is scary and unsettling," she said, trying to keep her voice calm. Gentle. "But a lot of police officers are looking for Julio. They'll find him soon, and our lives will get back to normal. Okay?"

Both girls nodded, but Gaby saw the skepticism in Bella's expression. "I won't let anything happen to you," she said fiercely. She'd die herself before she let Julio touch them. "We're safe, and that's not going to change. So watch the game until you fall asleep, and we'll do something fun tomorrow. Okay?"

Both girls nodded sleepily. Gaby kissed them both again and stood up. "I'll be right next door in the other bedroom," she told them. "It's got a huge bed. If you get nervous about being in a strange place, come and find me."

"Why would we get nervous?" Bella asked. But the tiny tension lines around her older daughter's eyes smoothed out.

"Just saying," Gaby said lightly. She glanced at the screen, where the baseball game played silently. "Sleep well. I love you both."

She turned off the overhead light and closed the door, standing outside for a moment. The low murmur of the girls' voices trickled out, but Gaby couldn't hear what they were saying. Which was okay. She was glad her girls were friends. Glad they talked to each other.

She leaned back against the door for a moment. To steady herself. Then she pushed away, stood straight and headed toward the living room. She had a few questions for Alex.

* * *

Alex sat on the couch, watching Gaby close the guest bedroom door softly behind her. She looked worn down. Pale. Hanging on by a thread.

Gaby slumped against the door, her eyes closed. He'd seen that same look in countless crime victims – as if shock and fear had sucked up every ounce of energy in her body.

Like Gaby had to gather herself to take another step.

Alex clenched a fist. Abrietto had done that. He'd tried to break Gaby's spirit. Hurt her. He'd forced her out of her home.

Alex needed to figure out why that douche bag kept returning to Gaby's house. What did he want?

He'd pointed a gun at Gaby, but hadn't fired it. Why? If all he wanted was Gaby dead, it would have been easy. Punch out the glass. Point the gun. *Bang.* No more Gaby.

But he hadn't shot her. He'd tried to grab her.

Why?

The questions kept floating through his brain, the answers just out of reach. Maybe Gaby had some ideas. Maybe there was something she knew but didn't realize she knew. If he wasn't so distracted by her, maybe he could think more clearly. He saw Gaby in distress, and his brain short-circuited.

As she pushed away from the door and walked slowly toward him, her gaze touched on everything. The cherry table in the dining room. The two antique Oriental carpets. The art on the walls.

When her gaze caught his, she looked wary. Guarded. As if she wasn't sure she really knew him.

His own fault. She hadn't expected this cold, sterile apartment, and she must feel out of place. Uncomfortable. His condo was nothing like her house. The place she lived was warm and welcoming. Cozy. A place where a family lived.

This place? It was a mausoleum, full of painful memories and old ghosts. Part of him had known she'd wonder about this apartment as soon as he'd suggested she and the girls stay with him. But, focused on keeping them safe, he'd ignored the tiny warning signal. Told himself where he lived didn't matter.

It did, of course. This condo was a part of him Gaby had never seen. Few of his friends had. His home screamed 'money', and he was uncomfortable with that message. He didn't want to be judged because of his *stuff*. He wanted to fit in with his buddies on the police force. Grab a beer at a cop bar, watch the game, talk some smack.

She'd probably have questions about that phone call from his mother, too. He'd have to tell her about his cold, distant parents and their pain-in-the-ass party.

He closed his eyes for a moment. One thing at a time.

Truth? He was a little embarrassed about this apartment. It wasn't him. Wasn't the way he wanted to live. He would have told her about his background eventually, but he hadn't been in any hurry. Where they came from didn't make any difference. It was where he wanted to go with Gaby that was important.

He wanted her to see *him*. The person, the cop, the guy who was crazy about her. All the other stuff wasn't important, and that included this fancy condo.

What he felt for her, what she felt for him – that was what mattered. Not the size of his bank account.

Don't be so naïve, a tiny voice whispered. Of course it mattered. Gaby would think he'd hidden it from her. And he had, he acknowledged. He'd hidden a lot more, as well.

He stood up as she stepped into the room and held out his hand. She hesitated for a nanosecond, then reached out and took it. He tugged her down onto the couch beside him and curled an arm around her shoulder. Snugged her up against him. Cupped her injured hand in his, so he wouldn't jostle it.

And then he said, "Okay. Hit me with the questions."

She turned to study his face, so close that her breath tickled his cheek. Then she swiveled on the couch so she faced him, but let him keep hold of her injured hand. He was grateful she hadn't withdrawn that, too.

"What was that phone call about?" she asked, rubbing her thumb on the back of his hand. "You sounded...upset."

He'd expected her to lead with questions about this apartment and its display of wealth. He closed his eyes and took a deep, shuddering breath of relief.

"It was my mother, as I'm sure you heard. She was reminding me about their party on Sunday. That I'm expected to show up."

The party was a yearly event. In his sister's memory. Which was the only reason he always went.

Tonight, he'd been tempted to tell his mother that he was bringing three guests, just to watch the horror on her face when he showed up with a woman and two children. But he wouldn't do that to Gaby or Bella or Cece.

"Then you should go," Gaby said immediately. "We'll be fine. Maybe I'll take the girls to the zoo if it's nice. Or to the mall. They always love going to the mall."

"You guys can't go anywhere alone," he reminded her gently. "But you're welcome to stay here while I'm gone. I won't be at the party for long. Just enough to put in an appearance."

She studied him for a moment, and he tried to make his expression neutral. Hide the distaste he felt for his parents. "Why do you dislike this party so much?"

Was he so obvious? He hoped not. "Where do I begin?"

If he told her about the party, he'd have to tell her about everything – his parents, the way he was raised. Theresa.

He wanted to tell her, he realized. He wanted her to know everything about him. Just like he wanted to know everything about her.

He'd resisted telling Gaby about the ugly parts of his life, afraid they'd scare her away. But over the past few days, he'd seen the depths of Gaby's strength. She could handle anything. Including the nasty corners of his life.

He knew about the skeletons in her closet. It was only fair she hear about his.

He jumped up from the couch and began to pace. "There's a lot you don't know about me," he began.

CHAPTER 15

Gaby settled back into the cushions, her face relaxing in a tiny smile. "You think?" She gestured around the room.

"Yeah. That's all part of it." Alex blew out a breath and stopped moving as he watched Gaby. Relaxed a little when she looked only curious and not upset.

"I was telling you the truth the other day when I said I wasn't raised like you were. It was clear you were loved. And that you loved your parents back. You may not have had a lot of *stuff*, but you were happy. You had a good childhood."

His gaze touched all the expensive furniture and art in his living room. They might be beautiful, but they couldn't compare to the warmth in Gaby's house.

He waited, and she nodded slowly. "Yes. My brother and sister and I didn't notice how little we had, because we were happy. Loved. Cherished."

A tiny spurt of jealousy flashed through Alex, but he ignored it. "My sister and I were just the opposite. We had all the stuff we could possibly want, but nothing of our parents' attention. I'm sure they loved us in their way, but they didn't have time for us. Theresa and I always wondered why they'd bothered to have kids. It was clear, even when we were young, that we interfered with their lifestyle."

"I didn't know you had a sister," Gaby said quietly. Almost as if she was hurt he hadn't shared that.

He swallowed hard. Again. "Theresa died eight years ago. While I was in the Navy. Drug overdose."

Gaby gasped. Pressed her hand to her mouth as she stared at him, blinking rapidly. Was she trying to hold back tears?

Then she stood up and reached for him. Wrapped her arms around his waist and held him tightly with her good hand. Touched his spine lightly with the bandaged hand. "Oh, Alex. I'm sorry," she murmured into his neck. "So sorry."

"Thanks," he said, closing his eyes and breathing her in. He buried his face in her hair, comforted by the way she held him. As if she was trying to share his pain. "We were close. It was just the two of us, you know?"

"I'm so glad you had her. And that she had you. That *someone* was there for you."

"Yeah, we were tight." *And I failed her.* His throat closed with shame, but he swallowed hard and continued, "After I graduated from high school, I didn't want to leave her at home by herself, with no one to watch over her, so I went to college locally. Lived at home. After September 11, I enrolled in the Navy."

Holding Gaby tightly for a moment, he thought back to the idealistic, naïve kid he'd been. He'd had so much. He'd thought it was time to give back. How his need to *do* something had warred with his guilt for abandoning his sister. "Theresa was going off to college in the fall, and I convinced myself she'd be fine once she escaped that house."

"But she wasn't?" Gaby murmured.

He forced himself to let her go and step away. He couldn't hold her while he told her the rest. He needed to be strong. Tell her what had happened. Assure her he would never abandon her the way he'd abandoned Theresa.

If he held Gaby while talking about Theresa, he might break down and cry.

"She was okay for a while," he said, pausing until his voice steadied. "She had friends, enjoyed her classes, started to make a life for herself. She wanted to be a high school teacher.

"She wrote to me every week and told me everything that was going on – about her friends, her classes, living in a dorm, the clubs she joined. She sounded...good. Happy. Like a normal college kid."

Those letters had been his lifeline during BUD/S training to be a Seal. During his deployments to Afghanistan and other dangerous parts of the world, they'd reassured him that his sister was thriving. That she didn't need her big brother to protect her.

Gaby touched his face, her fingers cool against his skin. Comforting. She cupped his face in both hands, the bulky bandage smelling like the brown stuff the paramedics used to clean wounds. "But she wasn't doing well?"

Alex closed his eyes. "She did great for a while. But then, during her junior year, she met a guy." Even now, he couldn't think about Jesse Collins without imagining his hands around the bastard's neck. Squeezing until the lights went out. Keeping Theresa alive.

Taking his hand, Gaby tugged him back to the couch. Pulled him down beside her and took both his hands. "What happened?" she asked softly.

"She began to party with him. Drinking, drugs. I'm sure she drank before she met that fucker, but after they met, all her letters were full of Jesse and the parties they went to. The bars where they spent every evening. Gradually, the letters started coming less frequently. At the end, I got one every couple of months.

"I took leave and came home. She introduced me to the guy. Jesse Collins. I wanted to wipe the floor with him, because I could see Theresa was in trouble. She'd lost weight. Her skin was pasty. The happy, outgoing college kid I remembered was gone. She wasn't…she wasn't my sister Theresa anymore.

"So I went to my parents. Told them something was wrong, and they had to step in. I couldn't stick around, so they had to take care of her. I was afraid she was doing drugs, but she denied it. I only had a week, and I spent all of it with her. She made an effort to act normally, but I knew she was anything but normal."

"What happened?" Gaby asked. She'd knelt on the floor in front of him, clasped his hands in hers. Leaned up and wiped the tears from his face. Kissed his cheek.

"Theresa had dropped out of college before I came to visit, but hadn't told my parents. She was living with Collins in some rat hole in the city. My parents thought that buying her this apartment would keep her away from the 'bad elements'."

He watched Gaby's gaze scan his living room. Touch on all the things that held painful memories.

Then she swung her knowing gaze back to his. "But it didn't, did it?" Gaby murmured.

"Of course not. They just moved the party into a nicer place."

He pulled Gaby onto the couch and wrapped his arm around her shoulders. He needed to be touching her. Holding her for the next part. "She died of a heroin overdose when she was twenty-five. By the time I got home, Collins had rabbited. The cops were damn good, though, and when they found his fingerprints on the syringe, they hunted him down. That's when I met Connor. He wasn't a detective yet, but he worked on Theresa's case.

"My parents' money counted for something. They hired the best lawyers in the city to keep after the prosecutors, and Collins was finally charged with manslaughter. He served eight years. Just got out of prison."

"So this was your sister's place?" Gaby asked.

"Yeah. She left it to me in her will, along with what was left of her share of our trust fund from our grandparents." He let his gaze scan the room, until it rested on the rainbow afghan.

"There's some of Theresa left in here. That aghan on the couch? Our grandmother made it for Theresa when she was a baby. She always loved the colors. Loved that our Gommiei had made it for her."

He stared at the quilt, remembering a smiling little girl with blond pigtails wrapping that rainbow around her shoulders and dancing around her room. Closing his eyes for a moment to hold that picture of his sister in his head, he murmured, "The quilt on the bed in the spare room was Theresa's too."

Forcing his eyes open, he turned back to Gaby. "I guess it makes me petty, but I live here because it pisses my parents off. They were...unhappy when I joined the Navy and became a SEAL instead of taking a job in my father's business. They didn't think I should have been rewarded for my disobedience by inheriting this apartment. They wanted it back. But Theresa had gotten one of my parents' lawyers to write the will, and it was rock solid."

"I don't think it's petty," Gaby said immediately. She trailed her fingers over his face, wiping away tears he hadn't realized had leaked out. "I think it makes you feel close to your sister. It comforts you.

"That's why you became a cop, isn't it?" Gaby was stroking his face, soothing him, and he leaned into her touch.

"Yeah. I wanted to help people, kids especially. Keep them from going down the path Theresa took. I couldn't do that while I was a SEAL. No way could I interact with kids in the villages in Afghanistan. Being a SEAL? It was important work, it needed to be done, and I'm damn proud of my service. But I wanted to focus on something else."

He stood up, drawing Gaby with him. "So now you know why I live in this fancy mausoleum. Sometimes I think about selling it. About moving away from the ghosts. But I…can't."

"You think you'd be abandoning your sister?" Gaby curled her arm around his waist. Pressed closer, and he closed his eyes. Breathed in her scent.

Alex buried his face in Gaby's hair and savored the comfort. "Maybe," he finally said, letting her thick waves swallow his words. "Probably."

Gaby turned into him, pressing herself against him from chest to thigh. She grabbed his shoulders and shook him lightly, until he lifted his head and met her gaze.

"Don't you think Theresa would want you to be happy?" Her voice was even. Gentle. But her eyes reflected his pain. "Do you think she'd want you to carry around this guilt? Don't you think she'd want you to sell this place and go somewhere that held no ghosts?"

"Maybe." He smoothed his hand over her head, let the silk of her hair trickle through his fingers. "But I can't. Not yet."

"When, then?" Gaby tilted her head as she watched him. She wasn't challenging him. Wasn't pushing, he realized. Maybe she was merely trying to help him see clearly.

"I don't know, Gaby," he finally said, scanning the elegant, carefully decorated room. Stopped at Theresa's afghan. "This still seems…right."

"Okay." Gaby stepped away from him but slid one hand down his arm. She tangled her fingers with him. "Let me check on the girls, then we need to clean up the dinner mess."

Alex watched her walk toward the guest bedroom, her hips swaying in her dark pants. His hands felt empty without her, and he wanted to snatch her back. Keep her close.

She was an amazing woman. Only hours ago, her ex-husband had tried to break into her home. He'd threatened her with a gun. But tonight, she'd been totally focused on *Alex's* problems. *His* pain.

He'd never known such a generous woman.

When she shoved her hair behind her ear, a flash of pale skin at her nape made him ache to press his mouth to that vulnerable spot. To ease the neck of her green shirt to the side and kiss the tiny bumps of her spine.

Gaby cracked the door to the darkened bedroom. Waited a moment, then tiptoed inside. Bella and Cece were lucky to have Gaby. Someone they could count on, no matter what.

A few moments later she reappeared, slipping into the hall and closing the door silently behind her. She held his gaze as she walked toward him. "They're both sound asleep."

Taking his hand, she led him toward the kitchen. "Show me where you keep your cleaning supplies," she ordered.

"Gaby, we don't have to do this tonight. And you're not doing any cleaning. Not with this hand." He picked up her bandaged hand and kissed the tips of her fingers.

She stopped. Turned to face him. "Are you kidding me? I'm not leaving that grease stain on your carpet. I don't care if you can buy twenty new ones. That's a beautiful carpet, and I don't want to ruin it."

"Fine," Alex said, his shoulders finally relaxing at the sight of Gaby standing in front of him, her hands on her hips and her head barely reaching his shoulder as she ordered him around. When this evening began, he wouldn't have imagined Gaby teasing him about having money. Wouldn't have imagined smiling, either. "We'll clean it up together."

She beamed up at him, grabbing his hand. "Thank you, Alex. Now show me where you keep your bucket and your carpet cleaner."

"You think I'm going to let you get your hand wet?" He snorted. "Suzi Chapman would skin me alive. You can carry the dishes into the kitchen. One at a time, so you don't have to use that hand."

Fifteen minutes later, Alex filled the dishwasher with

detergent, closed the door and started it. "All the chores are done, Ms. Slave Driver. Are you happy?"

Gaby leaned against the kitchen island, her hair tumbling over her shoulders, and grinned up at him. "Yes. I'll go to bed a happy woman. Thank you for indulging me."

Her cheeks were flushed, her eyes sparkling. Everything about her was light. Joyful.

In spite of the threats that had consumed her life, right now she looked carefree.

He wanted to taste that happy smile on her face. Hold her body against his. The image of Gaby sliding into *his* bed sent desire crashing through him. He wanted to sweep her up in his arms and carry her into his bedroom. Pull her down onto the sheets. Peel off her clothes. Make love to her all night long.

"I bet I could make you go to bed even happier," he managed to say. His palms itched to caress her. To feel the silk of her skin, the weight of her hair, the heat of her body.

Her breath hitched as she stared at him. Her pupils dilated. Her eyes darkened. A red flush rose from her neck to her face.

Her breath stuttered in her chest. "Alex..." She drew in another shaky breath. "The girls...they might look for me during the night."

"I know. I'm not going into that bedroom with you, even though I want to. Want it more than I want to take my next breath."

As he watched, Gaby's chest rose. Fell. Rose again. He reached for her slowly, giving her a chance to back away.

Instead, she stepped into his arms. Pressed her body to his and lifted her face. "Kiss me, Alex. Kiss me so I can taste you while I sleep alone in your bed."

He closed his eyes, trying to control the way his body reacted to her words. But when she drew him close, he gave in. Let himself show her how much he wanted her.

He crowded her against the island at her back. Slid one thigh between her legs. She made a tiny, needy sound and curled one leg around his. Drew him closer. Pulled his head down to hers.

Covering her mouth with his, he sucked gently on her lower lip. Scraped his teeth over her incredibly soft skin. When she gasped, he slid into her mouth.

Gaby clutched his back as he kissed her, tiny moans escaping as he slid his tongue over hers. He explored her mouth, tasting the faint tang of pizza sauce, pepperoni and mushrooms, the tannin of the tea she'd had after dinner. But beneath it all was Gaby, the sweet, slightly spicy taste he'd dreamed about since the last time he kissed her.

As she kissed him, she wrapped her arms around his neck and tugged him closer. Tore her mouth away from his and trailed delicate kisses over his cheek. Brushed her mouth over his stubble, and the tiny rasping sounds made him press closer. She tugged gently at his earlobe, then nipped it gently.

"Touch me, Alex," she begged, her breath ruffling the fine hairs behind his ear. "I want to feel your hands on me. I want my hands on you." Goosebumps rose down his arms. His chest.

Other parts of him rose, too. Insistent. Demanding.

He wrapped her shirt in his fist, but fought the urge to tear it off her. "Are you sure about this, Gaby? Today was..."

She put her uninjured hand over his mouth. "Today was horrible. *This* is wonderful. I want you, Alex. I have for a long time. I can't..."

He kissed her palm, making her gasp. Stutter to a halt. When he touched his tongue to the web between her thumb and index finger, she shuddered.

Before he realized what he was doing, he'd unbuttoned her shirt. He froze, but she didn't push him away. Slowly he parted it, drinking in the sight of her creamy olive skin. Her breasts, covered by a silky black bra. No lace, nothing fancy, just the pale crescents of her breasts rising from the tops of the cups.

He stared for a moment, running his hand over them. Drinking in her tiny cries. The way she jerked helplessly when his finger brushed over a nipple.

Dropping to his knees, he pressed kisses to her soft abdomen. Her breath stuttered. She gasped. Trembled in his arms. When he slid a finger beneath her waistband, she froze.

"We can't," she said, breathless, shaking her head as if just waking from a dream. "The girls."

"There's a squeaky board in the dining room," he said as he slid the button through the hole. Grasped the flange of the zipper. Lowered it tooth by tooth. "They can't sneak up on us. We'll hear them."

Her fingers dug into his arms. "Are you sure?"

"Positive." He pressed a kiss to the tender skin beneath her waistband, surged at the needy sound she made. "There's another squeaky board in the hall between the bedrooms. Double warning."

"I'm not...I'm not going to make love with you for the first time on that granite counter," she said, her voice low and breathy. As if she was having trouble forming the words.

"Okay. We'll save that for another time." Sliding his hands into her waistband, he cupped her ass in both hands. Her skin was soft, her muscles hard. He squeezed, thrilled when her hips twitched against his. When he slid his fingers further down, she let out a long, low cry.

"Gaby, you're driving me wild," he murmured against her abdomen. He let her go long enough to tug her pants down her legs. She grabbed for the waistband and held it in her clenched fist.

"We can't," she said, panting.

"I just want to touch you," he murmured, tugging the pants out of her hand. "That's all."

As the black fabric gathered on the floor, she stood before him in a scrap of black silk that barely covered her. It matched the bra she wore. And why hadn't he taken that off?

He glanced up, saw her chest heaving with her rapid stuttering breaths. *Later.*

Pressing his mouth to the swell of her pubis, he slid the silk down her legs. Sat back and looked his fill.

She was already wet. For him. He touched her gently, and she stuffed a fist into her mouth to muffle her cry.

He wanted to hear every sound she made. Every tiny cry, every moan, every scream.

Soon, he promised himself. Not tonight, with the girls sleeping in the spare bedroom. But soon.

Rising, he unhooked her bra. Let it fall open as he cupped her breasts in his palms. "Beautiful," he whispered as he tested their weight. He pressed a kiss to the valley between them, then curled his tongue around one hard nipple. When he sucked it into his mouth, she jerked against him. Stuffed her fist into her mouth again.

Releasing her nipple with a moist pop, he covered her mouth with his. "I want to swallow those noises you make," he murmured into her mouth. "Savor every note of them."

As he slid his hand between her thighs, he slipped his tongue into her mouth. She quivered beneath his hands, making inarticulate little sounds that vibrated against his tongue.

He pressed one finger against her clitoris, loving the way she arched against him. Circling it with his thumb, he slid two fingers inside her. She exploded in his hands, pulsing against him as he drank in her screams. Her orgasm went on and on, and he got harder as he imagined what it would feel like to be inside her as she came.

Finally, trembling, she slumped against him. He curled his arms around her, holding her as he let his mouth wander down her neck. He sucked on the tendons there, biting them gently, then moving on.

When she'd recovered, she reached for him. "My turn."

Her fingers brushed his cock, and he pressed into her palm for a moment. "Next time," he murmured.

"Now," she retorted. "I want to taste you. You got to watch me come. I want to watch you."

Alex closed his eyes and pressed closer for a long moment. He felt every one of her five fingers circle his cock. Finally, though, he pulled her hand away.

"Believe me, Gaby, I want that, too. But I think we've pushed our luck far enough for one night. If you put your mouth on me, I won't be able to stand up. I'd fall onto the floor, and the crash would wake up the girls."

She giggled, and he drank in the sound. After the day she'd had, he'd made Gaby *giggle*.

He felt as if he could fly. Leap tall buildings. Catch a speeding train.

As he stared at her, she touched his crotch again. He jerked, then realized she was re-zipping his pants. He hadn't even realize she'd lowered the zipper. "I want you so much, Gaby. But I'm a patient man. Being a SEAL teaches a man how to wait."

He reached down and pulled up her panties. Then he slid her pants back up her legs. Fastened the button. Re-hooked her bra and buttoned her shirt.

"There," he said. "You're good to go. Ready to kiss the girls goodnight and go to bed."

Her dark gaze searched his face. Lingered on his mouth. "Really? You take me completely apart, then tell me it's time for bed before I can even touch you?"

"Tonight," he said. "Only tonight. After this, all bets are off."

Gaby tilted her head and watched him for a long moment. "I've never met a man like you, Alex Jennings," she finally said. "Never even knew a man like you existed."

She cupped his face in both hands. Above the bandage on her left hand, her fingers stroked his temple. She kissed him one more time, then stepped back. Her smile was so bright it could light the city. "Thank you, Alex. I...you..." She closed her eyes.

Opening them, she kissed him once more, then stepped

away. "And fair warning. I'm not going to wait very long for my turn to watch you."

CHAPTER 16

Gaby lay in Alex's bed in the darkened room, thin strips of moonlight spilling into the room through the partially closed blind. This bedroom faced a courtyard, but the muffled sound of traffic from Lake Shore Drive was a soothing hum in the background.

Alex had retreated to his office after...after whatever it was that had happened in the kitchen.

Don't be such a wimp. You know exactly what happened. He made you come so hard your head nearly blew off.

Yeah. That.

She listened to Alex as he exited his office. The floor squeaked as he got closer, then squeaked again as he reached her door. She relaxed into his insanely comfortable mattress. He'd been right. They would have had a warning if either of the girls came looking for them.

He wouldn't lie to her. Not even for sex.

Although, technically, he hadn't had any. Sex.

A deficiency she intended to correct as soon as possible.

Once this nightmare was over and their lives were normal again.

Alex's footsteps stopped outside her door. In the small

space between the door and the floor, she saw the shadows of his feet. Two dark ovals on the golden floor. She prayed he'd open the door. Begged him not to do it.

She wouldn't be able to resist if he came into this room. She'd drag him into her bed and curl into him all night.

And that couldn't happen. Not now. Not with the girls next door, unsettled, and Julio out there somewhere, waiting to pounce.

After a moment, his feet disappeared. The door of the bathroom across the hall closed softly. Water ran in the sink. The toilet flushed. In a few minutes, Alex re-emerged into the hall.

This time, he didn't pause as he passed her door. The space between the door and the floor went dark as he turned off the lights. His feet kept moving until the door to his office closed with a quiet snick.

She wanted to run down the hall, avoiding those creaky boards, and drag him back to her bed. *His* bed. She half-sat, then fell back onto the mattress. She was the one who'd started...everything tonight. She was the one who had to be strong now.

She strained to listen, but didn't hear another thing. The condo breathed around her, the tiny creaks and sounds from an old building comfortable. Familiar. Her own house made similar noises at night.

Alex's pillows smelled like fresh air and sun. Like him. Gaby pulled one to her chest, curled into it and finally fell asleep.

* * *

By the time Gaby stepped out of the bedroom the next morning, the girls' bedroom was empty and she heard them with Alex, talking in the kitchen. Tugging her tee shirt over her hips, she smoothed her hands over her jeans and followed the sound of her daughters' giggling.

She hoped she'd be able to face them, and Alex, without

blushing or stuttering or generally acting like an idiot.

When she reached the kitchen, Cece was carefully lifting forkfuls of capers out of their jar and setting them on a paper towel folded onto a plate. Bella was slicing an avocado, and Alex was arranging thinly sliced smoked salmon on a plate.

"Hey, Gaby," he said, looking up and smiling easily at her. "We were afraid we'd have to eat breakfast without you."

"Alex said we didn't have to wait," Cece told her, the fork dripping liquid onto the plate. "Because we needed to keep up our strength for all the fun we're going to have today." She beamed at her mother as she scooped up another forkful of capers.

Predictably, Bella rolled her eyes as she put the sliced avocado onto another plate. "Alex just wanted to grab the best bagel for himself," she said. "The poppy seed. I told him that was your favorite, but he didn't care."

"Wow," Gaby said as she pressed a kiss to Cece's head, then Bella's. "Are we going to have to wrestle for that bagel, Alex?"

His eyes darkened as he held her gaze. Then he fumbled in the bag and pulled out another poppy seed. "Look what I found. Another poppy seed.'"

"Ha," Cece cried happily. "He was just teasing you. Just like he teased me about the fish pizza yesterday."

Gaby shoved her hands into her pockets as her heart raced and her palms got sweaty. She glanced at Alex and couldn't look away, undone by the desire in his eyes. "Yeah, Alex is a tease."

He lifted one shoulder and took a sip of coffee. Behind the cup, his eyes darkened even more. "I usually deliver what I've promised."

Bella's head swiveled from Alex to Gaby and back again, and her eyes narrowed. After a too-long pause, she said, "You promised breakfast, and everything's ready. Are we going to eat, or what?"

"We're going to eat." Alex picked up the plate full of bagels. "Cece, will you bring the capers to the table? Bella, why don't you take the avocado and the cream cheese?"

"What about me?" Gaby asked.

"You can grab your coffee." He nodded at her bandaged hand. "How does it feel today?"

"Better," she said, realizing it didn't throb like it had the day before. She looked from Bella to Cece. "Maybe you two can help me change the bandage after breakfast." The bandage was bulky, and she'd caught both girls eyeing it last night. She wanted them to see how small the actual cut was.

"We'll all help. Make it a family project," Alex said as he lifted the plate of bagels and headed for the dining room. Cece followed, chattering away to him.

"He's not part of our family," Bella muttered, grabbing the plate of avocados.

"Bella." Gaby put a hand on her arm as the girl tried to walk past her. "Can you give it a rest? I know you're stressed out and worried. You're not in your own home. You're scared about Julio. But just for today, can you act at least a little grateful that Alex let us stay here?"

Bella scowled and stared at the creamy green avocados. "I'm grateful."

"Then act like it. Please." Gaby let her go, drew in a deep, shuddering breath and picked up her coffee. The lovely flutter in her belly from the coded words she and Alex had exchanged was gone, replaced with a hard jolt of reality. However much she wanted Alex, she had to think about her daughters first. And it looked as though Bella was going to be...difficult.

Taking a sip of coffee to steady herself, she let the hot caffeine kick in before she walked to the dining room. The girls had left a place for her next to Alex, and a poppy seed bagel rested on her plate.

"Thanks," she murmured, glancing at Alex out of the corner of her eye.

"You're welcome." His knee nudged hers and lingered,

and she had to rein in the tiny shudder. The girls were watching. "Looks like everyone got what they wanted."

Except you. Memories of what had happened in his kitchen the night before unspooled in her memory as she stared at her plate, unseeing. Finally, she pressed her knee against his, then moved it away. Picked up her knife and smeared cream cheese on her bagel.

She couldn't allow herself to think about Alex that way today. She had to focus on the girls. On what they needed from her.

Glancing at Alex again, she bit into the bagel. It tasted like cardboard in her mouth.

* * *

She and Alex leaned against the wall in the theater lobby, a careful distance apart, and waited while the girls stood in line to use the restroom. Gaby waved at Cece, and out of the corner of her eye saw Alex glance at his watch. He'd done that a few times during the movie, too. "Something wrong?" she asked quietly.

"Just trying to figure out what to do tomorrow when I go to that damn party. You and the girls want to hang out with Raine and Connor for a few hours? I want to call them before they make other plans."

"What I'd like to do is go to that party with you," she said without thinking. Snapped her mouth shut. "Sorry. I didn't mean to invite myself. But I hate to think about you going alone. Someone should have your back."

Alex's tense mouth relaxed into a smile. "I thought I only needed someone to watch my six when I was a SEAL. Shouldn't be necessary for a family party."

"Not most family parties," she agreed. "But it sounds as though you're going into hostile territory."

His smile widened. "Yeah, Oakvale is definitely hostile territory." Cece and Bella disappeared into the rest room, and Alex took her hand. Twined his fingers with hers. "I'd love to have your company. But I won't subject Bella and Cece to that. Bad enough that I'd consider taking you along."

Gaby tightened her fingers around his. "Julio didn't follow us anywhere today." They'd gone to the zoo before coming to see the latest Disney movie. Bella had rolled her eyes and whined about going to see a kids' movie, but Gaby could tell she wanted to see it. She just hadn't wanted to seem like a baby.

And as the movie ended, Gaby had smiled when she spotted Bella furtively wiping her tear-stained face with the back of her hand.

"No. I paid really close attention. Drove a roundabout route to the zoo, and I'm certain no one followed. Same for this movie. I'll watch again when we go out to dinner."

"So if you can be sure Julio doesn't follow us there, maybe we can leave the girls with Raine and Connor for a few hours tomorrow afternoon, and I can go to the party with you."

Alex turned to face her. "You'd do that for me?"

"Of course I would," she said immediately. She'd do just about anything for Alex. Facing down his parents was nothing. "How bad can a few hours be?"

"You have no idea," he said, his voice grim.

"Hey, I've got a crazy man trying to kill me," she said. "Can't be worse than that."

He brought her hand to his mouth and pressed his lips to her palm. She let her hand linger for a moment, then gently tugged it away. The girls would be returning from the ladies' room any minute. "You're amazing, Gaby." He swallowed. "Thank you."

"Give Raine and Connor a call and see if that's okay with them. We'll stop by my house tonight so I can pick up something to wear. Let the girls see that everything's back to normal."

"Are you sure?"

"Absolutely."

He pressed a quick kiss to her lips, then pulled his phone out of his pocket. As he began to speak, Bella and Cece stepped out of the restroom.

"I'm hungry, Mama," Cece said, leaning against her hip.

"Really?" Gaby tucked the hair away from her face. "After that giant tub of popcorn you had?"

"Bella ate most of it," Cece said, glowering at her sister.

"Yeah, well, if you didn't eat it one piece at a time, you would've gotten more," Bella retorted.

Gaby closed her eyes. They'd bickered all day today. She understood why – they were on edge and anxious, and it was their way of coping. But she was getting a pounding headache. "Think of it like this, Cece. When we have dinner, you'll be able to enjoy yours. Bella will still be full of popcorn."

"Gaby?" Alex called from behind her.

She turned around, and he gestured her over. She turned to the girls. "Stay right here for a moment, please."

When she reached Alex, she positioned herself so she could watch the girls. Alex hit the 'mute' button on his phone. "Raine wants to know if we'd like to leave the girls with them tonight. They're having a sleepover with a bunch of the tae kwon do girls. Some of the girls talked about having a sleepover after Bella left yesterday, and Raine wasn't sure if she should call Bella and ask her to join them. She figured you'd want her close. But since we're leaving the girls with them tomorrow, she thought maybe you wouldn't mind if they came over early for the slumber party."

Gaby watched the girls, leaning against the wall the same way she had done with Alex. From the looks on their faces and their hand gestures, she suspected they were talking about the movie. Something Bella would never do in front of her mother.

Hard to pretend she was too cool for Disney if she was analyzing it with her sister.

"What do you think?" she asked, turning back to Alex.

"I think, if we're careful and make sure we're not followed, that they'd be safe. Connor will be there. They were just about to order pizza, but we can stop for dinner on the way over to their apartment. I'm sure you don't want them to have pizza three nights in a row."

He slid one finger over the back of Gaby's hand. "It would be a normal thing for them," he said quietly. "They wouldn't have to worry about Abrietto or someone breaking into their house or hurting them or you. They'd spend the evening with their friends. But it's your decision."

Gaby watched the girls. She wanted to keep them close. Somewhere she could watch them all the time. But was that fair to them?

"Connor will be there the whole time?"

"Absolutely. I already asked."

"Then…then let me ask them," she said, swallowing.

Five minutes later, they burst out of the theater, Bella practically running for Alex's car. "Hey," Gaby called. "Hold up, Bella. Walk with us."

Bella turned immediately and walked back to them without an eye roll or a scowl. Cece nudged her with her elbow. "Can I come, too, Bella?"

Bella shrugged. "I guess. You'll be bored, though. We'll be talking about b…stuff you don't care about." Bella leaned closer to whisper, but Gaby heard her say, "And if you tell Mom *anything*, I'll never speak to you again."

"I won't, Bell. I promise."

"Okay, then you can come."

"Can't you guys walk faster?" Bella said to Gaby and Alex.

"The car's three spots down," Alex said. "And we're stopping to eat before we go to Connor and Raine's. Something healthy."

He nudged Bella with his elbow, and she smiled up at him. Gaby's heart rolled over. Her girls were crazy about him, too.

"Not fast food," Gaby added, her voice thick, trying to

ignore the melting sensation in her chest. "So don't even ask. We're having a *real* meal."

CHAPTER 17

An hour later, Alex waited at the door of Raine and Connor's apartment as Gaby kissed Bella and Cece good-bye. She held each of them close until they squirmed away, hurrying back to the eight other girls sprawled over the floor. In the kitchen, Raine was serving pizza and salad onto plates, and Connor was pouring glasses of milk.

Gaby moved to stand next to him, her gaze on her daughters, and he nudged her shoulder with his. "They'll be safe," he murmured. "They'll have a good time. We'll pick them up tomorrow, on the way home from the party." He wanted to wrap his arm around Gaby, reassure her, but he knew better than to do it in front of the girls. Not only would Bella be mortified, but all of her teammates would tease her unmercifully.

She nodded, still watching the girls. Raine came out of the kitchen carrying a tray full of plates. She handed them out, then hurried over to him and Gaby.

"Don't worry," she said. "We'll be super careful. They'll be fine. And if Connor thinks anything is off, he'll call immediately." She glanced at the group of girls. "How far away is your party?"

"It's in Oakvale."

Raine jerked back, as if he'd said a vile word.

"Are you kidding me?" she muttered, glancing over her shoulder. As if afraid the kids would hear her. "Who do you know in that hellhole?"

"Uh…my parents?" he said.

Raine winced. "Sorry. Didn't mean to imply anything about your parents. I'm sure they're lovely people."

"They're not." He tilted his head, studying Raine. "You grow up there, too?"

"Lived there during high school. Escaped as fast as I could." She narrowed her gaze. "Jennings. I remember that name."

"Did you go to Country Day School?"

Raine rolled her eyes. "Didn't everyone who lived in Oakvale?"

"Yeah." He'd wanted so badly to go to the public high school, but his parents wouldn't even consider it. "You might have known my sister. Theresa. Although I think she was a few years older than you."

Raine shrugged. "Possible."

Connor came over after delivering milk and slipped his arm around Raine's waist. "Why are you scowling at Jennings? Do I have to kick his ass for you?"

"You wish you could," Alex said immediately, trying to ease the tension.

"Not necessary. Oakvale is going to kick it for him tomorrow."

Connor grimaced. "You're going up there?"

"Not for long," Alex assured them. He'd get the Oakvale story out of Raine later. He nodded toward Bella and Cece, sprawled on the floor, talking while everyone else ate pizza. "Thanks for doing this."

"Yes, thank you," Gaby added. "They needed some normal."

Raine glanced at the chattering girls. Smiled. "They'll get plenty of that." She opened the door. "Have fun at the party. And don't worry about the girls. They'll be fine."

"I know," Gaby said, giving her a hug. "I wouldn't have left them if I wasn't sure of that."

After quick goodbyes, which the girls barely acknowledged, they left Connor and Raine's apartment. The sun was setting, framing the courtyard in a golden glow, but the pale buds of the crabapples in the courtyard were obscured by the shadows.

"Nice apartment," Gaby said, her gaze touching the trees and the bushes along the brick walls. She lingered on the locked courtyard gate.

"Yeah," he said. "Secure, too." He wanted to take her hand, but was careful not to touch her. Who knew who might be watching from Connor's window?

As they stepped onto the sidewalk and headed toward his car, Gaby slipped her hand into his and swiveled her head from side to side. Her grip was so hard, her nails dug into the backs of his hand.

"No one followed us here," he said softly. "I made sure of it."

"I know," she murmured. "But the back of my neck is itchy. As if someone is watching."

Alex paused, untangled their hands and bent down, as if tying his shoe. He let his gaze scan the cars and vans around him. No one visible in any of them. Rising, he took Gaby's hand and spun her around, bending close as if kissing her.

"Look at me," he ordered. "Pretend like you're hot for me. Stare at my mouth. My eyes. Don't look behind me."

Her grip on him tightened. "What did you see?" she breathed.

"Nothing yet. Which is why we need to pretend to be completely enthralled with one another."

"I think I can manage that," she murmured.

Alex's gaze snapped to hers. She was staring into his eyes, a dreamy expression on her face. He suspected he looked equally starry-eyed.

"Good," he managed to say. "That's perfect."

"We're going to be alone tonight," Gaby said, her eyes lighting up as she leaned closer. "I wasn't thinking about that before."

He'd thought about it. But he'd tried to ignore the way his blood hummed through his veins. Kept any hint of *want* off his face so Gaby could make the right decision for her and the girls without any pressure from him.

He brushed his mouth over hers savoring her taste, as he cataloged each car on the street. All empty. Finally, when he was sure no one was watching, he eased away from her mouth. "Yeah," he said as he wrapped his arm around her waist and led her to the car. "You have any thoughts about what you'd like to do?"

She bumped his hip with hers. "One or two."

"We could watch a movie," he said, glancing down at her. Hiding a smile at her frown. "Go out for a drink. Maybe go dancing."

"We'll figure it out," she said, slipping one finger inside his waistband, a mischievous grin flirting with her mouth. "I'm sure something will come up."

"I'm sure it will," he muttered, squirming in his suddenly too-tight jeans.

A car door slammed behind them, close enough to make him spin around, sexy plans forgotten. An engine revved on the next block, and he watched as a dark SUV turned the corner and disappeared.

Drawing Gaby into the shadows next to an apartment building, he stood in front of her and watched. But nothing moved.

A rustling from the front of the apartment had him turning toward the sound. Reaching for the gun he'd left in the trunk of his car. Finally a yellow cat emerged from the bushes. Green eyes stared at them for a long moment, then the cat trotted in the opposite direction.

"Let's go," he said, taking Gaby's hand and hurrying her to his car. After she was seated, he popped the trunk, took off his jacket and threaded his arms through his holster. Slid the gun into it beneath his left arm.

Half an hour later, they pulled up in front of Gaby's house. He'd taken a long, circuitous route to get here, and he was certain no one had followed them.

Gaby reached for the car door, and he put his hand over hers. "Hold on a minute," he said, scanning all the vehicles on the street. It was twilight on a Saturday evening, and there were a lot of empty parking spots. Made it easier to check the remaining cars.

Finally he exhaled a long breath. No one lurking in any of them.

"We're not going to linger. In and out. Get what you need, and get back to my place." He was eager to get her behind safely locked doors. In a place where Abrietto couldn't get to her.

Gaby's sense of being watched back at Raine and Connor's building had made *him* itchy. He'd called Con, told him to keep a sharp eye out, and Connor had assured him that he would.

Alex stepped out of the car, watching for movement. Buildings and trees cast shadows across the sidewalks and covered the fronts of the houses in darkness. All those indigo shadows made perfect hiding places.

Julio probably wasn't here. Why would he be? It was clear Gaby's house was empty.

And the car that had driven away near Connor's apartment was probably someone who lived in one of the apartment buildings.

But Alex wasn't taking anything for granted.

Finally, he opened Gaby's door and helped her out. They hurried up the steps, and Gaby unlocked the front door. Flicked on the lights. Locked it carefully behind them.

The house smelled clean. The sharp tang of disinfectants filled the air, and as they got closer to the kitchen, the smell became stronger.

He tightened his hold on Gaby's hand as they reached

the kitchen. She stood in the doorway for a long moment, staring into the dark room. Finally, she turned on the lights.

The room was spotless. Nothing out of place. No signs of yesterday's carnage.

The door was perfect, as well.

Alex had told Matt to get a new door and send him the bill. It would have been impossible to remove every trace of blood from the seams of glass and wood. Gaby might not be able to see them, but *he'd* know they were there.

"Wow," she said, running her hand over the door. "It looks...like nothing happened. Like it's a brand-new door."

She unlocked it and opened it to make sure the lock had been changed. Froze.

She bent and peeled off the sticker. Clutching it in her hand, the tacky glue sticking to her fingers, she turned to Alex. "This *is* a brand-new door, Alex. Why did Matt do that?"

Alex sighed. Tugged her back into the house, locked the door and hung the key on the wall hook. "It was my call. I would have told you eventually. I didn't want even one molecule of Julio left on your door. Matt's going to send me the bill."

"Alex..." she began, but he held up his hand.

"I know you would have been fine with the old door. But I wanted you to have a new one. A door that didn't have awful memories for you. I'm not going to apologize for getting it. And I'm not going to let you pay for it, either."

Gaby tilted her head as she watched him. Finally she smiled, her eyes soft. "Thank you, Alex." She ran her fingers up and down his arm, and he couldn't stop the shiver. "I'm not angry with you. I'm not going to yell, or insist you let me pay. I think...I think it was an incredibly sweet thing to do. Thank you."

"Really? You're not upset?"

She shook her head and slid her arms around his neck. "Nope. I was dreading looking at that door. Afraid I'd see little specks of blood on the wood." She closed her eyes, and Alex assumed she was remembering what the old door had looked like yesterday. Then she pressed closer. Tightened her arms around him. "You're so thoughtful."

"That's me," he said, keeping his voice light. "Perfect boyfriend material."

Gaby froze for a moment, then pressed closer. "Yeah. You are."

"Gaby, I want...," he began, but she pressed cool fingers against his mouth.

"Later, Alex. I want to get my things for your parents' party and get out of here. We have better things to do tonight that hang around this house."

Her eyes were dark with promises, and suddenly he couldn't wait to get home. "Where's your bag?" he asked. "I'll get it."

She smiled and took his hand. "Upstairs." She headed for the stairs, still holding his hand. She led him into her bedroom and opened the closet.

Those electric blue shoes he'd noticed yesterday were sitting on the floor. Staring at them, he cleared his throat. "You going to wear those tomorrow?"

She glanced at the shoes. Then at him. "You want me to?"

"Oh, yeah. I want to see you in those heels."

She picked them up off the floor. "I love these shoes," she said, cupping them in her palm. "They were ridiculously expensive, but I watched until they went on sale. Then on clearance." She brushed a finger over one of them, leaving a tiny line in the suede nap. "I haven't worn them in a very long time."

Sorrow flickered across her face for an instant, then she looked at him. Smiled. Set the shoes on her bed and turned back to the closet.

She drew out one dress, then another. Frowned. Put it back.

Finally she zipped open a dress bag, studied the dress and pulled the bag out of the closet. Laying it on her bed, she tucked the blue shoes into the bottom of the bag, zipped it up and swung the bag over her shoulder. "Let's get out of here," she said, heading for the stairs.

Alex hurried to catch up with her, plucking the dress bag from her hand.

He hustled Gaby out of the house, pausing to check her block. The street was empty except for the shadows, and all the cars were dark and quiet. All he heard was the distant whine of traffic a few blocks away.

He loaded Gaby and the dress bag into his car, swept the street one final time, then started the engine. Alternating between the rear view mirror and the windshield as he pulled away from the curb, he accelerated quickly on the quiet street.

No one followed him. No cars waiting in the alley, either.

He drove steadily, his gaze constantly checking behind him. On both sides. He looked for cars parked along the curb that pulled into traffic too quickly. Cars that turned onto the street without pausing at a stop sign. As he merged into traffic on the Kennedy Expressway, no cars followed him up the ramp.

He let himself stand down, although he checked the rear view mirror often. After two miles, no one had switched lanes with him. No one hung back. They were clear.

Gaby had been watching him since they left her house, but she hadn't said a word. She must have heard his sigh as he relaxed back into the seat, because she set her hand on his thigh. The bandage felt bulky against his leg, but her fingers were nimble. She caressed tiny circles on the denim of his jeans, using just the right amount of pressure. Blood rushed south, and he shifted on the leather upholstery, uncomfortable.

As her hand crept higher, he sucked in a sharp breath and swerved toward the shoulder. Swallowing hard, Alex took her hand, pressed it to his mouth, then set it on her leg. "As much as I'm enjoying that, I want us to make it back to my place in one piece," he said.

"Sorry." Her low voice made every nerve in his body quiver.

"You don't sound sorry," he said, gripping the steering wheel more tightly.

"Oh, I am," she promised. Her words vibrated through the car like a purr. "I'll make it up to you. I promise."

"Not another word," he said through clenched teeth. "Please. Let me focus on driving. On...on watching."

She glanced over at him with a wicked smile. "I like watching, too."

Banging his head against the headrest, he shook his head to clear his brain. "*God*, Gaby. *No. Talking.* I'm begging you."

She folded her hands together in her lap, her eyes twinkling. She looked playful and naughty and pleased with herself.

She looked pretty damn perfect.

His skin tingled as if she was touching him, and he glanced over to find her watching him, her eyes dark pools of want. Need. The whine of the rumble strip on the shoulder jerked his attention back to the road.

He needed to focus, damn it! Pay attention to the traffic. The cars around them. Even though he was pretty sure they were clear, he couldn't take anything for granted.

Neither of them spoke as he drove into the underground lot at his condo. He slammed his door a little too hard. Yanked her dress off the hook in the back seat. Opened Gaby's door and helped her out.

Twined their fingers together as he hurried her toward the elevator.

As the old elevator lurched and began its unhurried trip to his floor, Alex wanted to punch the control panel. Make it go faster.

Instead, he clutched Gaby's hand and stared at the red numbers ticking off the floors. Time slowed. Stretched out. By the time the doors eased open, it felt as if he'd traveled around the world on foot.

The scratch of metal on metal as he tried to unlock his door screeched through the silent hall. Gaby was standing too close, the heat from her body burning into his back. Once he managed to unlock the door, he tugged her in behind him. Kicking the door shut, he activated the locks. Yanked open the closet door. The wooden hangers banged together with a hollow sound as he hooked the dress bag over the metal rod.

Then he pulled Gaby against him. "No talking now, either."

CHAPTER 18

Gaby's heart thundered against her ribs, the sound roaring in her ears. She was sure Alex could hear it in the cocooned silence of his apartment.

As if the rapid hammering of her heart was his signal, he gripped her shoulders, whirled her around and pressed her against the wall.

Half his face was in shadow, the other half dimly illuminated by the lamp in the corner of the room. But even in the semi-darkness, his eyes were deep wells of hunger. As if the need he'd been suppressing for far too long had burst free and consumed him.

Just as he intended to consume her.

"Gaby." He covered her mouth with his and devoured her. It was the only word his fuzzy brain could produce. Swallowing her incoherent cries, he drew her lower lip into his mouth. Teased it with his tongue until she opened to him. And when she did, his tongue claimed hers, drinking her in as if, lost in a desert, he'd finally found water.

Desire rose inside her in a wild rush. Her skin was too tight. Her body was too hot. She needed his skin against hers, his hardness against her softness. Needed to hear the sound of their bodies slapping together, easing the urgent ache that exploded like a skyrocket, sending sparks everywhere.

Her tongue dancing with his, she yanked his shirttail out of his jeans and ran her hands up his back. His muscles rippled beneath her fingers as he boosted her higher in his arms. She wrapped her legs around his waist and surged against the heat and length of his erection, squirming until it was exactly where she needed it.

Tiny cries erupted from the back of her throat, dirty, pleading sounds she'd never imagined she could produce. She was so close. If Alex didn't stop, she was going to come before they'd even gotten their clothes off.

"God, Gaby," he panted, shoving her shirt to her neck and opening her bra. He groaned as her breasts fell free. Swirled his tongue around one nipple as he reached for her jeans. "Need you." He tugged on her nipple, sending lightning flashing through her. "Right now."

"Yes," she said, fumbling between them to unbutton his jeans. Reaching inside, she wrapped her hands around his thick, rock-hard penis. He jerked in her hand, and she wanted to slide down and lick him. Memorize his taste. Pull raw sounds from his mouth. She was so close to begging Alex. She wanted to make him beg, too.

Instead, she struggled free. Yanked her jeans and underwear down one leg. With the denim and satin dangling from the other leg, she lifted up to him again. Wrapped both legs around him again. "Now, Alex. Please. I need you inside me."

He shoved his own jeans down, far enough to release his penis, then reached for his pocket. The quiet crinkle of foil made her fumble between them for his hand. "We don't need that," she murmured, tugging it away from him and dropping it on the floor.

Her movements made his penis glide through her folds, and his hips flexed against her. He groaned again. "You sure?" His voice was a low, throaty growl.

"Yes," she whispered. "I am."

Wrapping his arms more tightly around her, pressing her against the wall, he slid into her. He fastened his mouth to hers as he thrust into her, his tongue moving in time with his hips. "Alex," she mewled. "Oh, God." Trapped against the wall, she couldn't move the way she wanted to. But it didn't matter. Holding her with one hand, Alex reached between them and pressed on her clitoris as he thrust, and she exploded in his arms.

Dimly, she felt his hips stutter against hers, heard his cry of release. Her orgasm went on and on. His, too, as he continued to move. Finally he slowed, then stopped. He turned and slid down the wall, still clasping her in his arms, until they sprawled together on the floor.

He pressed her head into his chest, and his heart thundered beneath her ear. She panted, trying to catch her breath, her hands still gripping him tightly.

His cheek was nestled against her head, and her knees gripped his hips. He was still inside her, and she didn't want to move. Alex surrounded her, enveloping her with his scent. The connection they shared buzzed between them like a live wire, twisting tighter and tighter until she felt as if she was fused to him.

His heart slowed. Her breathing returned to normal. Her shirt, bunched around her throat, was too tight. Her jeans, still attached to one leg, trailed across the floor like a flag of surrender.

Finally, Alex lifted his head. Eased her away so he could look at her. "Gaby." Regret was heavy in his expression. "I'm sorry. I didn't want to fuck you tonight. I wanted to make love with you."

Her hands trembled as she trailed her fingers across his face. "Alex. Please don't say you're sorry. I was as out of my mind as you were. I wanted that as much as you did." She pressed her mouth to his, nibbled his lip, then rested her forehead against his. "That's what happens when you...when you *yearn* for someone for so long. You lost control. So did I. And it was perfect."

He wrapped his arms around her and pulled her close, her bare chest against his shirt. "Have you been yearning for me, Gaby?"

"God, yes, Alex." She nuzzled closer, breathing in his clean air and sunshine scent. "I've wanted you for so long."

His sigh stirred her hair and sent shivers through her. "I've wanted you, too, Gaby. But you deserve so much more." He stroked his hand over her hair, soothing her. Settling her. "I want to cherish you. Worship you."

"I want to cherish you, too, Alex." She burrowed between two buttons on his shirt and pressed her fingers into his warm skin. Felt the hard muscles beneath it. "And I plan on doing a lot of worshipping tonight. Although it's hard to imagine how anything could be better than that."

His mouth curved on her head, and his warm breath made her shudder. "Was that a challenge, babe? Because I love a challenge."

Her heart fluttered against her ribs. She was sure she felt it move. "It was the truth, *babe*. No more, no less."

"Then I accept the challenge." He lifted his head and leaned away. "This condo is soundproof. And I'm going to make you scream, Gaby. A lot."

"Hmm," she hummed against his chest. "I bet I can get some screams out of you, too." She nibbled on his nipple, smiled against his skin when he shuddered.

His penis moved inside her. Thrilled with her effect on him, she flattened her tongue on the hard nub. "Maybe the screaming should start right now," she murmured into his rock hard muscles.

In response, he cupped her face in his hands and stared down at her. "You didn't care about the condom, Gaby. How come?"

She circled his wrist, pulled his hands toward her mouth and kissed one palm. The other. Then pressed them to her face again. "I'm on the pill."

"Really?" Alex let go of her face and brushed her hair

behind her ears. "How come? I'm pretty sure you haven't been dating anyone."

"Of course I haven't dated anyone since Julio." She trailed her fingers over his face, touched the side of his neck and felt his blood racing. Just as her blood raced for Alex. "I never stopped taking them after Julio was gone. You know how he was. I was terrified he'd come back and rape me and I'd get pregnant."

"Okay. I get that." He leaned back against the wall, pulled her against him and began stroking her hair. "But it's been a year."

Here it was. Now he'd know how much of a sap she was. But she didn't care. This was Alex. The only man who'd ever made her sappy. She knew he wouldn't use it against her.

She pressed her cheek against his. "I was kind of hoping I'd need them again. With you."

Alex stilled. "You've been thinking about this for a year?"

"Yes," she whispered. "I have."

Alex eased her away. Stared down at her, wonder in his gaze. "And you trusted me enough to let me go bareback?"

"Yes." She put her hand on his chest, felt his heart beating against her palm. "I trust you completely, Alex."

"Even with something as important as this?"

"Yes."

He closed his eyes and wrapped his arms around her. "I don't know what to say, Gaby. I'm...I'm...wow."

She nestled closer, a little uncomfortable that she'd shown him so clearly how she felt about him. Trying to recover, she said, "Maybe we can move on to the screaming part of the evening?"

She felt him smile against her cheek. "I'm all over that, babe."

Swinging her into his arms, he rose to his feet effortlessly, as if she weighed nothing. "That was impressive," she murmured as he walked toward his bedroom.

"What?" He glanced down at her, puzzled.

"Standing up while you were holding me."

He nuzzled her hair as he stepped into his bedroom. "Little trick I learned during my days as a SEAL."

"Do you have other tricks you can show me?" she asked, pressing her mouth to his neck.

"I have lots of tricks." He trailed his mouth over her cheek. "I'll show you all of them tonight."

Without turning on the light, he set her on the bed. She bounced up when he reached for the buttons on his shirt. "I want to do that," she said, easing his hands away.

"You want to undress me?"

"Yes. So I can worship you."

He looked down at her, smiling in the dim light. "Can I do one thing first?"

"What's that?"

"Finish taking your pants off. I'm afraid you'll trip on that leg of your jeans that's been trailing after you."

Gaby looked down and saw her jeans bunched around one ankle, one leg curling to the side like a tail. She reached down to pull it off, but Alex brushed her hands away. "Let me."

He crouched in front of her and eased the jeans and underwear away. Then he sat back and studied her, his hands smoothing over her legs. Cupping her knee. He pressed a kiss to the inside of one thigh. Then the other.

"I could spend all night just looking at you," he said, his voice low and velvety as his hands crept higher. "Touching you. Finding all your favorite places."

He stopped his hands inches from where she really wanted him. Brushed one finger over the hair between her legs. Down the crease of one thigh. Then the other. "What about here, Gaby?" He stroked over her again. "Is this one of your favorite places?"

One touch, Alex's dark, throaty voice, and she was a puddle in front of him. A throbbing, trembling mess.

Wildfire danced across her skin. Her legs shook. She grabbed Alex's shoulders and hung on. Her mouth could form only one word. "*Alex*," she breathed.

He looked up at her, still fully clothed, his eyes dark. "I want to taste you, Gaby. I want the taste of us together in my mouth. Lie down."

"Not yet," she replied, lifting trembling hands to his shirt. "You've seen me naked. I want to see you, too. I need to touch you. Taste you."

She wanted to rip off his shirt. Tear out the buttons and slide it down his arms. To torture herself, and Alex, she pushed the buttons through their holes slowly. Brushed the backs of her hands over the front of his jeans before easing the shirt down his arms.

He stood still as a statue, watching as she undressed him, his unbuttoned and unzipped jeans tented in front of him. She dropped the shirt on the floor, putting her palms on his hard, flat abdomen. His muscles twitched beneath her fingers. When she drifted lower, he circled her wrists with his fingers. "Not yet, Gaby."

She tugged her hands free. "I need to see you, Alex."

Gripping his jeans, she lowered them to the floor. Tugged his boxer briefs down, as well. Finally she knelt on the floor and pulled his clothing off one leg, then the other. Then sat back on her heels and looked at him, naked in front of her.

His broad shoulders tapered down to narrow hips, and his abdomen was muscled and flat. She'd thought 'six pack' abs were something only found in romance novels, but she was staring at the real thing. Further south, his cock rose thick and long from a thatch of dark blond hair.

"Alex," she breathed. "You're so beautiful." She'd never seen a more beautiful man. And he wanted *her*. As much as she wanted him. Her heart trembled in her chest as she reached for him. But he slid his hands over hers.

"My turn," he said.

Gaby glanced down at herself. Her shirt covered her

naked breasts, her open bra bulky and bunched up beneath it. Alex reached for the hem, drawing it slowly over her head. He tossed it on the floor, dragged the straps of her bra down her arms, and dropped it on top of her shirt.

Both of them stood naked in the dimly lit room. She was stripped bare in front of Alex, and she let him look his fill. She wanted him to see all of her. Her flaws. Her imperfections. Her faults.

She reached out and touched Alex's hip, found it warm and hard beneath her fingers. Slid her palm over the curve of his ass. Felt him tremble, the same way she trembled when he touched her.

"I want to look at you all night," she said. "Touch every bit of your skin. Taste every inch of you." She could be herself with Alex. Tell him what she wanted. She trusted him. Knew he'd accept her, no matter what.

"I want that, too," Alex murmured, lifting his hands to cup her breasts. "And we will. We have all night, Gaby."

He leaned behind her and dragged the quilt and top sheet to the foot of the bed. Then he slid his hands beneath her and lowered her to the sheets.

He pressed his mouth to hers, and she struggled to get closer. Kissed him back as he tiptoed his fingers over her ribs, spread his hand on her abdomen, brushed his thumbs over her breasts. While she squirmed against him, he slid down her body and took one nipple in his mouth.

She arched off the bed with a tiny cry, and he lifted his head and grinned at her. "The first time, but not the last," he said, leaning down and swiping his tongue slowly over her other nipple. She felt him smile against her skin when she made a needy, desperate sound.

By the time he kissed his way down to the apex of her thighs, she had lost count of how many times she'd cried his name. "Now, Alex," she panted. "I want you now. Please."

Instead of sliding into her, he slid lower and covered her with his tongue. Sucked her clitoris into his mouth and swirled his tongue around it, and she shattered with a keening scream.

She was still quivering when he rose up and slid inside her. Impossibly, she felt herself trembling on the edge of the cliff again. Wrapping her legs around Alex, pressing her heels into his back, she held his gaze as she moved with him, climbing higher and higher. Together.

There was no first-time awkwardness. No hesitation, no adjustments to make. They moved together as if they'd done this for years and knew everything about each other. Finally, still staring into her eyes, Alex thrust hard into her with a wild cry.

She followed him over, wrapping her arms around him to hold on as her climax shattered her.

By the time she regained her senses, Alex had flipped her over so she was lying on top of him. One of his hands traced lazy patterns on her back, and the other gripped her hand tightly. As if he never intended to let go.

He pressed a kiss to the side of her head, and she felt a caress of air as the sheet and quilt fluttered over her and settled on her skin. "Sleep, Gaby," Alex whispered. "I've got you. You're safe."

Yes. She was safe with him. He'd protect her heart as fiercely as he protected her body. "I love you," she whispered against his skin as she tumbled into sleep.

* * *

Alex stared at the light slanting through the blinds as he held Gaby tightly to his chest. She was sprawled over him, her hair trailing over his shoulder, the top of her head tucked into his neck. He was pretty sure she hadn't meant for him to hear her say she loved him.

"I love you, too, Gaby," he murmured into her hair, his eyes prickling. He'd waited so long for Gaby. Spent so many days thinking about her. So many nights dreaming about her.

The reality was a hundred times better than any of his

dreams.

He never wanted to let her go. And once they caught Abrietto and put him in prison, Alex would make sure Gaby knew exactly how he felt.

About her. Bella. Cece.

Those girls were as precious to him as Gaby herself. He wanted to protect them, too. Love them. Give them everything he didn't have growing up – a father-figure who would always be there for them. The guy who'd show up for all of Bella's tae kwon do meets. The man who'd speak French with Cece. The man who'd read to them. Spend time with them on his days off. Adore them the way he adored their mother.

His arms tightened around Gaby as his eyes fluttered closed. Once they caught Abrietto, they could focus on the future. On being happy. On making a family together.

CHAPTER 19

Alex woke abruptly, aware something was different. Not wrong, just not the same.

Then he saw a fan of dark hair across his belly. Gaby. And her mouth was very busy. His cock sprang to life.

"You're awake," she hummed, lifting her head to grin up at him. The waves of her hair brushed over his cock, making him bite his lip to keep from moaning. Gaby tilted her head at him.

"Do you have any idea how many times you made me scream last night?"

Alex lifted onto his elbows so he could watch her. "I lost track."

"So did I." She held his gaze while she curled her tongue around him. Released him with a little pop that made all his blood rush to his groin. "It's my turn to make you crazy. Make you squirm." She took him in her mouth again. Slid her tongue along his length. "I want to make you scream."

"You're on the right track," he managed to say.

Dropping back to the bed, he tangled the fingers of one hand in her hair. Gripped the sheet tightly with the other. Closed his eyes to keep from watching her when he felt his control slipping.

"Let go, Alex," she whispered, swirling her tongue around his tip. "It's not always going to be about me. Sometimes, it's going to be about you."

Hearing her talk about a future with him, about making love with him again, was enough to send him crashing over the edge. To lose control enough to make him gasp, "Gaby!"

His cries bounced off the walls, then settled on the two of them as they curled together. Contentment wrapped them in a protective cocoon, shutting out everyone and everything but each other.

His precious Gaby. He'd been waiting for her for so long. Dreaming about her for so long. And the reality was a thousand times better than any of his dreams.

Hours later, Alex rolled over and watched Gaby. Her hair was tousled and tangled as she sprawled on his bed, her eyes half-open. "I can't move," she said, her mouth curling into a smile. "And it's all your fault."

"I'll accept the blame for that." He sat up and scooted closer. Bent down and kissed the small of her back. Those little indentations on either side of her spine drove him crazy, and he dragged his tongue over them. Savored her taste. The hint of salt on her skin. The scent that was unmistakably Gaby.

"Let's get a shower, then I'll fix you breakfast."

"Hmm, don't want to move. I want to lie here and smell you."

"Smell me?" He lifted his head. Sniffed. "Am I stinky?"

"No." She smiled, and he wanted to see that soft, satisfied look on Gaby's face for the rest of his life. "The pillow smells like you. I hugged it all night when you weren't here to hug. Now I want to savor the real thing."

He smoothed his palm down her back, stroked the cheeks of her ass. Lingered.

Without moving, she said, "You keep that up, we're not making it out of here in time for breakfast."

He squeezed once more, then reluctantly sat up. Glanced at his clock. Groaned. "You're right. We have to leave for my parents' place in less than two hours."

Gaby slid up and leaned against the headboard, tugging the sheet to cover her breasts. "It doesn't take two hours to shower and eat breakfast."

He wanted to tug that sheet away from her. Show her what he intended to do to her. "It does if we take the kind of shower I'm thinking about."

Gaby smiled, letting her gaze drop to his fully-erect cock. Then she glanced at him from behind the curtain of her hair.

"That sounds really good," she said, her voice low and throaty. "I have a lot of places that need to be massaged."

"I was hoping you'd say that."

* * *

Two hours later, Alex turned onto the Kennedy Expressway, staying in the right lanes so he could merge onto the Edens. To go north to Oakvale.

"Tell me about this party," Gaby asked, putting her hand on his thigh.

He covered it with his own hand. "They have it once a year. To raise money for programs that help kids get into drug rehab. There are so many kids whose parents can't afford it or don't have enough insurance."

He tightened his hand on hers. Let go when the road curved and her white bandage flashed in the sunlight. Reminding him to check the rear view mirror. He'd forgotten all about Abrietto last night. "All their rich friends come and write big checks. It makes them feel righteous."

Gaby turned her hand and twined their fingers, the bandage a tiny bump between their palms. A reminder of that bastard Abrietto and how he needed to be dealt with before Alex and Gaby could move forward together. "It sounds as though your parents are doing something good. Raising money that's needed for kids who get hooked on drugs."

"They're trying to look good," he said, remembering all the times his parents had ignored Theresa. "Pretend like they were good parents."

"Maybe they're trying to make up for what they *didn't* do when you and Theresa were kids," Gaby murmured. "Maybe this is your parents owning up to their mistakes."

"Do you always see the good in people?" he asked.

"When I can." She shrugged. "I don't know your parents. I want to give them the benefit of the doubt."

"I really don't want to talk about them," he said. "Can we talk about Abrietto instead?"

Her hand tensed beneath his. "Now there's a mood killer."

"Better to talk about this now, when the girls aren't here." He glanced over at Gaby, waited until she nodded reluctantly.

"I've been trying to think this through. Do you have any idea why he isn't making tracks out of the city? Why he keeps coming after you?" He let her hand go, rested his palm on her thigh. To comfort her. Reassure her that he'd protect her. "He had a gun the other day. He could have killed you. But he didn't. What does he want?"

She slid around on the seat to face him. He glanced at her face, but she didn't seem upset. Just...pensive.

"I thought about that, too. Why didn't he just break the glass, pull out the gun and shoot me? Instead, after he broke the glass, he tried to grab me. He wanted something."

"Any idea what it was?" Alex asked.

She swallowed hard and turned to stare out the windshield. "He was going to rape me the first day. Maybe that."

Rage at Abrietto made him clutch her thigh. Too hard, he realized as she flinched. "Sorry, babe." He brought her hand to his mouth and kissed her fingers.

"He knew you'd called the cops. Knew he wouldn't have time to...for that. What else would he want?" He glanced over at her. "You mentioned that he wanted money that first time he was in the house. Did he ask for money on Friday?"

Her fingers twitched, as if she was reliving those moments when she'd grabbed the knife. "I don't remember," she finally said. She shot him an apologetic glance. "I'm sorry. I was too busy trying to keep out of his reach to pay attention to what he was screaming at me. And all that blood..." She swallowed. "So much blood."

He kissed her hand again. "We'll find him," he assured her. "We have uniforms checking on all his known associates. Flashing his picture at the SRO's. He has to be staying somewhere."

She lifted one shoulder. Let it drop. "Maybe it *is* money. That first day he was yelling at me to give him money. I'm not sure why he thought I had cash to hand him. I told you how he forged my signature and stole most of the money out of the checking account I keep for the girls. He knows I put that checkbook in a safe deposit box. He knows it's not in the house."

"Maybe he figured that you'd brought it back to the house after he went to jail."

"Maybe," she said, her voice filled with doubt.

He squeezed her hand again, then let her go. "Enough about Abrietto. This is our exit," he said.

"Okay." She shifted in her seat, her hands clasped tightly in her lap. "Tell me what to expect."

As Alex talked about the party, told her it would be at his childhood home, mentioned some of the people who'd be there, she watched the scenery flying past. She'd never been to these northern suburbs, and it looked like she'd landed in a foreign country.

Trees arched over the road, providing a green canopy for the cars beneath them. On one side, she spotted a huge house, sitting far back from the road. The soft red of its bricks was the same color as the roses blooming in front of the house.

The next house was white stone, each piece different, all fitted together carefully. Every house they passed had a meticulously tended lawn spreading out in front of it. Many of the properties were hidden behind brick or stone walls. Through the openings for driveways, she saw the stately buildings, some of them covered with ivy, their manicured gardens filled with sculptured trees and bushes. A few of the estates had flower gardens, but they were roses or other formal, prickly bushes. Meant to be looked at and admired, but not touched.

Finally Alex slowed in front of a house with an open gate. Cars lined the driveway all the way up to the door, a uniformed police officer directing traffic. Instead of turning onto the driveway, Alex parked on the side of the road next to the wall.

"You're not going inside?" she asked, surprised.

"Faster getaway out here," he said, his face grim. "I've learned from experience it's best to have my car handy."

She leaned over the console and pressed a kiss to his mouth. "You're not alone this time," she promised. "We'll face it together."

He swiveled in his seat and cupped her face in his hands, kissing her again. Deepening it, until she swayed across the console, trying to get closer. Finally he let her go and took her hand.

"I wish we could go home right now," he said. "Collect Bella and Cece and go back to my place. Order in some food, watch television. Laugh. Have fun. Just *be*."

"We'll do that later," she promised. "As soon as we're done here, we'll call Raine and Connor and get the girls."

"That's what I want," Alex said. "To hang out with you and Bella and Cece. I want real life. Not this..." he waved his hand toward the house. "This carefully controlled, artificial existence."

Gaby smiled and kissed his hand. "Nothing controlled or artificial about the Stefanos."

"Exactly." He pressed a quick kiss to her mouth, then

reached for the car door.

Her phone rang, and she picked it up. Raine. Her heart pounding, she pressed the call button. Then put the phone on speaker so Alex could hear. "Raine. Is everything okay?"

"Everything's fine," Raine assured her, and Gaby's shoulders relaxed. "The girls had a great time last night. Stayed up way too late, ate too much popcorn, watched too many cheesy movies." She hesitated for a moment. "They want to go bowling," she finally said. "I've corralled five mothers to go with us, so there's almost one adult for every kid. Is it okay if Bella and Cece go, too? If not, Connor will stay here with them."

Gaby glanced over at Alex. He said, "Raine, which bowling alley are you going to?"

"Bel-Air Lanes. Not too far from our apartment."

"I know it. It's pretty small. A family place. Not the kind of bowling alley where people hang out at the bar. It's mostly just bowlers." He glanced at her. "Gaby? What do you think?"

"Do you think it's safe?" she asked.

"It's public, but the chances of Abrietto being there are pretty slim. He doesn't seem like the bowling type."

Gaby stared down at her hands. Remembering the way the hair on the back of her neck had lifted when they were leaving Raine's yesterday, she wanted to say no. Wanted Connor to keep the girls locked up in his apartment. Where they'd be safe.

But there would be lots of adults. Lots of people watching Bella and Cece. "Are you going to tell the other parents what's going on with my girls?" she asked.

"Just that there's a situation and we need to keep a close eye on them," Raine assured her. "Believe me, Connor won't take his eyes off them."

"May I talk to Bella for a moment?"

"Sure." Raine heard her call, "Bella? Your mom wants to talk to you."

"Yeah, Mom?" Bella sounded impatient. As if she wanted to hurry back to her friends.

"I'm nervous about this," Gaby said. "If I let you go, you have to promise to stay close to Raine and Connor. Pay attention to what's going on around you. And keep an eye on Cece. Don't let her wander off. Don't *you* wander off."

"I won't, Mom. And I'll make sure Cece understands." Gaby heard voices in the background. Then Bella said, "Connor will have his gun. And he said he's going to put leashes on me and Cece."

Gaby could hear the smile in her daughter's voice. She hadn't heard that in a while. "Okay, baby, you can go. Just, please, be careful."

"I will, Mom. Talk to you later."

After a pause, Raine said, "You sure you're okay with this, Gaby?"

"I trust you and Connor to keep them safe," she said. "And we'll be there soon. We're at the party now, and Alex doesn't want to stay too long."

Alex leaned closer to Gaby, resting his hand on her shoulder. "We'll give you a call when we're on our way home," he said to Raine. "If you're still at the bowling alley, we'll meet you there."

"I'll throw the girls' stuff in the van then, just in case," Raine said.

"Okay. Thanks."

Alex kept his eyes on her as he said goodbye to Raine. He didn't take his hand off her shoulder, though, and she pressed hers against it, trying to tell him to leave it there. She needed to feel that connection with him. That reassurance that the girls would be safe.

As soon as Gaby slipped the phone into her purse, he murmured into her ear, "We don't have to stay here. Let's start the car and head back to the city. We can go to the bowling alley ourselves, if that would make you feel better."

Gaby drew in a deep, shuddering breath. "I'm anxious," she admitted. "But Julio isn't some kind of freak with superhuman skills. He's just a common thug. And not a very bright one. Connor will be there." She summoned a smile and squeezed Alex's hand. "Let's go to your party."

Trying to set aside her fears, she stepped out of the car. The sun warmed her shoulders, and the grass was lush even out here, on the shoulder of the road. She tiptoed over it to keep her heels from sinking into the soft dirt, and once they stepped onto the driveway, she reached for Alex's hand.

"The weather's nice, so they'll be set up in the back yard," he said. He glanced down at her shoes. "We'll walk through the house, though. Easier than walking across the grass."

A man in a black suit opened the front door. Smiled at Alex. "Welcome home. It's good to see you, sir," he said.

"Thanks, Cameron," he said, smiling back. "Good to see you, too."

Alex tightened his grip on Gaby's hand and she returned the squeeze, glad she was here for him. Alex was helping her face her demons. She was thrilled she could do the same for him. No one should have to face the ghosts of their pasts alone. Especially when they were unhappy and painful ones.

As they stepped into the house, she slowed, gawking. Oriental rugs as beautiful as the ones in Alex's apartment covered the floors in the hall and the open door of what looked like a living room. Portraits hung on the wall. Relatives of Alex, because she could see the family resemblance. One man had Alex's long fingers, the ones that had caressed her.

A woman had his sharp cheekbones, just like the ones that made Alex so handsome, the cheekbones she'd kissed last night.

Glass sculptures sat on table tops, elegant, flowing shapes in brilliant shades of blue and green and yellow and purple. Light struck the swooping purple sculpture, breaking the light into rainbows reflected onto the wall. She'd bet her next paycheck that they'd been made by some famous artist.

As she and Alex walked down the hall, the air was scented with beeswax and lemon. The hardwood floors were a beautiful, reddish wood that glowed in the light.

The furniture gleamed with polish. Everything carefully chosen and put together. Even in her best dress, she felt drab. Ordinary.

This place felt more like a museum than a real home. It was impossible to picture two children growing up here. Where would they play? Surely they didn't sprawl on those gorgeous rugs to read or do their homework.

She slipped her fingers between Alex's and pressed her palm to his. She didn't want him to think about all the sad memories he'd shared with her. She wanted him to know he wasn't alone.

They passed through the kitchen, which was bustling with caterers in white uniforms and servers wearing grey. No one gave them a second look. Then they stepped onto the patio.

Gaby had worn her nicest dress and her fancy blue shoes. She'd applied makeup carefully. Curled her hair. But watching these perfectly made up women, their hair and clothes and jewelry all expensive and elegant, she suddenly felt out of place. Her dress was from a well-known designer, but she'd bought it from a resale shop. Her shoes from a clearance rack.

She'd bet that none of these people even knew what a clearance rack was.

Then she straightened her shoulders and lifted her head. Alex wanted her here. That's all that mattered. So she'd enjoy this glimpse of how the one percent lived, then she'd go back to her regularly scheduled life. With Alex.

"Alex, darling." A woman with white blond hair and diamonds around her neck hurried up to Alex and air-kissed both his cheeks. "It's good to see you."

"You, too, Mother," he said. Gaby heard the tension in his voice. She wondered if his mother had picked up on it.

"I'd like you to meet Gabriella Stefano. Gaby, this is my mother, Beatrice Jennings."

"Nice to meet you, Mrs. Jennings," Gaby said, holding out her hand.

Alex's mother hesitated as her gaze swept over Gaby, then she smiled. "Lovely to make your acquaintance too, Gabriella." Her handshake was brief as her gaze shifted to her son. "I didn't realize you were bringing a guest, Alex."

"I didn't think one more would matter."

"Of course not. But you might have let me know. I would have arranged a luncheon before the event. Just your father and I, you and Gabriella."

"Some other time," Alex said easily. "Gaby didn't want to leave her girls for too long, and I know how focused you like to be before this party."

Alex's mother narrowed her eyes when Alex mentioned the girls. As she studied Gaby, her nostrils flared, as if she'd smelled something distasteful. Finally she turned to Alex.

"You're right. There are a million details to supervise." She glanced over Gaby's shoulder. "There's Julia Carleton. I need to speak to her." She tilted her head and studied Alex, her mouth tightening. "I always thought you and Julia would make a fine couple, dear. You're both police officers, from the same background…"

She glanced at Gaby, and Gaby got the message. *You're not from the same background. You and my son* don't *make a fine couple.*

Beatrice touched Gaby's arm. "If you're interested in donating to Theresa's Fund, dear, the details are on the table in the corner."

"Mother," Alex said sharply. "Gaby isn't here to *donate* to your cause. She's here for me."

"Of course, dear. Does she know about Theresa?"

"Gaby knows everything, Mother."

Beatrice's mouth pinched as she studied Gaby. "I see. Then I definitely look forward to getting to know you better, Gabriella."

As Beatrice fluttered past them, Alex glanced over his shoulder and froze. "Julia really is here. What the hell?"

Gaby turned and saw Alex's mother talking animatedly to a young, red-haired woman. "You know her?"

"She's a Chicago cop. A detective. She was a couple years behind Theresa in high school, but..." He shrugged. "It's a small community." He scowled in the direction of his mother and the redhead. "Why the hell would my mother invite her?"

Gaby leaned against Alex's shoulder and studied the redhead. "She already told you, don't you think?" she murmured. "Your mother thinks you and Julia would make a nice couple."

Alex shook his head. "That just proves how little my mother knows me. Yes, we both grew up in Oakvale. And I like Julia. We've worked together a few times. But she's not my type. She's too driven. Too many hard edges. Julia and I would kill each other after a couple of weeks."

Alex looked down at her. "*You're* my type, Gaby. You have the biggest heart of anyone I know. You're the best mother I know. And there's no artifice in you. You're real, inside and out."

Gaby's heart warmed. Alex thought she was real. While this place where he'd grown up...it didn't look real. It looked like make-believe-land.

Like she imagined a Hollywood movie studio would be. Beautiful houses, beautiful people, beautiful lives. But behind the scenery? All a façade.

How had Alex turned out so...so normal? If she hadn't seen his apartment, she would never have guessed he came from this.

She leaned against him. "I'm so impressed, Alex," she murmured.

"With this?" He frowned as he looked down at her. "Really, Gaby?"

"Not with this. With *you*. That you're the person you are after being raised like this."

She cupped her hands around his face. "I *see* you, Alex. You're real. You're not this place. Not your parents. You are so much more. You don't rely on your money to get by. I'm guessing that no one but me even knows about all this." She stared into his eyes. Wanted to kiss him, but she wouldn't do that to Alex in front of all these people.

"You love without considering class or money. You're so generous, and not just with your money. You're generous with your time and with your heart. You're the man who loves two little girls who have no claim on him."

She stroked her thumbs over his cheeks. "You do a difficult job, and you do it well. You're not entitled. Arrogant. None of the things I've always associated with the one-percenters."

"The SEALs beat that right out of me," he said with a smile. "On the teams, you don't get anything because your parents have money. You earn everything you get."

"I think it's more than the SEALs," she murmured. "I think it's who you are."

Alex twined her hands with his and kissed the back of one hand, then the other. "I see you, too, Gaby," he said, his low voice washing over her like a cool, clear stream. "You're so much more than the woman who was caught in a bad marriage. You're raising Bella and Cece on your own, and doing a damn good job of it. They're happy, loving, well-adjusted kids. Yeah, Bella is a typical teen, but beneath all the swagger and the smart mouth is a good, kind young woman. You're the strongest woman I know, in spite of all the struggles you've had. I see you, and I love you for who you are."

Her heart melted in her chest. And as though Alex could feel her wobbly legs, he tightened his grip on her hands. Scanned the crowds. "Let's go find my father, so I can introduce you. Then I want to get out of here. Go back to the real world with you and Bella and Cece."

"I'd like that, too," Gaby said, eager to have her daughters close to her. Bella and Cece and Alex. That was all she needed.

Fifteen minutes later, as they both slid into Alex's car, he turned and kissed her. Touched her face lightly as he made love to her mouth. Then he leaned his forehead against hers. "I love you, Gaby. Completely. With everything I am."

"I love you, too, Alex," she said, her heart swelling until she was sure it would burst out of her chest. "I never planned on falling in love again. But you were always there when I needed you. You didn't let me push you away. And once I knew you?" She smoothed both thumbs across those cheekbones she loved. "I realized you were the man I'd always been looking for."

They kissed each other again, and it felt like a promise. A pledge. Finally, Alex sat up reluctantly. "Let's go. I want to pick up Bella and Cece and crash at my place. Spend the evening watching a movie and eating popcorn."

"Bella will probably insist on watching the Bearcats," Gaby said as she buckled her seat belt.

"That's my girl," Alex said with a grin as he fastened his seatbelt. "God, Gaby, I'm so crazy about both of them."

"I think they're equally crazy about you."

He glanced over at her. "Are you sure Bella won't have a problem with us being together? She seemed a little upset when she thought we were dating."

"She was territorial. You were her friend first. Once she gets used to the idea, I'm pretty sure she'll be thrilled."

"I hope so." He squeezed her hand, put the car in gear and headed back toward Chicago.

Toward home.

They'd just merged onto the Edens expressway when Alex's ringtone filled the car. Alex pressed the Bluetooth button on the dash to connect and said, "Hey, Raine. We're on our way back. We should be there in thirty minutes."

"Thank God." Raine's voice was loud in Alex's quiet car. She sniffed, as if she'd been crying. "Crank up the speed, Alex, and light 'em up. Bella's missing."

CHAPTER 20

Forty-five minutes earlier

Bella watched the stores and houses flash past as they drove to the bowling alley in Ms. Taylor's van. Last night had been fun. She'd been able to forget all the bad stuff that had happened this week.

And being with her friends and Ms. Taylor in the van felt normal. Like they were going to a meet, except that Detective Donovan sat next to Ms. Taylor. And Cece was in the back seat.

Katya was chattering about the cute guy in her math class, and Bella relaxed into the seat, happy to talk about the kind of stuff they gossiped about at tae kwon do. Boys. Clothes. Teachers.

"I remember Jason," Bella said, nodding. "He's great. And he's a nice guy." Jason wasn't as great as Piotr. Or as hot. But Bella was happy for her friend.

Katya wasn't the only one who had a new boyfriend. Bella remembered the way her mom had looked at Alex last night. "I think my mom has a new boyfriend, too."

The van rolled to a stop at a traffic light, and Raine turned around to smile at Bella. "That's great, Bella! Anyone we know?"

They all knew him. She shrugged one shoulder. "Maybe."

Raine's smile widened. "I hope you're right. He's a great guy, and they're perfect together. Your mom deserves to be happy."

Ms. Taylor turned around and the van started moving again, but Bella stared at the back of her head. *Your mom deserves to be happy.*

Ms. Taylor was right – Mom *did* deserve to be happy. And Alex *was* a nice guy. Why had Bella been so mean to her mom about him? He wasn't anything like that asshole Julio. And Alex had been nice to her and Cece. Not fake nice, like Julio had been in the beginning. Genuinely nice.

He'd taught her about baseball. Watched the 'Cats with her. Talked to Cece in French, which made Cece light up like a music video.

He'd been good to their mom, too.

Bella huffed out a breath. Maybe…maybe it was okay if Alex and her mom were dating. As long as they didn't start with the mushy stuff. At least not in front of her. That would just be gross.

A white van passed them. There was writing on the side, but something about the driver caught Bella's attention. She leaned closer to the window, squinching her eyes to get a better look at him, but the vehicle was already past them.

She leaned over until her cheek rested against the window, but still couldn't see the driver.

"Bella?" said Detective Donovan. "What's wrong?"

"Nothing," she said, flopping back onto the seat. If she told Detective Donovan that she thought the driver looked like Julio, they'd turn around and go home. They wouldn't get to go bowling.

"Then why were you making that face?" He turned around more so he was staring right at her. "It looked as if you were trying to see the truck's driver."

"I didn't...I couldn't see him."

"Why did you want to see him?"

Bella squirmed in her seat.

He held her gaze. "Do you think it was Abrietto, Bella?"

She couldn't look away. And she couldn't lie to him while he was watching her with that...that kind of scary face. She swallowed. "I'm not sure."

"But it might have been?" He swiveled around and grabbed his cell phone. Typed something in.

"Maybe." Not being sure was stupid. She'd promised her mother she'd pay attention, and she hadn't. She'd been talking to Katya instead.

Detective Donovan spoke into his cell phone. "I need a license check on a white panel truck, commercial plate, number VR 5306."

Bella stared at the vehicle. It was too far ahead of them to see the driver. She leaned closer to the window, willing the truck to slow down. To get stuck behind another car.

But it turned onto a side street, bouncing over a speed hump, then speeding up again. She saw something about plumbing written on the side. Then they passed the street and lost sight of the truck.

"I need that ID now," Detective Donovan barked into the phone.

"Got it, Detective." The van was silent. Still, as if everyone was holding her breath. It was so quiet that Bella could hear the dispatcher. "The vehicle is registered to Frank Kutowski Plumbing."

She rattled off an address, and Detective Donovan said, "Please send a patrol car over to that address. For a..." he glanced at the girls, "a well-being check."

"Will do."

"Have the officers call me as soon as they have any information." He rattled off his phone number and ended the call.

Ms. Taylor said quietly, "It was a plumber. He could

have had an emergency call."

"Could be," Detective Donovan answered as his phone pinged. A few moments later, he held up his phone which displayed what looked like a driver's license. "Take a look at this guy, Bella. His address is about six blocks from your house. Do you recognize him? Has he done plumbing for your mom?"

Bella leaned forward to study the picture. "I'm not sure…he doesn't look familiar." She straightened her back when she heard how tentative she sounded. "We haven't needed a plumber lately, though."

"Did Abrietto ever mention a guy named Frank Kutowski?"

"No." She swallowed. "But I never paid much attention to anything Julio said."

Ms. Taylor glanced over her shoulder and gave Bella a tiny smile. "Good for you, Bella."

"Okay." Donovan studied the street in front of them. In back of them. Every side street they drove past. "Chances are everything's fine. It was probably just a guy who had a slight resemblance to Abrietto. Maybe the shape of his nose, or something like that." He turned and looked at Bella again. Held her gaze.

"But if there's anything I don't like about what the patrol officers find, we're going to cancel the bowling. Go back to our apartment."

"No," Bella said, her voice a little too loud. "That's not fair to everyone else. Why should they have to miss bowling because of me?" She *hated* that asshole Julio. He wrecked *everything*.

"Because we need to make sure you and Cece are safe," Donovan explained patiently. "That's our number one concern."

He smiled at her, but she got it. He was in charge. They'd do what he wanted to do.

"Fine." She turned back to Katya and tried to resume their conversation about Jason, but her heart wasn't in it.

She was waiting for the ring of Detective Donovan's cell phone.

They were pulling into the parking lot at the bowling alley when it finally chimed. Bella stilled. All talking in the van stopped. Ms. Taylor pulled into a parking spot.

The car next to them was playing "Forever" by Drake, so loud that Bella could feel the vibrations in her feet. She could see Detective Donovan's mouth move, but she couldn't hear what he said.

"Forever" faded as the car pulled out and drove away, and Donovan swiveled around in his seat. "No one was home. The neighbors said someone was in the house this morning, because the lights were on and now they're off. They said Kutowski takes emergency plumbing calls, so that's probably who was in the van." He studied her for a moment.

"I don't like that you were freaked out, Bella," he finally said.

"I've been freaked out since that first day," she retorted. "When Julio came back and almost hurt my mom. This is no different." She didn't say anything more. She was afraid if she pushed, Donovan would push back. Cancel the bowling trip.

"All right," Donovan said after a long silence. "Stay in the car for a few minutes."

He stepped out of the car and stood in the parking lot, studying everything. The way his head swiveled back and forth on his neck made him look like the owls they'd studied in biology class.

He finally walked into the bowling alley, and no one in the van spoke. They all stared at the doors, watching for him to come back. The silence was heavy. Fearful. Like it had been at home, *before*, when everyone was afraid of what Julio might do.

It seemed like forever before Detective Donovan came out. He swung back into the passenger seat and turned to face them. "Okay, we'll stay. But we're playing one game, then we're leaving. I don't want to hear anyone complain. Got it?"

Everyone murmured yes, then they got out of the van. Ms. Taylor and Detective Donovan put Bella and Cece in between them as they walked to the door, and Cece slipped her hand into Bella's. Bella held on tightly.

By the time the rest of the girls and the mothers arrived and they all got shoes and picked their balls, Bella felt better. Calmer. There was a kid's party going on, and a bunch of ankle biters were running around, yelling and screaming. The other girls rolled their eyes, but Bella liked seeing the little kids.

All the kids in the bowling alley were reassuring. Ordinary.

She wanted *ordinary* more than anything else right now.

Half-way through their game, Bella was winning their group. She threw her ball down the alley and got all but two pins. "Yes!" She pumped her fist. She could get the other two.

But she threw a gutter ball. Stomping back to the place where the balls came out, she waited for her ball and grabbed it. It was too heavy. And it was ugly, too. All dark green and brown.

The rack that held the extra balls was against the wall. Right behind their group. She hurried over and set her old ball in an empty spot. Picked up a pretty blue one, but it was too heavy. A pink one was too light.

She'd just found a blue and yellow ball that felt right when an alarm started blaring. *Deet. Deet. Deet.* It was so loud and piercing that it made the air pulse and hurt her ears.

She dropped the ball back into the rack. Then she smelled the smoke.

Cece. She had to get her sister out of here. She turned to hurry back to the lane, but someone slapped a hand over her mouth, wrapped an arm around her waist and hoisted her into the air. Ran around the corner to where the restrooms were.

Where no one could see them.

By the time they noticed she was gone, it would be too late. Terror crashed through her in an icy wave, and she gagged at the man's smell. Garlic and onions and BO. Like he hadn't taken a shower in a long time.

She tried to turn around to signal Detective Donovan, but they were out of sight. The guy was running down a corridor next to the rest rooms.

Bella kicked back, as hard as she could, and the guy grunted. Squeezed his hand more tightly over her mouth. So she kicked again. Harder. He stumbled, then shoved through a door that said 'No Exit. Alarm will sound.'

They burst into the cool air, and Bella began clawing at the arm around her throat. Dug her fingers into him, as hard as she could. Kicked again. Squirmed.

"Knock it off, you little bitch."

Oh, my God. Julio.

He set her on the pavement and his hand closed over her nose and mouth, cutting off her air. Freaking out, she struggled and kicked as he dragged her along.

Memories of Ms. Taylor's self-defense lecture flashed through her mind, and Bella reached behind her and tried to gouge Julio's eyes.

His hand tightened on her nose.

She needed to breathe! Her vision darkened and she saw spots of light. Asshole Julio was choking her to death.

She tried to kick him again, but she was too weak. She clawed at his arm. Opened her mouth and bit his hand, sinking her teeth into the fleshy part beneath his thumb.

Julio grunted and took his hand away from her mouth. She gulped air into her lungs, opened her mouth and screamed.

Suddenly he let her go. Bella stumbled on the asphalt of the parking lot, regained her balance and tried to run. She took two steps before Julio grabbed her collar, hoisted her into the air and shoved her against the side of the truck. Then he slapped her. Hard. Her head jerked back and pain exploded in her skull and her cheek.

As her head spun, he fumbled in the pockets of her cargo pants. "Where's your cell phone, you little bitch?"

"Cece took it!" she managed to say as she twisted away from his searching hand. "She wanted to play a game." Her fingers curled with the need to touch her phone, stashed in the pocket on the lower leg of her pants, to make sure it was safe. Instead, she kicked out, trying to hit his knee.

Julio picked her up and threw her into the back of the van, then slammed the doors. She landed hard on the metal floor, shoulder first. She lay there for a moment, stunned. Her face was on fire, she was so dizzy she wanted to puke, and her shoulder ached from its impact against the floor.

Moments later, the floor rumbled as Julio started the engine. He backed out of the parking spot, shifted the gears and sped up.

The van smelled like oil and metal. Grease. Two big red tool boxes rested in the middle of the space. Cardboard boxes lined the walls, bearing pictures of machines. One said 'Dispose-all'. The closest one said 'sump pump'. Racks high on the walls held white pipes in different lengths and thicknesses.

The white panel truck she'd seen. It had belonged to a plumber.

Julio *had* been the driver.

Fumbling in the pocket on her lower leg for her phone, she rolled into the corner, where the boxes partially hid her from Julio. Her hands shook so hard she dropped the phone on the floor with a metallic thump.

Her teeth chattered with terror and she couldn't stop shaking. Couldn't *think*. Julio would come back here and see her phone. Take it away. She had to call for help.

Her hands were trembling too wildly to hold the phone, so she propped it on her leg. Pressed the speed dial for her mom's phone. Then held it to her ear with both hands, hoping Julio wouldn't hear her mom answer.

"Bella?"

"Mom," she whispered, so relieved to hear her mother's voice. Then began to cry silently. "Julio has me," she hiccupped, then sucked in a shaky breath. "I'm in the back of a van. Kut something plumbing. Help me!"

She heard the faint sounds of her mom talking. Then Alex said, "Don't say a word, Bella. You're a brave, smart girl. Leave your phone on, but hide it. We'll have them trace you. We're on our way, Bella, and we'll find you. I promise. We won't let Julio hurt you."

"Okay," she whispered. She held the phone to her ear, needing to hear her mom's voice. But Alex must have heard her shaky, frightened breathing.

"Put the phone in your pocket, baby," Alex said. "Don't let him see it."

She didn't want to put the phone away. She needed the connection to her mom. To Alex.

"Please, baby. Put it away," Alex said.

"I will," she whispered. She clutched it to her chest for a moment, holding it so tight that her fingers ached, then she slid it into the pocket. It took three tries to get the button through the hole.

Her fingers touching the edge of the phone through the thin material of her pants, she sprawled against the wall of the van, panting and shaking. Completely helpless.

No. Not completely. She knew taw kwon do. Ms. Taylor had taught them self-defense. She could do *something*.

She leaned forward until she could see the back of Julio's head, his dark hair shaved short, and felt a fierce satisfaction. They must have shaved it at the jail. Julio had been really proud of his hair. He spent more time than Bella did in front of the mirror.

"How did you know where I'd be?" she called to him.

He glanced in the rear-view mirror, and even from here, she saw his smirk. "I was waiting at that bitch teacher's place – I owe her for putting me in prison. Your mother thought she was so smart, leaving you with that bitch. But it was easy to follow you to that bowling alley. I saw you watching me in that truck, so I circled back and followed at a distance. Who's the smart one now?"

You're not as smart as you think you are, asshole. You didn't find my phone, did you? "Why did you kidnap me?" she called to him.

"I didn't kidnap you, you little shit."

Then what do you call it?

Her phone was still on. Alex and her mom would hear what he said. The thought steadied her a little. "Why did you take me away from the bowling alley?"

"Your bitch of a mother has something I need."

Julio didn't have much of a vocabulary. She sat up and leaned against the wall. She was fighting back. That made her feel a little better. A little steadier. "She doesn't have any of your stuff. She threw it all away."

He turned to glance at Bella, and his expression scared her. He wanted to hurt her. "She has money. I need money. We're going to make a trade."

"My mom doesn't have any money." Bella frowned. Why would he think that? "She barely makes enough for food. We have beans and rice at least twice a week. We never eat anything good." Except when Alex was around. But Julio didn't need to know about Alex.

"Shut your mouth, *puta.*"

Bella didn't know much Spanish, but she knew that word. The mean boys in her school called some of the girls *puta*, and she'd looked it up. *Prostitute.*

Julio turned right and sent her sliding into the wall. Her foot grazed a piece of plastic in the corner of the van, and a light flashed behind the plastic.

The tail lights.

Bella stared at the piece of plastic, her heart racing. She'd just finished a book about a girl who was kidnapped. She'd been thrown into the trunk of a car, but she'd kicked the tail light out and stuck her hand through the opening. Waved and waved, until she heard the police behind her.

Bella leaned around the boxes and looked up at Julio.

He was driving fast, the truck swaying from side to side. But she didn't think he was watching her.

Squirming backward, trying to stay hidden behind the boxes of pumps, she pressed her foot against the plastic and shoved. Nothing happened.

She drew her leg back and kicked. Again. A tiny crack appeared in the plastic, and Bella pretended she was in a tae kwon do match. She gathered herself. Focused on that piece of plastic. Then she threw all her weight behind another kick.

The plastic broke with a crack, and Bella froze. Peeked from behind the box. But Julio didn't look back.

Where was he taking her?

Fear shivered through her, and she kicked at the tail light again and again until she felt her foot break through.

Laying on her belly, she stared through the hole she'd created. Saw cars on the road behind her.

Taking a deep breath, she stuck her hand through the hole. Waved as if her life depended on it.

Her fingers got cold. Sharp stings burned her hand. What felt like a stone hit her index finger, and she had to stuff her other hand in her mouth to keep from crying out.

But she kept waving. Because her life *did* depend on it.

CHAPTER 21

When Gaby heard Bella's voice on her phone, she started to cry. *Thank God. Her baby was alive.* Able to call her. She sobbed once, swallowed the sound. She didn't have time to fall apart. They needed to concentrate on finding Bella.

Alex dropped his own phone, still live with Raine, into Gaby's lap. "Tell Raine to hang up and have Connor call me. Put my phone on vibrate." He nodded at the phone she clutched tightly. "Keep Bella on the line, and listen hard for Abrietto's voice."

He glanced at her and his fierce expression lightened for just a moment. "She's a smart girl. Smart enough not to let Abrietto have her phone. What's Bella's phone number?"

Gaby swallowed the ball of tears in her throat and recited it to Connor.

"Good. I'll have Connor start tracking it. We'll find her."

Alex's calm voice and quiet commands were oddly reassuring. As if he knew what to do and had no doubt they'd rescue Bella. Her chest tight with fear, Gaby relayed the instructions to Raine and ended the call on Alex's phone.

She hit the button for vibrate, then pressed her own phone to her ear to listen.

All she heard was the rumbling of the van. Then she heard a sniff. Another.

Her hand tightened on her phone. That bastard Julio had made her strong, fearless Bella cry. She'd kill Julio herself if he hurt a hair on her daughter's head.

This was her fault.

She shouldn't have let Bella and Cece go to the sleepover with Raine. Had a secret, yearning part of her known she and Alex would spend their night alone making love? Had she let that influence her decision?

A tiny whimper escaped, and Alex glanced at her. "I know what you're thinking," he said. "Stop it. This wasn't your fault. You did everything possible to keep her safe. None of us had any idea Abrietto would find them at the bowling alley. Don't beat yourself up, Gaby."

"I shouldn't have let them go to Raine's," she whispered. "I should have kept them with me."

"It's easy to say that now. But no one could have foreseen this. They were with an armed cop. There were seven adults watching ten kids. You can't prevent everything, babe."

He brushed his hand over hers, then returned it to the steering wheel. "We'll get her back. I promise you."

"You can't promise that." Gaby's throat swelled with tears she refused to shed. She wouldn't feel sorry for herself while her daughter was terrified and alone.

"I just did."

Alex pressed his foot to the accelerator and the car leaped forward.

Beneath the humming of the wheels, Gaby heard Bella clear her throat. Then, her voice wobbling, she asked Julio why he'd kidnapped her. *Good girl, Bellabug.*

Gaby listened to their exchange, and Bella finally fell silent. Gaby wanted to yell to Bella that they'd find her. Promise they'd keep her safe. But she clenched her teeth together to keep from opening her mouth. Finally, when neither Bella nor Julio spoke again, she put her hand over the speaker of her phone.

" Remember when I told you about the checking account I have? The settlement money from Antony's death? Julio wants it," she told Alex. "That's why he took Bella. To trade her for my money."

A muscle in his jaw twitching, Alex flipped on the lights and siren and pressed the accelerator harder. Houses, a shopping center, a greenhouse all flashed past in a blur. Cars pulled onto the shoulder as they flew down the expressway. Gaby glanced at the speedometer and swallowed. Eighty-five miles an hour.

He was getting her back to Bella.

Faster.

Alex's phone vibrated against her leg, and she handed it to Alex. She kept her own phone pressed to her ear and heard something crack. Shatter. Her fingers tightened on the phone, but she didn't hear any more.

It sounded like the phone bounced against something hard. Had Julio found it? Thrown it away? Closing her eyes, Gaby took a deep breath, forcing the air into her tight chest. She listened intently, but heard nothing but the hum of the car.

How was she supposed to get money today? She'd give Julio whatever he wanted, but the bank was closed on Sunday. And she was pretty sure he wanted more than she could get from an ATM.

Alex was murmuring to Connor, but he must have heard her stifled cry. He reached over and squeezed her hand. Let her go immediately to return his hand to the steering wheel.

Gaby told herself she couldn't fall apart. As much as she wanted to curl up into a ball, that wouldn't help Bella. It wouldn't help Alex, either, who needed to concentrate on helping Connor finding her daughter.

Julio wouldn't hurt her, she told herself. She was valuable to him. He wanted money. Bella was the key to getting that money.

Maybe he would *hurt her. Julio was mean. Vindictive.* The tiny voice in her head was relentless. It conjured too many pictures, each one worse than the next.

She wanted to scream at Alex to go even faster. To get her to Bella before Julio could hurt her daughter. But she bit her lips together and swallowed the words. He was already driving way over the speed limit. Alex had the lights and siren on, and the other drivers were getting out of his way. He was focusing on the road, controlling the car, and she didn't want to distract him.

Suddenly he turned to her. "Gaby. They traced the phone. They know where he is. They're sending squad cars to intercept them."

"Thank God." Gaby put her head in her hands and sobbed.

* * *

The wind knocked Bella's hand back and forth against the broken pieces of the tail light. It hurt, but she clenched her teeth and ignored the pain. Someone would notice. Someone would call the police. Any minute now, she'd hear sirens. They would stop Julio and arrest him.

Suddenly Julio spewed a string of ugly words she didn't understand and wrenched the steering wheel, sending the truck careening around a corner. The vehicle shuddered, and Bella held her breath, afraid the truck would tip onto its side. But it righted itself, and the truck leaped ahead, as if Julio had pressed on the accelerator.

Bella eased her hand back into the truck, shocked when she saw it covered with blood. Swallowing at the tiny cuts that criss-crossed her hand, she closed her eyes to block out the sight, then lay on the floor, peering out the hole where the tail light used to be.

She could see only a tiny slice of what was behind her, but she saw the flashing lights of a police car. It was getting closer, and Bella closed her eyes and sucked in a deep, shuddering breath. They'd found her.

Easing away from the hole, she shoved her bloody hand through it once more and waved wildly. "I'm here! I'm here!" she wanted to shout, but had to pray that the police saw her hand and understood.

Julio wrenched the car around another corner, and another sharp pain shivered through Bella's hand. Then she heard the first siren. In front of the truck.

Then more, from behind the truck. Tears of relief fell to the floor, running down the grooves in the corrugated metal floor. Bella swiped them away and pulled her hand back inside. The police would make Julio stop, and she had to be ready.

She had to open the door and jump out before Julio got back here to grab her. The door handle was shiny silver. If Julio had locked it, she was in trouble. She wanted to pull on it to check, but was afraid the doors would swing open. If Julio stomped on the brakes, she'd fly out the door.

She glanced toward the front of the truck and found Julio watching her through the rear view mirror. "Don't you move, you little bitch! You hear me? You stay right where you are."

Bella knew from experience that any defiance would enrage him, so she nodded. Kept her head down. Curled onto her side to watch the police cars converging on the truck.

Suddenly she slid on the floor and banged into the door. Julio had braked hard. The truck flew over a speed bump and landed with a hard jolt, tossing her body a few inches off the floor, then slamming her down again.

Everything ached – her back, her head, her arms. Her bloody hand stung and throbbed. But as the truck slowed even more, she sat up. Crouched, ready to open the rear door as soon as the truck stopped.

They careened over another speed bump, then she heard two loud popping noises. Two more. The truck lurched from side to side, wobbled, slowed. Finally came to a shuddering stop.

Bella reached for the handle and yanked it up. Nothing happened. She glanced at the front of the truck. Julio was climbing into the back of the truck, baring his teeth with rage.

Her hand shaking, she shoved the handle down. Pushed hard, and the door flew open. Sobbing with fear, she dropped to the street and landed on her hands and knees.

Julio was behind her, yelling at her. She pushed off the asphalt and tried to run, but he grabbed her shirt and yanked hard. Arms flailing, she crashed into Julio's chest.

* * *

Alex roared off the Kennedy Expressway at Addison and turned left, listening to the running commentary from Connor. "The patrol cars have spotted them." A pause. Then Connor said, "God, Gaby, that girl of yours is smart. She broke out the tail light and she's waving her hand. Didn't need it, since we have a trace on her phone. But, damn! That kid is something else."

Gaby leaned toward the phone, her face sheet white. "Is Cece all right?" Alex heard the tears in her voice and wanted to reach out and comfort her. But he didn't dare take his hands off the steering wheel as he veered around cars, one set of wheels bumping up on curbs when necessary.

"She's safe, Gaby. All the other girls went home with their moms. I sent Cece back to our apartment with Raine. They're inside, with the door locked. Safe."

Thank God Cece was safe, but all Alex could picture was Bella and Julio. Once the car stopped, what would that bastard do? Would he hurt her, because he couldn't punish Gaby except through her daughter?

Alex needed to calm down. He was a police officer, for God's sake. He knew the drill.

But this was *Bella*. She wasn't an unknown victim, she

was Gaby's daughter. A kid he was crazy about. Alex gripped the steering wheel more tightly. "Where the hell are you, Donovan?"

"Mia picked me up. We've caught up with the patrol cars chasing the truck. Abrietto turned down Argyle, and squad cars are setting out stingers. Gaby, those are spike strips. They'll puncture the tires and make the car stop."

It was all coming to a head, and Alex needed to get Gaby to her daughter. Stepping on the accelerator, he dodged one car, then another, then spurted ahead. "We're on Addison," he said. "What's the closest intersection?"

"Oakley. Make a left. The stingers are three blocks up."

Alex glanced at the dashboard clock. "Should be there in two minutes. Less, if the fucking cars would pull over."

"We've got this, Jennings. Keep Gaby safe."

"She needs to be there for Bella," Alex said, his teeth clenched together, focusing on the street in front of him. Oakley was two blocks away. One block. *There.*

He stomped on the brakes as they reached the intersection and swerved into a left turn. Two blocks ahead of him, six or seven squad cars were tailing a white panel truck. He heard the loud, echoing bang of the stingers doing their job, then the van lurched to a stop. Nothing happened for a moment, then the back door flew open and Bella fell out. Landed on her hands and knees, then stood up to run.

Abrietto leaped from the truck, and Bella flew backward.

* * *

Bella's breath huffed out as she collided with Julio, and he grabbed her arm. He missed her left, though, and she spun around to face him.

Dimly, she heard the shouts of the police officers behind them. Julio reached behind his back. Bella spotted something dark in his hand, and all the practice she'd done in tae kwon do took over.

As Julio held her arm high in the air, Bella swung, twisted and broke free. Stumbling backward, she was turning to run when she saw Julio raise his hand. Pointed the dark thing at her.

A gun.

"Back down or I'll shoot her," Julio yelled to the cops. He was looking at the police officers crouched behind the doors of the squad cars instead of looking at her.

Anger rushed through Bella. *Julio thought she was helpless?* That, since he had the gun, she wouldn't be able to stop him? Protect herself from him?

She remembered what her mother had told her so many times. *If a man tries to hurt you, kick him in the balls. As hard as you can. That will stop him.*

Bella knew how to kick.

Judging the distance, Bella leaped up and slammed her foot between Julio's legs. She connected with a dull thump.

As she danced backward, Julio crumpled to the pavement with a shrill scream. His gun clattered across the asphalt, and Julio scrabbled for it. A police officer scrambled forward and snatched it up.

Her vision clouded red, Bella stared at the man writhing on the ground. Julio would have hurt her. Just like he'd hurt her mom so many times in the past.

Raising her leg, she kicked him again in the same place, throwing all her weight behind it. "That's for all the times you hurt my mom, you asshole," she yelled.

Julio's scream was so high-pitched that her ears hurt. She drew her leg back for a third kick when someone wrapped arms around her and yanked her away.

"I've got you, Bella. You're safe. Your mom is here, too."

Alex. She spun around and threw herself into his arms. "Alex," she sobbed.

"You're safe, Bella," he said, his arms closing around her. "I've got you."

Shaking so hard that her teeth chattered, Bella clung to

him, weeping into his shirt, all the terror and fear gushing out of her in a hot flood. Alex just held her, one hand rubbing her back, murmuring reassurances to her.

Behind her, Bella heard, "Bella! Bella!"

Her mom. She tore out of Alex's grasp and turned around, searching frantically for her mother. In her best black dress and her blue shoes, her mom was running toward her. Bella stumbled toward her, and moments later was enfolded in her mom's hard embrace.

Pressing her face into her mother's neck, crying against her skin, she inhaled her familiar, gingery scent. Hot tears ran down her face and onto her mom. She felt her mom's tears falling onto her head and running down her cheeks.

She started to shiver, and couldn't stop. Finally, her mom eased away from her, brushed tears from Bella's face. Her mom touched Bella's cheek, biting her lip as she touched the sore spot where Julio had hit her.

Her mouth quivering, her mother touched Bella's throat. Her arm. Clasped her bloody hand between her own soft hands. "What did he do, baby?"

"He slapped me." Bella didn't want to think about Julio. So she burrowed closer to her mother, wrapping her arms around her and holding her as if she'd never let go. Her mom stroked her back, her hair, her arms, murmuring in that low, gentle voice she used when Bella was upset.

Bella used to think it was babyish. Stupid.

Right now, it was the sweetest sound she'd ever heard.

Eventually, her mom leaned back and took Bella's hand. Started crying again. "We have to get you to the hospital. Have you checked out."

Alex put his arm around her mom's shoulders. "Paramedics are waiting for Bella. Let's let them take a look at her, babe. Okay?"

Her mom leaned into Alex and nodded, and Alex squeezed her against him.

Bella jerked up her head and stared at Alex. Then her mom. They *were* together. She remembered how jealous she'd been. How much she'd resented her mom for taking Alex away from her.

She'd been such a stupid kid. She'd had no idea what was important.

Then Alex reached for her. Hesitated as he watched her, his hand hanging in the air.

Bella folded herself against him, and Alex tucked her against his other side. As her mother cradled her bloody hand, Bella wrapped her other arm around Alex's waist and clung to him, her face buried in his shirt. Then, sandwiched between the two adults she loved most in the world, all three of them headed for the ambulance with the flashing lights.

CHAPTER 22

Gaby sat in the back of the ambulance, still shaking, clutching Bella's good hand. The paramedic was bent over the bloody one, delicately cleaning it. She held a magnifying glass over Bella's hand and studied all the tiny cuts. "I'm looking for pieces of plastic," she told Bella.

Bella nodded but didn't say anything as she watched the paramedic work. Out of the corner of her eye, Gaby saw Alex in the street, talking to Connor. He'd stayed where she could see him, Gaby realized.

He looked away from Connor and met her gaze. Smiled. Then turned back to Connor.

He'd stood where he could see *her*, too.

A wave of love crashed over her and she turned back to Bella, overwhelmed. Alex had gotten her here in time. Bella hadn't been alone when she jumped out of that truck. She didn't have to be comforted by strangers.

Tears rolled down her cheeks and dropped onto her chest as she tightened her grip on Bella's hand. Her daughter glanced over at her. Frowned. "Why are you crying now, Mom? Everything's good."

"I know," Gaby whispered. "I'm...I'm just so relieved.

And so sorry Julio was able to take you. Hurt you. I shouldn't have let you go to the bowling alley. I should have asked Connor and Raine to keep you at their place."

"That's dumb," Bella said. "Who knew ass...jerk Julio would find me at the bowling alley?"

Gaby squeezed her eyes closed as she tried to block the images scrolling through her head. Bella in the back of the truck, terrified. Hurt, beaten up and bloodied. All because of Julio.

"You were so strong, baby. So brave. And so smart to kick him like that."

Bella's fingers gripped Gaby's hand harder. "I did what you told me to do. I kicked him where it hurt."

Gaby hiccupped a laugh. "That you did, Bellabug. Twice. It was a beautiful sight."

The paramedic looked up at Gaby and Bella. "My partner's taking a look at your kidnapper," she said. "Sounds like he might have a ruptured testicle."

A vicious burst of satisfaction erupted in Gaby's chest. "Good. He deserves it."

Bella frowned. "What does a ruptured testicle mean?"

"It means you kicked him really, really hard," the paramedic said as she applied ointment to the worst cuts on Bella's hand. "Hard enough to turn his testicle into mush. If it's bad enough, they'll have to surgically remove it."

Bella's good hand tightened on her mother's. "Am I in trouble for that?"

"Of course not, honey." The paramedic paused and looked right at Bella. "Kicking him was self-defense." She covered Bella's palm and fingers with gauze. "One of the cops told me he had a gun."

The matter-of-fact words should have reassured Bella, but her daughter's eyes were wide with fear. Her hand trembled in Gaby's. As the paramedic wrapped white tape over the gauze on Bella's hand, Gaby leaned out of the truck. "Alex?" she called.

He hurried over and climbed in. "What's wrong? Is

Bella okay?" he asked, his gaze flicking between her and Bella.

Gaby rubbed circles on Bella's back, feeling the tension in her muscles. "Bella's worried about the way she kicked Julio. It sounds like he might have a ruptured testicle, and she's afraid she'll get in trouble for kicking him."

Alex crouched beside Bella, steadying himself with one hand on Gaby's shoulder. He wrapped his other hand around Bella and Gaby's joined hands. "That was self-defense, Bella. No way are you getting into trouble for that. Even after he was down, Abrietto was reaching for the gun. And a ruptured testicle? No one deserves it more than that asshole. Sorry, Gaby," he added, glancing at her.

He didn't look sorry at all. Gaby resisted the need to rest her head against his shoulder and turned back to her daughter.

Bella's face had relaxed. Not quite smiling, but she stared at Alex as if impressed by his bravery for swearing in front of Gaby.

"Special circumstances," Gaby murmured, trying and failing to hide a tiny smile as she glanced at him. "One day dispensation."

Bella did smile at Alex then. "Lucky you," she said. "Saved you fifty cents. I've paid a lot of money into the swear jar." She leaned closer to Alex and lowered her voice. "She's never caught me saying the five-dollar word, though."

"Guess I better watch my mouth, then," he said. "I don't want to bring down the wrath of your mother."

Gaby blinked hard but couldn't hold back the tears. Bella and Alex were teaming up. Against her. She bit her lip to hide her smile and wiped the tears away from her cheeks.

A loud ripping sound echoed through the back of the ambulance, and Gaby saw the paramedic patting the last piece of tape into place on Bella's hand. "You should take her to your doctor tomorrow, Ms. Stefano," the woman said, putting the tape and gauze back into a big tackle box. "Have him or her take another look at that hand. She might need antibiotics."

"I will," Gaby managed to say, swallowing her tears. "I'll call first thing in the morning."

The paramedic smiled at Bella. "You're an amazing kid, Bella. It was really great to meet you."

Bella flushed and darted a quick look at Gaby, then shrugged at the paramedic. "I do tae kwon do at school. I remembered what Ms. Taylor taught us."

"Smart, too." The woman adjusted a piece of the tape, then gently patted the bandage that completely immobilized Bella's hand. "You're all set. Keep that hand elevated tonight. Put a plastic bag over it if you take a shower, and seal the bag around your wrist with a rubber band."

Still holding Bella's uninjured hand, Gaby stepped down from the ambulance and steadied Bella while she descended. Alex stood on the other side, hand held out to catch Bella if she stumbled.

He'd catch any of them if they stumbled, Gaby realized, her eyes filling again.

And when *he* needed catching, she'd be there for him.

As soon as Bella was on the pavement, he slung an arm around her shoulders. "You good now?"

Bella leaned into him for a moment, and Gaby saw her sniff. Swipe her nose across her upper arm. "I'm good," Bella said, her voice a little shaky. "But can we get Cece and go home?"

"Of course we can." Alex kept his arm around Bella, and she didn't try to squirm away. Thank God. He kept Bella safely tucked into his side as they walked to his car, and on Bella's other side, Gaby curled her arm around her daughter's waist.

Bella cuddled closer and some of the tension in Gaby's back eased. The heavy weight that had been pressing on her shoulders lifted.

When they reached Alex's car, Gaby slid into the back

seat with Bella. Alex caught her eye in the rear view mirror and smiled. It felt as though he'd reached out and touched her. Gaby took a deep, steadying breath. Buckling herself into the middle seat, as close to Bella as she could get, she held her daughter's injured hand between both of her own as Alex pulled away from the collection of squad cars and the ambulance.

They hadn't gone far when Alex finally broke the silence. "Bella, you're going to have to talk to the police about what happened," he said gently. "Do you want to do it now, or wait until tomorrow?"

Bella huddled closer to Gaby, and Gaby felt her shivering. "Tomorrow?"

"It's up to you. But the sooner you talk to them, the more you'll remember."

"I think Bella needs to go home right now," Gaby said, too sharply. Swallowing, she tried to soften her tone. "She needs to decompress a little." She turned to her daughter. "You'll remember everything, won't you?"

"Yeah." Bella swallowed and shivered again. "I was really scared," she whispered.

"I know you were," Gaby said. "I was, too. Terrified." She knew, too well, what Julio was capable of.

"I didn't mean to push," Alex said, and she met his gaze in the rear view mirror again. He mouthed, "I'm sorry."

Gabys expression softened, and she nodded. Alex was right – Bella would remember more if she talked to the police today.

"Maybe I could write everything down when we get home," Bella said. "So I don't forget any of the details."

"That's a great idea, Bella," Alex said. "It'll help us, but writing it all down might help you, too. A therapist recommended it to me once, and it was a good idea."

Bella frowned. "When did you have to see a therapist?"

Gaby saw Alex's hands tighten on the steering wheel, and she reached for Bella's good hand. "That's a really personal question, baby. Something Alex might not want to share."

"No, it's okay." The car rolled to a stop at a traffic signal, and he twisted in the seat so he could see Bella. "My younger sister Theresa died several years ago. I wasn't home at the time." He swallowed. "I was in the Navy, on the other side of the world – and it *killed* me to think about her alone and scared. For a long time, every time I turned my head, she was there.

"I had a hard time dealing with it. The therapist I saw helped a lot."

"Your sister died?" Bella stared at the back of Alex's head, frowning.

"Yes, she did. Of a drug overdose." Alex's voice was calm, but Gaby heard the pain in his words. She wanted to reach into the front seat and touch him.

But she stayed where she was. Bella needed her, too.

"That's so sad," Bella said, subdued. "It would be awful if Cece died."

"Yes. It was hard."

"I'm sorry," Bella said in a small voice.

"Thanks, Bella," Alex replied. "That means a lot to me."

A moment later, Bella said, "You were in the Navy?"

"Yes, in Special Ops." The light changed and Alex began driving again. "Until I decided I'd rather be a cop and help kids learn tae kwon do."

Bella leaned forward on the seat. "Do you know tae kwon do, too?"

"I do."

"So you were, like, one of those guys who got Bin Laden? A SEAL?"

Gaby saw Alex smile. "I was a SEAL, but I wasn't on that team."

"That's so cool!" Bella leaned over the seat. "There was a movie about those guys. Everyone else on the tae kwon do team saw it, but Mom wouldn't let me." Bella slid her gaze toward Gaby, and Gaby drew in a breath, grateful to Alex for changing the subject. For giving Bella something to think about besides her ordeal.

"Maybe you and I could see it together," her daughter continued. "Since you were one of those guys."

"Maybe not right now, Bella," Alex said easily. His gaze flashed to Gaby's. *Don't worry*, his eyes said. *We're a team. I've got your back.* "It's pretty violent."

"Huh." Bella slumped against the seat. "It would be a way to get to know you better," she said.

"Sorry, Bella. Not happening."

"I used to think you were a fun guy, Alex." Bella scowled at the back of his head. "I've changed my mind."

"Still not taking you to that movie, kid."

Her daughter slumped against the seat, her eyes narrowed at the back of Alex's head.

Gaby wanted to cradle Alex in her arms and whisper her thanks to him. He'd shared a painful part of his past, and Bella had been able to think about something besides Julio and what had happened to her. At least for a few moments.

A white panel truck, similar to the one Julio had used, flew past them on the left. It stopped at a red light, though, and Alex's car was beside it.

Bella stared out the window at the truck, and Gaby put her arm around her daughter and tugged her closer. "The police have Julio," she murmured. "He's back in jail where he belongs. He can't hurt you anymore."

Bella swallowed, but kept her gaze on the truck.

Gaby sucked in a sudden, sharp breath and tightened her hold on her daughter. Had that bastard Julio done more to Bella than throw her in the back of that truck? "Bella, besides slapping you, did Julio hurt you in any other way?"

Alex stilled in the front seat, but she couldn't look at him. She was completely focused on her daughter.

Still staring at the white truck, Bella said, "After he took me out of the bowling alley, he held his hand over my face and mouth. I couldn't breathe. I was afraid he would…"

"Afraid he would do what, sweetheart?" Alex asked.

Bella's shoulders tightened. "Afraid he would smother

me." She glanced at the back of Alex's head, then quickly looked away.

"What else, baby?" Gaby asked softly, swallowing the ball of fear that lodged in her throat. Maybe something had happened that Bella didn't want to talk about in front of a man.

"He slapped me, then he threw me into the truck and took off. He was driving so fast that I kept slamming into the side of the truck. Or the door. It hurt." She rolled her shoulders, as if testing for pain.

Her mom took Bella's hand and brought it to her mouth. "I'm so sorry he hurt you, Bella. And so glad you were smart enough to save yourself." She leaned away from her daughter, studying her expression. "Is that all, sweetheart?"

"Yeah."

"We can talk about it later, if you'd like," Gaby said.

The traffic light turned green and the white truck sped off in front of them. Moments later, another car turned onto the street and their view of the truck was blocked.

Bella finally looked over at her, frowning. "There's nothing else to talk about."

"He didn't touch you other than the slap?"

Comprehension filled Bella's expression. "He didn't rape me," she said in a low voice. Her lip quivered and she swallowed several times. Glanced toward Alex. Alex didn't react. Didn't give any indication that he'd heard.

"If he had, I would have killed him with my bare hands," Gaby said. "I would have torn him apart."

"Why didn't you do that when he hurt *you*, then?"

Gaby sucked in a breath. Let it out. She should have had this conversation with Bella a long time ago. "I should have. I should have thrown him out of the house the first time he hit me."

"You threw *me* out," Bella said, staring at her bandaged hand.

"Bella…" Gaby swallowed the hard ball of shame and regret. "I will regret that night for the rest of my life. I never meant for you to run away. Those two hours you were gone were the longest of my life. I was trying to get you to go to a friend's house. I wanted you to be safe, in case Julio somehow got out of jail and came back. And I pretended to be angry because I knew if you thought I was protecting you, you wouldn't leave."

"Of course I wouldn't have." Bella lifted her head to stare at her mother, her expression fierce. "I would have kicked him like I did today. Kicked him until he screamed like a baby."

Gaby wrapped her arm about Bella, holding her close. Rocking her. "That was never your job, Bellabug. That was *my* job. I just wasn't strong enough to do it."

She leaned away from her daughter. "The therapist I saw after Julio was arrested helped me a lot. She helped me find my strength. I'm a lot stronger now." She kissed Bella's injured hand. "You've always been strong, Bella. I love that about you. And I'm so proud of you."

She set her hand on Bella's back, massaging it. "We're almost at Raine and Connor's," she murmured. "We'll get Cece and go home. Okay?"

Bella nodded, and Gaby stroked her back, trying to comfort her. Bella must have been so terrified. But she'd done what she had to do to stay safe. "You were smart. Clever. I'm so proud of you, sweetheart."

"Don't be," Bella muttered. "I went to change my ball without telling Connor or Raine. I thought it would only take a second. That's when Julio grabbed me."

Dear God. "Don't blame yourself, Bella. What Julio did was all on him. *His* fault. Not yours."

Alex looked in the rear view mirror and caught her eye. Nodded. His eyes softened, and she read his expression easily. He wanted to comfort her. Comfort both her and Bella. But for now, he'd focus on getting them home as quickly as possible.

"I should have told Raine or Connor what I was doing."

"Yes, you made a mistake. But…" As she scrambled to

find a way to reassure Bella, Alex spoke.

"Everyone makes mistakes, Bella." Alex turned and smiled at Bella, and the stiffness in her daughter's shoulders softened. "The important thing was that you used your head. It was smart to call your mom so the police could track your phone. Smart to kick out the tail light and wave your hand. Connor told me dispatch got more than ten 911 calls about a hand waving from the back of a truck." The car rolled to a stop at another light, and he glanced over his shoulder again.

"And it was really courageous of you to kick Julio like that, especially when he had a gun." He reached back to tuck a strand of Bella's hair behind her ear. "I'm sure he was sorry that he'd taken you. Especially when you kicked him the second time. He's going to hurt for a long time. And if he loses a testicle?" Alex shrugged. "He should consider himself lucky. He deserves a lot worse than that."

He touched her bandaged hand. "You made a mistake, but you made up for it. So let it go, okay? Think about how strong you were. About how you kept thinking, even when you were terrified. Not about the mistake you made."

Bella stared down at her gauze-and-tape-wrapped hand. Picked at a loose end of tape. "I'll try," she said, her voice so soft Gaby barely heard her.

They pulled up in front of Raine and Connor's apartment building, and Bella opened the door and got out. Hurried to the courtyard gate and tried to open it. Shook it when she realized it was locked.

"Hurry up," she called as Alex handed Gaby out of the car. He squeezed her hand, and she clung to him for a moment. Then she let him go and hurried over to Bella.

"Ring the bell in that box to the right," she told Bella.

Fifteen minutes later, they were back in Alex's car. Cece had thrown her arms around Bella as soon as she'd walked into the apartment, and Bella had been clutching her sister's hand ever since.

Gaby sat in the corner of the back seat, watching Cece

stroke Bella's bandage. "Ms. Taylor told me what happened," she said to Bella. "What you did was amazing. I wouldn't have known what to do."

"You will if you join tae kwon do club." Bella nudged her sister's shoulder. "Ms. Taylor will teach you that stuff."

"I'll join." Cece nodded like her head was on a spring. "As soon as I'm in seventh grade. Alex, will you still come to the meets when I'm on the team?"

"Of course I will, Cece. Do you think I'd miss watching you?"

"Good," she said happily. "I'll get Frankie to join, too."

"You'll be better than Frankie," Bella said. "She doesn't pay attention."

Gaby let out a long breath and glanced at Alex. He'd turned the rear view mirror so he could watch her, and he smiled at her. He opened his mouth, but before he could speak, Cece tugged at her hand. "What about our stuff at Alex's house?" she asked.

"I'll drop you all off at your house, then I'll go to my place. I'll pack your things and bring them back," Alex said. "Would that be all right?"

Bella shot forward in her seat and punched his shoulder with her good hand. "Don't you dare look at my diary," she said.

"Not even a peek?" Alex teased.

Bella scowled at him. "Don't even joke about that, frogman."

One side of his mouth curved up at the nickname. "Bella. I wouldn't dream of invading your privacy." Alex's voice was the perfect combination of reassuring and affectionate. "I'll just pack it with the rest of your stuff."

God, he was so good with Bella. He knew exactly how to handle her prickly teen-aged moods. She watched him in the rear view mirror, memorizing the gentleness in his eyes, his soft smile. For her daughter.

His eyes flashed to Gaby's in the mirror, and she smiled at him. "Thank you," she mouthed.

When they got to her house, Alex carried Bella and Cece's bags into the house. They watched as the girls climbed the stairs. Gaby's heart ached as she watched how slowly Bella was moving. Maybe a soak in the bathtub would help her.

The girls' voices drifted down the stairs, and Alex drew her into the kitchen. "How are you holding up?"

Gaby gripped his hand. "Now that we have both girls back, and we're home, I'm fine." She leaned against him and wrapped her arms around his waist. "It was hard for you to talk about Theresa," she said. "I could tell. But thank you for doing that. And talking about being in the Navy, about that stupid movie she wanted to see, distracted her. You were wonderful, Alex."

"I'm crazy about both of your girls," he said, pulling her against him. He wrapped his arms around her and she curled into him. Leaned on him. He brushed his mouth over her hair. "As crazy as I am about you."

"They adore you, Alex." She reached up and kissed him. "And so do I," she whispered.

"Your nightmare with Abrietto is over. After what he did today, he's never getting out of prison. I want to spend the rest of my life showing you how much I love you, Gaby. Making a life with you and Bella and Cece." He brushed her hair away from her face. "Now that we've found each other, I can't let you go."

"I hope not," Gaby said. "Because if you try, I'll run after you and drag you home."

Alex cupped her face and smoothed his thumbs over her cheeks. "Home is where you and the girls are. True north. Where you are? That's where I'll be."

He kissed her again, and Gaby leaned into him. Wrapped her arms around his neck and pulled him closer. As their kiss became more needy, more frantic, Alex pulled away. "Not the right time for this," he murmured.

He was right. Gaby swallowed and loosened her arms. "I know."

"I'll get the girls' things and be back as soon as I can." he said, running his finger down her nose. "How about I pick up some Chinese on the way back?"

"That would be great." She gripped his shirt and pressed another kiss to his mouth. "I'll see you soon."

"You will," he murmured against her lips.

"Oh, my God," Bella said. "Are you two going to be those disgusting, kissy-face parents that everyone gossips about? Embarrassing me at every meet?"

Alex pulled Gaby closer and she saw him grin at Bella. "Every chance we get, Bella. Embarrassing their children is in the parents' handbook under 'job description.'"

Bella rolled her eyes, but Gaby saw the smile struggling to break free when Alex said 'their children.' "Just watch yourself around Cece. I don't want her scarred for life."

Alex opened his arm and Bella threw herself into the hug. "Me, too," cried Cece, and she squirmed between Alex and Gaby.

The four of them swayed together, clutching each other tightly. Gaby's throat swelled. Thickened. She blinked her eyes, but she couldn't stop the tears from falling on her daughters' heads.

Here in the quiet of her kitchen, wrapped around Alex, Bella and Cece, she had everything she'd ever wanted. Her two children, and the man she loved with every molecule of her being. There was no place she'd rather be.

She was the luckiest woman in the world.

EPILOGUE

Six months later

Gaby frowned as she studied her fiancé. Instead of watching the smiling people on the dance floor, or looking at the deliriously happy bride and groom, he stared at the wall behind Raine and Connor. It was like he was a million miles away.

Alex had been behaving strangely for the past week – not hearing when she spoke to him, not teasing the girls, frowning when he thought no one was watching.

He'd been even more off since they arrived at Raine and Connor's wedding. As they walked up the stairs at the Chicago Cultural Center and into the Preston Bradley Hall, he hadn't even glanced at the gorgeous mosaics on the wall or the stunning dome in the ceiling. The only time he'd relaxed or smiled had been when Bella walked down the aisle in her junior bridesmaid dress.

Gaby's throat had tightened when she'd seen Bella. When Bella glanced at her and Alex and Cece with a luminous smile, Alex had beamed at her. Now, as they danced, Alex's shoulder practically vibrated with tension beneath Gaby's hand. And instead of looking at her, Alex stared into space, a muscle in his jaw twitching.

It wasn't how she'd imagined this wedding would be – the magnificent, ornate venue with the view of Millenium Park, sharing Raine and Connor's joy with all their friends, dancing with the man she loved.

Enough. Grabbing his hand tightly so he couldn't wriggle away, she tugged him off the dance floor and into a corner of the room. Partially hidden behind a large potted azalea bush, she set her hands on his shoulders. "What's wrong, babe?" She swept her thumbs over his cheeks, his barely-there whiskers scratching her skin. "You've been acting strange all week. And now we're dancing in this gorgeous, romantic room and you're a million miles away."

Alex sighed and reached up to take her hands. "I'm sorry, Gaby." He slid his fingers through hers as a half-smile lifted his mouth. "I've always been good at hiding what I was thinking." He lifted her hand and pressed a kiss into her palm. "I guess you're better at reading me than I am at hiding my shit from you."

Tightening her fingers around his as dread squeezed her chest, she said, "God, Alex. You're scaring me. What's wrong?"

"*Wrong* isn't exactly the word I'd use. I'd say I'm more nervous." He cleared his throat. "Scared, maybe."

"You?" Holding onto his hands as if they were the only steady thing in the world, she lifted to her toes and brushed a kiss across his mouth. "The man who used to be a SEAL? The guy who faces down murderers every day at work? You're *scared?*"

"Terrified," he said.

Gaby glanced down at the ring on her left hand. "More scared than when you asked me to marry you?" That day, his hands had trembled so badly he'd dropped the ring on the floor as Cece giggled behind him. Bella had rolled her eyes so theatrically that Gaby had had to stifle a laugh.

"Way more scared. Then, I was pretty sure I knew what you'd say." He stared down at her, and heat flooded her face. He'd known damn well she'd say yes that evening. He knew how much she loved him, because she told him every day. "Today, I don't have a clue."

Her heart thudded and anxiety settled on her chest. Wrapped itself around her lungs. Squeezed. "Now *I'm* scared. Are you sick? Did something happen at work? Is this about your parents?"

"None of the above." He closed his eyes, drew in a deep breath, then led her toward two chairs in the corner. "There's something I want to ask you, and I've been trying to figure out the best way to do it."

"Okay, you're freaking me out." She gripped both of his hands. "What is it, Alex?"

He drew in a deep breath. Let it out slowly. "I want to adopt Bella and Cece. I want them to be my kids. Officially. Legally. In every sense of the word."

Gaby sucked in a sharp breath. "Really?" Her heart stuttered, and warmth spread through her body. "Are you sure, Alex?"

"Of course I'm sure." He frowned. "Why are you surprised? You know how much I love them."

"I know you love them. I just…I wasn't expecting that," she admitted. She swallowed, remembering Beatrice Jennings' chilly silence when she and Alex announced their engagement to Alex's parents and introduced them to Bella and Cece. "Your dad was great when we told them we were engaged. But your mom didn't exactly jump for joy. I doubt she'll be thrilled she's getting two grandchildren in the deal, as well."

Alex's mouth thinned. "Then that's her loss." He closed his eyes and breathed deeply, as if struggling for control. "She's not exactly grandparent material, anyway. I doubt Bella and Cece will be having any sleepovers with her."

Gaby smiled at him and nudged them with her shoulder. "Yeah, I can't imagine Bella and Cece staying overnight in that house, spilling popcorn on that priceless Oriental carpet in the library. But there's more to adopting the girls than your parents' reaction."

Alex shrugged. "I've been doing some research. There are reams of documents to be filled out. Legal papers we'll have to file. Home visits from social workers to schedule. But the important part is already settled." Alex cupped the back of her neck and kissed her. "I love them. I'm pretty sure they love me, too."

"They do. And I'd love to have you adopt them. But we'll have to ask them. They're old enough to make this decision themselves."

"What if they say no?" Alex eyes clouded as he wrapped his hand around hers. "What if they don't want another father after Abrietto?"

"Julio was never a father to them," Gaby said. "I'll never completely forgive myself for bringing him into my family, but the girls would never compare you to Julio. They know you're nothing like him."

"Can we ask them tonight? When we get back to the hotel?"

"Yes, let's do that." She grinned at him. "Before they're distracted by that big swimming pool in the spa tomorrow morning."

Alex swept her into his lap. "God, Gaby, I love you so much. What did I do before I met you?"

She ran her fingers through her hair and smiled against his mouth. "Hmm, I bet you had to carry a stick to beat off all the women who wanted you."

Raine had told her about the women who'd hit on Alex at the tae kwon do competitions they both attended. According to Raine, those women had been determined. Relentless.

"After I met you, babe, I didn't take a second look at any of those women." He wrapped his arms around her and kissed her, and the familiar sharp need swept over her. She leaned into him and lost herself in their kiss.

"Hey, you two, let's keep this G-rated."

Gaby broke away and spotted Lizzy Donovan as she dropped into a chair a few feet away. "Hey, Lizzy. Why aren't you out there dancing with Mac?"

Lizzy rubbed her hand over her enormous baby bump. "Mac and I had a couple of dances, but I'm done. Any more, and this baby might pop out right there on the dance floor."

Alex laughed. "That would make for a pretty unforgettable wedding."

"Yeah, well, not going to happen." She arched her back as Tessa fell into the seat beside her, holding her sleeping three-month-old son.

"How are you holding up, Lizzy?" Tessa asked.

"Fine, as long as I'm not dancing." She leaned over and studied the baby. "How can Ryan sleep through this noise?"

Tessa laughed. "Are you kidding me? He's a Donovan. He's used to noise and activity." She nodded at Lizzy's enormous belly. "Have you decided on a name for her yet?"

"Still negotiating." Lizzy sighed. "Mac has an unfair advantage. His job involves a lot of negotiating. All I negotiate at work is my lunch break."

Alex's hand suddenly tightened on hers. "We need to dance," he said, his voice hard as he frowned at the dance floor.

Gaby turned to study the mob of people pressed together, swaying to a slow song in the center of the room. "Why do we *have* to dance?" she asked. Lizzy and Tessa's heads swiveled toward the dance floor, as well.

"Bella's out there. Slow-dancing with some punk. I need to take a look."

He tugged on her hand, and Gaby heard Tessa and Lizzy laughing behind her. She followed him into the crush of people, and Alex swept her into his arms. But he wasn't looking at her. He frowned over her shoulder. Narrowed his eyes. Swung her around so quickly she stumbled.

"What are you doing?" she asked.

"Watching them."

Gaby swung around and saw Bella dancing with a teen-aged boy. Both she and the boy, who she thought was a Donovan cousin from Wisconsin, were stiff and awkward. There was at least a foot of space between them.

"She's fine, Alex."

A muscle in his jaw twitched as he clenched his teeth. "That boy is touching her."

"He's got his hand on her waist." Gaby slid her hand down to press Alex's hand tighter against her body. "That's what you do when you dance."

Alex scowled. "I don't like some punk I don't know putting his hands on my kid."

Gaby hid her smile against Alex's shoulder. When she could look at him without laughing, she lifted her head. "She's fifteen, Alex. When they're fifteen, girls like to have boys touch them. Didn't you like touching girls at that age?"

Alex continued to stare at Bella and the poor boy. "I want his name. Where he lives."

Gaby swung Alex around so he couldn't see Bella. "Alex. You are *not* running a criminal history on him. Bella has barely forgiven you for doing that with Piotr."

Alex tried to turn to watch them again, and Gaby grabbed both of his hands. "Babe, I know this parenting thing is new to you. I love how protective you are of the girls, and deep down, I know Bella is, too. But you don't have to worry about her dancing with that kid. He's from Wisconsin. She's just practicing with him. Figuring out what to do when she's at that high school dance with Piotr in February. Okay?"

A laugh bubbled up inside of Gaby as she watched Alex glower at the poor kid, and she struggled to suppress it. "And I don't think you have to worry about her when she and Piotr are at the dance. After that little talk you had with him at the last tae kwon do meet, I don't think Piotr is going to step over any lines."

The dance ended, and instead of starting another song,

the deejay picked up the microphone. "Ladies and gentlemen, Raine and Connor are getting ready to leave. If you'll gather near the door, there are rose petals to throw as they try to slip out quietly."

Laughing and talking, the crowd of people moved toward the door, taking tiny gauze packets of rose petals from baskets on tables. Alex and Gaby positioned themselves where they could see Raine and Connor. Cece squeezed between them, opening her rose petals and sniffing them.

"They smell good," she announced, smiling up at Gaby, then Alex.

"They do," Gaby answered. "I bet Raine and Connor will think so, too."

Bella crowded against Alex's side. "I thought we were supposed to throw birdseed at weddings."

"Not inside, Bell," Alex said easily. "You'd have people slipping and falling all over the place. No one could dance." Gaby saw his eyes narrow. "You wouldn't want to stop dancing, would you?"

"No way," Bella answered. "This is so much fun."

Alex opened his mouth, and Gaby squeezed his hand. When he glanced at her, she shook her head. "Don't do it," she mouthed.

Connor and Raine appeared, their arms wrapped around each other's waists. They had eyes only for each other as they headed for the door, and Gaby smiled at her friends as she tossed her rose petals.

A cloud of red petals fluttered down on Connor and Raine and all the guests. Moments later, Connor and Raine disappeared. Cece and Bella scurried off, the rest of the crowd went back to the dance floor or the bar, leaving Alex and Gaby standing near the door.

Alex brushed a rose petal from Gaby's cheek, his fingers lingering for a heartbeat against her skin. "I can't wait to see you walking up the aisle toward me, Gaby," he murmured. "Let's get married soon. As soon as we can arrange everything."

She leaned into him. "I want that, too." She stared down at the heavy ring on her left hand and brushed her thumb over the diamond. "So much."

"Good." He curled his arm around her waist, and they both watched Bella and Cece dancing. "Let's get our girls and go home. I have a question I need to ask them."

* * *

Alex unlocked the door to their hotel room and waited for Gaby and the girls to precede him. The door to Bella and Cece's adjoining room stood open, and both girls headed for their room.

"Hey, Bella. Cece." His mouth was desert dry, and he had a hard time swallowing. "Can you stay in our room for a few minutes? There's something I want to ask you."

"Sure." Cece turned around and plopped onto the edge of the king-sized bed that filled the room. Bella kicked off her heels and padded over in her bare feet to sit beside her sister.

She narrowed her gaze at Alex. "You better not say anything about me dancing with Jacob. I saw you watching us."

"No, Bella, not a word about Jacob." He swallowed again, and Gaby slid her hand into his. Squeezed hard, then threaded her fingers with his. "This is something else.

"I was wondering..." He cleared his throat. "Your mother and I were hoping..." *Damn it, Jennings. You faced down the Taliban. But you can't tell these girls you adore that you want to adopt them?*

Gathering his courage, he said, "Bella, Cece, I love you both so much. In my heart and in my head, you're already my children, but I want to make it official. I'd like to adopt you. So I'm legally your father, too. What would you think about that?"

Bella and Cece both stared at him. Then they looked at

Gaby. "Mom?" Bella said.

Gaby let go of his hand and curled her arm around his waist. "I think it's a wonderful idea, but it's your decision."

Cece frowned. "Would daddy in heaven be sad if we had another father?"

Gaby let go of Alex, knelt in front of her younger daughter and swept her into her arms. Then she reached out and pulled Bella into her other side. "Your father loved both of you very much. So much that he'd want you to have a father who loves you as much as he did. He'd want you to have someone to take care of you, to watch the Bearcats games with you, to come to your tae kwon do meets. He'd want you to have someone who'll be there for you whenever you need him."

Alex knelt on the floor next to Gaby. "I don't need a piece of paper for that. I'll always love you. I'll always want to hang out with you. I'll always be there when you need me.

"I already feel like your father. I just want to make it official. Legal."

He glanced at Cece. At Bella. He couldn't read them at all.

Finally, Bella said, "I want to be a real family. Just like the Donovans."

"We're already a real family," Gaby said. "Nothing can change how we feel about each other. This will just make it legal. So Alex can call you in sick to school. Take you to the doctor if you need to go. Put you on his insurance at work."

Bella looked from Gaby to Alex. Tilted her head. "Would we have to change our names?"

"That's up to you," he said. "You can still be a Stefano. Or you can change to Jennings. Maybe keep Stefano as your middle name. Whatever you want."

"Could we call you daddy?" Cece asked.

His throat swelling, Alex managed to say, "If you want to, Cece. I would...I would love that."

Bella glanced at Alex, then looked away. "I think I'll stick with Alex," she said gruffly.

"And I'm good with that, too," Alex assured her.

Cece and Bella slipped out of Gaby's arms, and Alex closed his eyes as he hugged them close. A tear escaped to slip down his cheek as he embraced them, and Gaby kissed it away.

"How long will it take?" Bella asked.

"Your mom and I have to get married first," Alex said, sitting back on his heels. "After that? Maybe six months? I'm not sure. I'll make an appointment with my lawyer on Monday."

"So when are you getting married?" Bella asked.

"As soon as we can, Bella," Gaby told her, leaning against him, and circling his waist with her arm. "Neither of us wants to wait."

"Are we going to have a party like Raine and Connor?" Cece asked.

"Of course we will," Alex said. "But we don't want to wait to get married while we plan a big party. So maybe we'll run away and get married. Just the four of us.

"Then we can have a big party later. By the time it's planned, the adoption should be final. So it will be a double celebration."

Cece looped her arms around Alex's neck. "And then we'll live happily ever after."

The lump in Alex's throat got even bigger. "Yes." He looked at Bella. At Cece. And finally at Gaby. Holding her gaze, he murmured, "We're going to have the best happily ever after the world has ever seen. Because the three of you are everything to me. Everything I'll ever need."

Teary eyed, Gaby smiled at him and leaned in to press a kiss to his mouth. Cece grinned at him, her eyes as bright as the sun. Even Bella blinked her eyes too quickly. Then, allowing her smile to break free, she said, "If you're going to be our father, you need to get 'Cats season tickets. That's what fathers and daughters do, isn't it? Go to the ball game?"

Alex managed a watery half-smile. "Wow, Bella, you read my mind. You really *are* my kid. That's exactly what fathers and daughters do." He nudged her shoulder with his, a rush of love overwhelming him. "I'm gonna need you to help me pick out the seats, though."

Bella shrugged, but Gaby could see happiness shining through her. "That's easy, frogman. Best in the house. Let's do it tomorrow."

"No way! We're going to the meeting about the French camp tomorrow," Cece said, scowling at her sister.

"'Cats tickets are more important," Bella said, scowling at her sister. "Don't you want to go to the games next summer?"

"But the Canoe Island French Camp people are only going to be in town for one day," Cece wailed.

As her daughters squabbled, Gaby reached out and pulled both of them into her arms. "We'll have time for both." Their life as a family was just beginning, and the possibilities stretched out in front of them, each one better than the next.

"Our happily ever after is starting right now."

* * * * *

If you enjoyed **See Me**, pick up the next book in the series – **Catch Me**.

ABOUT THE AUTHOR

Two-time Rita finalist Margaret Watson published her first book in June, 1991. Since then, she has written thirty books for Silhouette Intimate Moments and Harlequin SuperRomance, as well as nine titles in the Donovan Family series.

Margaret's books have won or been finalists in many contests, including the Colorado Award of Excellence, Desert Rose Golden Quill, Holt Medallion, and National Reader's Choice.

When she's not writing, Margaret practices veterinary medicine. She lives in the Chicago area with her husband, three daughters and a menagerie of pets.

* * *

Thank you for reading See Me. I'm honored you chose one of my books, and I hope you enjoyed it!

- If you would like to receive an email newsletter when my next book is released, sign up at **www.margaretwatson.com**.
- Reviews help other readers find books they'd like to read. Please leave a review of this book at your favorite on-line retailer. I welcome all reviews.
- Please recommend this book to your friends and on discussion boards.